William Bruce Leffingwell

Manulito, or, a strange friendship

William Bruce Leffingwell

Manulito, or, a strange friendship

ISBN/EAN: 9783743381988

Manufactured in Europe, USA, Canada, Australia, Japa

Cover: Foto ©Andreas Hilbeck / pixelio.de

Manufactured and distributed by brebook publishing software (www.brebook.com)

William Bruce Leffingwell

Manulito, or, a strange friendship

MANULITO;

OR,

A STRANGE FRIENDSHIP.

BY

WILLIAM BRUCE LEFFINGWELL,

AUTHOR OF "WILD FOWL SHOOTING," "SHOOTING ON
UPLAND, MARSH, AND STREAM," ETC.

PHILADELPHIA:
J. B. LIPPINCOTT COMPANY.
1892.

Printed by J. B. Lippincott Company, Philadelphia.

CONTENTS.

CHAPTER X.

CHAPTER XI.

CHAPTER XII.

CHAPTER XIII.

CHAPTER XIV.

CHAPTER XV.

CHAPTER XVI.

CHAPTER XVII.

MANULITO;

OR,

A STRANGE FRIENDSHIP.

CHAPTER I.

UNREQUITED FRIENDSHIP.

"Fate made me what I am—may make me nothing,
But either that or nothing must I be;
I will not live degraded."

BYRON.

THE summer days had passed, the frosts of October nights had touched with gilded fingers the
trees and grass, the rich green of the summer-time
was gone, and the autumnal season was changing
to scarlet hues the leaves of the forest, and coating
with yellowish brown the blades in the meadows
and marshes. Among the trees, the evidences of
approaching winter were apparent; the leaves fell
in gentle quiverings to the earth; the wild ducks
were in the streams; the prairie-chickens had
"packed;" the advance guard of Canada geese
had appeared; and the busy squirrels were working industriously, garnering their winter stores.

In this early day the vast solitude seemed un-
inhabited by human life, and the quietude was
apparently unbroken, the soil untouched by the
foot of sacrilegious man. And yet, while the birds
flitted through the woods and the wild turkey
strutted in perfect abandon, and in the bottom-
lands the deer herded together in droves and
browsed in apparent safety, two hunters were trav-
ersing the woods, one, a white man, who was
nearing his little home in the sparsely-settled
country, the other, an Indian, just returning from
the village, and each ignorant of the presence of
the other.

Beneath the branches of the great hickory-trees
the dwarfish burr-oaks spread their ragged arms in
elfish grimaces, as they looked up at their majestic
neighbors. The squirrels seemed to be in every
hickory-tree, and, while the unshed leaves hid
them from view, the constant pattering of the
"shucks" on the carpeted earth and the falling
leaves betrayed their presence. At one place the
thickness of the timber temporarily ceased, and an
open glade received with frank warmth the caress-
ing beams of the October sun which streamed in
unbroken rays on the faded grass. The density
of the forest at the west would cause the most
unromantic mind to wonder at its apparent end-
lessness, and to conjecture what it contained. The
silence of death pervaded this wilderness, when
suddenly the bushes parted, and as if ushered

from some other world, there stepped into the open glade a magnificent figure, a perfect specimen of physical manhood. He was dressed in a semi-civilized costume, showing his desire to conform to some rules of conventionality and yet retain perfect freedom of action. In height, he was a trifle over six feet; in weight, perhaps one hundred and eighty pounds, but so perfect in his build that he looked slighter; he was erect, possessed of great strength, and as supple in his movements as a trained athlete. On his head he wore a gray turban cap with folding rim, while sewed on its front and flowing with a graceful swerve over it was a single feather, the pinion of the gray eagle. His jacket and trousers were made of buckskin, and his feet were encased in moccasins. He was apparently from twenty-five to twenty-eight years of age. His forehead broad and high. His eyes were of the deepest blue, and in their light the soul of frankness prevailed. Their glance won involuntary affection, captured the fealty of man and beast, and when their owner was pleading for the oppressed, or condemning some act, they shone with a grayish brilliancy that caused the most hardened criminal to tremble. His nose was large, yet in proportion to his features, and slightly hooked, an indication of the eagle when aroused. His mouth was a study, while through his beardless lips there shone in matchless evenness teeth perfect in form and of the purest white.

His chin was broad and prominent, showing decision, and his voice was sweet and mellow. On
the hunter's left arm the barrel of his rifle lay
carelessly, while his right hand grasped the stock
and his fingers rested against the trigger guard.
Over his shoulder there hung a magnificent specimen of the wild turkey. As he stepped into the
opening his dog was at his side, and he was one to
command both admiration and respect. His ears
were cropped, his size immense; in color he was a
grayish brindle, and in breeding he combined the
blood of the Scotch deer-hound, the blood-hound,
and the bull-dog. It seemed as if he had inherited
the good qualities of them all, for he was fleet as
the swiftest deer, his nose so sensitive that he dis-
cerned the faintest scent, and his pluck and fearlessness beyond parallel. All the affection this dog
felt for any human being was concentrated in his
devotion to his master, and even the ferocity of his
glance softened into gentleness as he looked into
his eyes.

They had not gone more than a few steps before
the south wind brought to the ears of the hunter
the faint " gobble" of a turkey. Quick as thought
he raised his finger warningly to the dog and
stepped back into the thicket. Plucking a green
leaf from an under bough, he placed it to his lips
and called three times in perfect imitation of the
hen-turkey's call; the gobbler answered, but the
hunter suddenly arose from his concealment and

exclaimed to his dog, "Come, Hector! what's the use of shooting more than we want? We've one, and that's enough. Besides, Manulito is out to-day and he will bring in a deer, for he said he was going down on the bottoms, and he will surely get a shot. If he does he will get his deer, for although his left hand is gone he is the best shot in this section,—of course," continued he, smilingly, "excepting you and me."

At this moment a partridge walked proudly into the opening within a few yards of the hunter. Astonished at seeing him, it sprang towards him, then wheeled and darted across the glade. The hunter's gun came to his shoulder. No sooner had the butt touched it than the explosion followed, the feathers drifted with the wind, and the partridge fell dead fully fifty yards from him. At his command the dog brought the bird, but its appearance was spoiled, for the ball had struck at the base of the neck, and head and neck were gone. As the hunter took it, he said to the dog, "It's a shame, Hec, to wantonly destroy life, and I don't often do it; but the bird was so frightened, was going so fast, and straight away, I thought I would see if I had forgotten my cunning, and just as soon as I saw the effects of my shot I was sorry for it. But that's the way it is with us hunters: we often attempt a difficult shot, but the pleasure of success is more than lost in our sincere sorrow over a wanton destruction of life."

As he spoke he was leaning against one of the largest trees. His dog seemed uneasy, and as he walked near his master, the hunter bent over him and struck him playfully with his cap. As he did so, the loud report of a rifle rung out, and the bark of the tree from which the hunter's body had temporarily moved scattered in broken fragments over the ground. With a deep growl the dog bounded in the direction whence came the shot, while the hunter, knowing his danger in his exposed position, sprang behind the tree. The dog disappeared, but soon returned with drooping tail and crestfallen look. The master's eyes filled with an angry light, his form seemed to increase in height, and his fingers clutched his rifle until it seemed he would crush it.

"What!" said he; "afraid? God knows, I never thought *you* would shrink when my life was in danger,—you, who have saved me at two different times, and strangled the enraged and wounded bucks that were trampling me and trying to gore me to death! And now you falter? I did not think that the man or beast lived that you feared. Ay, I thought for me you would brave flood or fire. I would do it for you, although you are but a dog. But——" and the hunter paused as a quick suspicion came to him, " can it be *possible* that *he* fired the shot? *He* whom I have always befriended, whose life I saved at the peril of my own? They have often told me of the treachery of an Indian,

but this one,—Manulito,—who taught me the mysteries of the forests, the secrets of woodcraft, until I, ignorant before, now surpass him in skill at his own craft. I cannot believe it, and I will not." Turning to his dog, he said, "You are a craven, and I cannot understand you. 'Tis true that you know Manulito well, and have hunted with him and me many times, but what of it? If it were he that fired that shot, you should have torn him to pieces. But then," said the hunter, " dogs, perhaps, cannot discriminate between right and wrong."

The hunter went to the place whence the smoke came and critically examined the spot. The dog seemed ashamed of his actions and stood still. While the hunter was on hands and knees searching for some sign of the enemy, Hector stole silently away, and was gone for perhaps a minute when the hunter missed him. He was about to call when he heard a sharp, joyful bark, which led him to where the dog stood wagging his tail. At first nothing was to be seen, but Hector placed his nose to the ground, and there, scarcely perceptible to the ordinary glance, was the faint impression of a moccasin. Perhaps the hunter would have been happier if he had not seen it, for he knew this track. Going back to the tree, he examined it, and taking his hunting-knife, extracted the bullet with the greatest care and placed it in his pocket.

It was now late in the afternoon, and as he started

homeward his thoughts were bitter, and the fierce passion that smouldered in his bosom found vent at times in the most violent outbursts.

"Oh, the ingratitude of man!" said he. "A dog will lick the hand that feeds him, and hold his provider eternally with sincerest affection; but man, base, unsympathetic man, is like a serpent, which, warmed into life by some human being, will turn at the first opportunity and sting the hand that kept it in existence. And thus it is with me. I have come near ending my life, shot down like some wild beast, without an opportunity of defence, and that, too, by one whom I had rescued from a death of the most cruel suffering."

As he thought of these things, his grief in discovering the baseness of his friend, his deep-seated anger as he brooded over this act, caused him to reel at times, and the proud, elastic step which had so often trod the forest with the noiselessness of the panther now awakened the stillness of the woods with its shambling gait.

"I would not have believed it!" cried he. "'Tis true I was forewarned,—that is, in a general way, —and often twitted of this strange companionship, and told that the Indian would commit some deviltry towards me the first chance he had. And how often I have upheld him, befriended him, plead for him, cared for him, clothed him, fed him! Why, at my house food and clothing were as free to him as if he were one of my own kin. The powder,

the ball fired at me, were gifts from my hand; his rifle, the mate to mine, I gave him, and so similar is it to mine that but two persons, he and I, can tell them apart. How pleased he was with it! and well he might have been, for a handsomer, truer one never reached this section of the country." And as he thought of this he set his teeth and brushed his hand before his eyes as if to dispel some horrible vision. "And to think," continued he, "that with *this* gun, *my* gift, the mate of the one I now hold in my hand, he should attempt to kill the man who had given it to him! It would have been murder, —murder most foul and accursed,—for it would have been done with malice aforethought. And the penalty, if he were detected, would be *death.* Ay, and *death* it must be, for before the setting of the sun to-morrow night he or I must die. I could shoot him down like the dog he is, but that must not be. He shall have a chance for his life, but, wide as the world is, he and I must not wander on its face; it is too small for both of us, and one must leave it forever. I would not feel safe with him living, for, having once attempted to kill me, the imagined wrong he holds against me will never be satisfied while I am alive."

2

CHAPTER II.

THE CHALLENGE AND THE DUEL.

" So the struck eagle, stretch'd upon the plain,
No more through rolling clouds to soar again,
Viewed his own feather on the fatal dart,
And wing'd the shaft that quivered in his heart:
Keen were his pangs, but keener far to feel
He nurs'd the pinion which impelled the steel."

BYRON.

THE sun had gone to rest, the stars were shining brightly, when the hunter reached his cabin. His loving wife and prattling babes greeted him affectionately; he kissed them fondly, while a great lump arose in his throat, for he felt that, perhaps, this would be the last time they would meet him at his door. But he hid from his wife the feeling that weighed so heavily on his mind.

"We are so glad to see you, Will, and have been waiting and watching for you."

"I was delayed," said he.

"Yes," she replied, "we knew you were, but Manulito said——"

"What!" thundered he, "Manulito, the Black Wolf, been here?"

"Why, darling," she replied, "he came some time ago, and is now in his room, and I am afraid

he has been drinking hard, for he is very ugly, and I told the children to keep away from him."

At the mention of the Indian's name the hunter with a great effort controlled himself, and, had it not been for the presence of his wife and children, a just vengeance would have been at once meted out. Why had the Indian come to the house after the happenings of the day? Did he think his murderous design had been carried out, and, with the cruelty inherited by his race, did he intend to pursue his purpose still further and exterminate the family, now that its head was gone? The hunter did not comprehend the situation, but, telling his wife he wished to go to the kitchen for a moment, left her, and a few steps brought him into the presence of his enemy. He listened, and found that the Indian was asleep. The spirit of revenge arose in his breast; he set his rifle against the wall and drew from its sheath his long hunting-knife. Cautiously he glided towards the sleeping Indian, then from the slumbering form drew the heavy blanket, exposing a form massive and muscular. The bare skin was discernible in the feeble light. He recalled all the cowardice of his sleeping foe, his attempt to assassinate, his ingratitude, his treachery, and if he spared him now, perhaps before the light of another day he and his little ones would be among the dead. Should he hand him over to justice? Justice in this new country had no mercy for an Indian, and the mere accusation of this popular young hunter,

supported as it would be by circumstantial evidence,
meant the conviction and death of the accused, provided summary disposition was not made at the
hands of the advocates of Judge Lynch, a court
that was in great favor in the new West. But
though his thoughts were bitter, and though he
knew he had to deal with one cunning and merci-
less, yet he could not kill him while asleep. The
hunter's body trembled in his emotion, for he had
resolved that on the following day he would bring
the Indian to an account, and settle forever the dif-
ferences existing between them. As he looked on
the sleeping body of his false and ungrateful friend
his eyes filled with tears, for he had placed in him
the most implicit confidence, and the memories of
the delightful days they had passed together afield
now crowded in fleeting visions to his brain. The
bitter pangs of unrequited friendship rankled in his
bosom, and with ill-suppressed emotion he glided
quietly from the room.

At supper-time his wife chided him because he
did not eat, but he allayed her anxiety. Supper
being over, he told his wife he was going to mould
some bullets, and again entered the room of the
Indian. Stepping quickly to the old hearth, he
touched the prepared wood, and at once there shot
up a strong light, quivering and wavering on the
opposite wall and on the floor, where, wrapped in
his blanket, the Indian still lay.

The hunter set the stock of the rifle on the floor,

folded his arms over the muzzle of the long barrel, looked steadily at the Indian, and said,—

"The journeys of the day have wearied Manulito, and he returns to his den and sleeps while the Gray Eagle hovers o'er him. I have seen Manulito from hour to hour pursue the wounded elk, and when the darkness of the night had overtaken him, return from many miles on the back trail, and still his limbs were not weary and his eyes were un-dimmed, but looked into the darkness with a clearer vision."

As the hunter first spoke, the Indian threw his blanket from his shoulder, looked in astonishment at the speaker, and then settled back in a noncha-lant manner as if to await developments.

"Manulito has lost his cunning," continued the hunter, "when he seeks the sacredness of a home he has but a short time before sought to destroy. Did Manulito have good luck to-day?" he asked in a sneering tone.

As the light grew stronger the features of the Indian were brought into distinctness. There was nothing evil in his face. On the contrary, its regu-larity, his aquiline nose, his perfect teeth, and his haughty, defiant looks caused one to admire, not fear, him. His crown was close shaven, except a tuft filled with feathers, and around his bronze throat a necklace of wolf-claws were strung; his body was naked to the waist, and the muscles of his chest and arms stood out like cords; his black

b   2*

eyes never before quailed beneath the glance of any
human being, but now, perhaps he felt his disgrace,
realized the cowardly attempt he had made to shoot
his best friend, and before the steady gaze of the
man he had betrayed his eyes fell; his confusion
was but momentary, however, for with a spring he
sat upright and exclaimed,—

"Manulito does not always find his game. The
autumn winds have dried the leaves and the trail is
hard to follow."

"Did Manulito,—he whom I have called——"
and the hunter straightened his tall form and set
his teeth together firmly,—"he whom I have
called *my brother*,—did he go to the bottom-lands in
pursuit of deer and turkeys? Or was this game too
small, and did Manulito leave the flowing prairie-
grass and follow the coursing stream, or traverse
the dense forest seeking *larger* game?"

"Manulito left the wigwam of him whom the
pale-faces call 'Silver Tongue' when the coming of
the day had chased to rest the departed night, and,
while the frost was cold and hard on the grass-
blades, sought the bottom-lands in pursuit of deer.
But Manulito was not light of foot nor true of
sight, and the day passed, and he is here without
venison."

"Yes," replied the hunter; "but were other than
you to say you were not light of foot, or your aim
not true, I would know they lied! Not light of
foot? Have you forgotten the time when you taught

me woodcraft, the secrets of the forest, the sheltered banks, how to trap the mink and beaver, how to trace in air the flight of the honey bee, how to tell the course of the winds, the points of the compass by the mosses on the old trees? Have you forgotten the time when, with the stealthiness of a tiger, you crept upon the buck which lay half concealed behind a log, and then with lightning speed sprung and buried your tomahawk in the frightened animal's brain before it could arise? How, when the wounded doe sought to escape, you dashed in and seized her from the jaws of the angry hounds? How, in the village races, you made but sport of those who contended against you? Not light of foot? No, no; don't say that! And then you say you are not true of sight. On the brightest day, when the sun is at his height and the earth is burning under his penetrating glances, I have seen you look in his face without flinching. Often on the prairie you have told with unfailing accuracy the presence of the deer when others could see nothing but sky and grass. In the forest, where the trees and leaves so perfectly blend together, you have called my attention to the ruffed grouse as he stood close to the body of the tree, looking like some old gnarled limb, or have silently picked from under some faded leaf the tiny quail that had escaped its mother. In the sky, where a dot of black flecked the dome of the heavens, you could discern the eagle from the buzzard,—the distance

ne'er deceived you, for the sky, the prairie, and the woods were all as open books to you. Then, do not say you were not true of sight, but rather confess that for some cause unknown to me you attempted to murder your best friend. I do not *believe* you were in the bottoms. I do not *believe* you tried to kill deer to-day. But I *do* know that one shot you fired you missed, and before the setting of another sun you shall account for it."

The hunter was now pacing the floor, and the Indian sat with his head bowed in his hands.

"What has Manulito to say?" thundered the hunter.

The Indian did not reply, but sat and swayed his body to and fro as if in great mental or bodily suffering.

"Listen," said the hunter, "and I will tell you a story, every word of which is true, and your missing hand will tell you of its truth.

"Five years ago there was one of the coldest winters ever known in the West; the snow fell heavily in November and stayed until April; one fierce storm was but the forerunner of others to come; stock perished from the cold; it was impossible for people to leave their houses at times, so the suffering and distress were great. One night a storm was at its fiercest, the wind blew with terrific violence, the snow was churned into the finest powder, while the trees roared as the wind tore through them, and gave to its violence the very limbs of

their bodies. Cattle were huddled together, some moaning in anticipation of their expected fate, others with backs to the wind, craving the protection of the stacks and barns.

" In a cabin, just in the edge of the woods, there lived a young hunter, his wife, and child. This night they sat close to the roaring fire and listened to the crackling of the hickory wood, while the screeching of the winds and the lowing of the cattle distressed and terrified the timid mother, and caused the prattling babe to seek the safety of its father's arms. Suddenly there rose above the din without the mournful wail of a hound. 'What's that?' the young man said, as he sprang to his feet and listened for a repetition of the sound. 'It's nothing but the wind wailing through the tree-tops,' exclaimed his wife. Then again it was heard, louder, clearer than before. 'Oh!' said he, 'some one is lost, is perishing in the storm, and the hound is bewailing his fate!'

" He walked to the door; all was darkness without, but he distinctly heard the howl of the dog, and located the sound. The wife begged him piteously not to go, the child repeated in baby accents the mother's appeal; but a life was at stake, and with an inward prayer for protection, he stepped into the darkness. But why continue the story, Manulito?"

The Indian arose as if to speak, but the hunter motioned him to his seat, and said,—

"He was gone perhaps half an hour; to his wife it seemed an eternity. She tried to look out into the impenetrable darkness, but could see nothing, and on her bended knees she besought her God— your Manitou—that her husband might return. Her prayers were answered, for she heard a sound at the door, and quickly opening it, found her husband, who, with a final effort, dragged into the house the body of a man, and fell exhausted at her feet. A strange dog was with them, a hound, nearly perished with hunger and exposure. This man whom the master of the house had imperilled his life to save was an *Indian.* His left hand was so badly frozen that it required amputation. All through the dreary winter the Indian was cared for in that home, and at length recovered his health. Would you not have thought, Manulito, that that Indian would *never* have forgotten their kindness? That his life would have been dedicated to them, and that he would have died to benefit those who nursed him back to life again? And yet he did forget all these things, and one day stalked this hunter and fired at him as he stood resting against a tree."

As the hunter finished his tale, he paced the floor, as if he had reached some decision that would be followed without deviation. The Indian, stoic though he was, tried at times to interrupt the story, but the hunter waved him to silence, and at last he remained quiet.

The fire had gone down, and a bed of brilliant coals shone in the hearth.

"Bring me your bullet-mould and your rifle," said he to the Indian.

As the Indian did this, the hunter took from his pocket a flattened and battered piece of lead, and said, " To-day some one fired this bullet at me; it missed me, but struck a tree against which I was standing. I had accidentally moved, and this movement saved my life. My rifle and yours, Manulito, have the largest bores of any to be found. If this bullet fills your mould, your gun sped the bullet."

By this time the lead was melted and poured into the mould. The Indian seemed indifferent, and looked on as if in idle curiosity. As the mould opened it disclosed a perfect ball, which the hunter cooled and placed in the muzzle of the Indian's rifle, showing it belonged to one of that calibre.

"What has Manulito, *my brother*, to say?" cried the hunter, in a sneering tone.

The Indian cast his blanket from him and stepped into the middle of the room, exposing a form fit for the gladiatorial ring, and said,—

"Manulito is here! In a moment of passion he sought to take the life of the Gray Eagle, and now thanks his Manitou, the Great Spirit of his fathers, that he failed. When the buck is killed the doe mourns, and when the doe dies the fawn perishes. The Great Spirit, at times, protects the buck that the doe and fawn may live and bless the earth with their young; but in the tribe of Manulito treachery is punished with death. Manulito is not afraid to die. Afraid to die!" said he, in derision, and his bosom swelled. He then walked over to the hunter and said,—

"Gray Eagle, Manulito forgot that you had saved his life, forgot all he owed you; but, prompted by the Evil Spirit, sought your life. Now he remembers all,—remembers how you met him at the door of your cabin, on the return from a hunt, invited him in, and said, 'The Wolf and the Eagle will always be friends.' Then you gave him this gun, and said, 'We are brothers, our guns are alike. I will teach you the mysteries of the books, and you are to teach me the secrets of the woods. We will hunt together, fish together, and when night overtakes us we will divide our blankets, and the stars and the Great Spirit will watch over us both.' But——" and the Indian hesitated, speaking in sorrowful tones, "Manulito has attempted the life of his brother and must die."

Saying this, he jerked his tomahawk from his girdle and thrust it into the hands of the hunter, dropped on one knee, and bowed his head to receive the expected blow. The hunter was at first too much astonished to speak, and stepped back with the uplifted tomahawk, as if in a trance; then, dropping it, shaded his eyes in horror at the thought of striking a defenceless man.

"Arise, Manulito," said he; "not now,—not now. I would not injure a man except in self-defence. The traditions of your tribe may require you to do this, but I cannot permit it. You shall have a chance for your life, a chance fair and equitable, such as an honorable white man accords his foe. To-morrow we will fight; yes, fight to the death. And when the sun has gone to rest, one of us, perhaps both, will be in the presence of his Maker. By right, you are entitled to the choice of weapons. I would prefer a duel in the open air; to meet as man to man, and, displaying our strength and skill, to let the weaker perish. I will not insist on this; but to-morrow, when the sun is at its height and our shadows are shortest for the day, meet me in Round Grove. The forest is broad and deep, and you and I can display our woodcraft, for from its depths one of us will never return alive. I will wage war with you then according to your mode, and let your natural cunning contend against mine, and the result will prove if I have profited by your instructions and can equal an Indian in his element. I will give no quarter, and expect no mercy. God knows, Manulito, I loved you as a brother. You have deceived me, and, as those who were the dearest friends become, when estranged, the bitterest enemies, so you and I meet in the grove for the last time. Am I not fair? And have I not the right to ask this meeting?"

B   3

At the conclusion of the hunter's speech, the Indian replied,—

"When the Evil Spirit steals into the heart of the red man the poisoned sting seeks his brain, and he knows not what he does. As the rivulet courses down the mountain and gathers force, until the stream is a river beyond the control of man, so anger, jealousy, and hate course from the heart to the brain, and, like the fuel thrust into the flame, burn and burn until the heart is on fire and the brain runs wild, and the man whose body is possessed by the Evil Spirit knows not what he does, and seeks to harm those he loves best. Manulito is a warrior,"—as he said this he dropped his rifle-stock on the floor with a loud noise,—"and as a warrior delights to fight, to seek, and to kill. His father was a great chief, and dwelt on the banks of the Mississippi for many years. The winters came and went, the Manitou blessed the earth with game, with corn, and the river was alive with fish. In the council, he spoke, and his words were as sweet honey and full of wisdom; while in battle, his arm was of oak, and his enemies fled like squaws at his coming. This was many seasons ago, and now Manulito stands alone, the last one of a tribe that once peopled the Valley of the Mississippi as the pigeons fill the woods. The Gray Eagle knows that Manulito hates the pale-face race, and why should he not? Where are his brothers, his sisters, his tribe, his lands? Broken and destroyed and held by those who came with fire-water and false promises to rob them of the lands which the Great Manitou gave them hundreds of years before. They fled before the pale-face tribes, and sought to find the place where the sun goes down to rest at night, hoping there to gain peace, and to hunt as in years gone by. But, like the warrior on the trail, or the hound following the wounded deer, the pale face forever overtook him. Manulito thought never to dwell with them; but one night, when the frost-king held the earth and the winds shrieked through the trees, tired and cold and unable to go farther, he sank into the snow and would have perished, but was saved by a white man. For many moons he dwelt with him; he learned to read, to write, to spell, and the things he once thought made squaws of men pleased him most. But"—and the Indian dropped his glance—"he learned to love the fire-water of the white man." Then, as if some burden was on his mind, he gazed intently into the fire, and continued, " It shall be as the Gray Eagle wishes, and to-morrow, at noon, Manulito will be in the woods."

" 'Tis well," said the hunter; " and understand, you are to seek me, and I will you, and all things shall be considered fair, whether to use the rifle, the knife, or the tomahawk."

" All men must die," said the Indian, " but no man can tell when his time will come. Should to-morrow be the time that the Great Spirit has

set for Manulito to die, he asks the Gray Eagle to
bury him in his blankets, his arms at his side, that
he may drive away the wild beasts in his journey
to thè Happy Hunting-Grounds. Manulito will be
in the grove at noon." Saying this, he strode
hastily from the room.

Left alone, the hunter sank into a chair and tried
to collect his scattered thoughts. The events of
the entire day were in his mind: the cowardly act
of the Indian, and then again his willingness to
give his own life as a forfeit, or rather to atone for
the attempted crime. He knew the Indian hated
the white people, although he had so many times
shown a deep affection for him and his dear ones.
He had felt that he knew the Indian, but the more
he thought of him the more perplexed he was.
He felt that perhaps he was too bitter, too hasty
in insisting upon a duel, in which it was now plain
the Indian did not wish to engage. He did not
attribute it to cowardice, for he knew too well
the courage of Manulito, and knew .he scorned
danger.

Wearily and sorrowfully he sought his rest, but
his eyes did not close in sleep. Long before the
break of day he was astir. As he left his home
that morning he said to his wife,—

"Hector has never missed following a trail. To-
day, at noon, unchain him and tell him to seek his
master."

He knew the dog would find him, living or dead,

and would return home for help or guard him until discovered.

How bitter the parting with his wife,—an outward calm, concealing the cruel suffering within! Oh, the folly of a duel! To heap years of bitter suffering on innocent heads! As he left the garden gate, there reached his ears the sound of a mother's voice blending in pathetic harmony with her child's, as they called " Good-by, papa dear; we will watch and wait for you." Love makes cowards of men, and it did of him. He longed to return to all that was near and dear to him, but honor demanded that he keep his word, even at the cost of his life.

CHAPTER III.

RECONCILIATION.

" No thought of flight,
None of retreat, no unbecoming deed
That argued fear; each on himself relied,
As only in his arm the moment lay
Of victory."

MILTON.

THE day was perfect, and the north wind gently moved the white clouds that floated above, clinging to the ceiling of blue in the distant skies. The long walk in the brisk morning air refreshed him,

3*

and all feelings of sadness yielded to one of quiet determination. Before leaving his home he carefully loaded his rifle, and, strangely enough, the first bullet he took from his pouch was the one he had moulded and marked with his initial the night before. "A life for a life," thought he, "and the bullet intended for me shall be tried at him." But he changed his mind, selected one without a blemish, and put the marked bullet again in his pocket.

As the sun was at the zenith and the shadows proclaimed the hour of noon, he entered the woods. He had often traversed them, and knew every spot, but now the air seemed oppressive, and he felt as if he were in a place where death stalked abroad and might appear at any moment. He watched with unusual caution, and his rifle was in position to fire instantly. The leaves rustled gently to the earth, and as they grated against those remaining on the trees, the slight sounds caused him to start in expectancy. Well he might, since one false movement might cause his death, for he had pitted his skill against that of a child of the forest.

He had worked slowly and with extreme caution for perhaps a mile, gazing intently, and scrutinizing every tree and bush before approaching it. So silently did he proceed that the birds of the forest noted not his approach. A flock of wild turkeys ran before him, and the gobbler, with arched neck and curved wings, strutted within twenty yards of him; then again, a buck and two does browsed unsuspiciously within close gunshot.

As the time passed and he neither saw nor heard anything of Manulito, he felt the necessity of greater caution and exercised it. He must have been in the woods an hour, when, approaching the huge trunk of an old tree which had been blown down, he settled quietly between its branches. As he sat there, it seemed at times as if he heard pattering on the leaves; in front of him the "put-put" of a turkey was heard, and the bird stepped plainly into view. While watching it his blood ran cold in his veins, as he heard a voice behind him, saying,—

"When the Eagle is weary he seeks his rest."

He knew he was at the Indian's mercy, and slowly turning his head, saw the stalwart form of Manulito standing over him with tomahawk in hand.

"The Eagle is tired," continued he, "and alighting to rest, his weariness dulled his sight and closed his ears. The Gray Eagle said there should be no mercy, whether with tomahawk, rifle, or knife. As the Gray Eagle sat beside this tree, Manulito could have touched him with his rifle or have killed him with his tomahawk, but the Gray Eagle is not to die by the rifle or the tomahawk. If it were so, he would now lie still in death with his skull cleft in twain. But the Gray Eagle shall fight for his life as the white man fights, face to face with his foe. Come," said he, "follow me to the open glade,—you know where it is; the spot where we ate our first venison. It was there we sat together and at night shared our blankets. Here it is now."

As he said this, they stepped into a beautiful grassy plot, surrounded by birch and willows, while at one side a silvery stream rippled along with half-suppressed murmurs. The Indian leaned his rifle against a tree, laid his tomahawk on the ground, and said,—

"On this spot, Gray Eagle, two brothers settle their only quarrel. We will fight with knives, and but one shall live. Should Manulito fall, bury him here, but sometimes *think* of him, and of the happy hours you and he passed together in the woods and bottom-land."

As the Indian finished, he threw his blanket to the ground, drew his knife, and stepped into the middle of the green, awaiting the approach of his adversary. The hunter drew his cap tightly on his head, and with knife in hand, stepped into the opening. The hunter was the taller of the two, with longer arms, but his strength was concealed beneath his tight-fitting buckskin shirt, which seemed strained to bursting as his arms moved up and down. The sun shone brightly on the Indian, and the copper skin of his massive arms and shoulders glistened in the light.

They eyed one another with deep attention, each watching for some weak point of attack, but none could be discovered. The Indian was apparently on the defensive. They seemed like two human tigers thirsting for blood, each recognizing the bravery and skill of the other. For fully ten minutes they tried for an opening, yet neither spoke a word, each feeling that he needed all his strength and breath in the final struggle. At last, as if intending to test his adversary, the hunter rushed forward, and before the Indian could strike, sprang back with the agility of a deer. The Indian did not attempt to follow him up; this was repeated again, then again, until the hunter said,—

"Must the Eagle swoop down on the Wolf and return without a bite?"

The Indian did not reply, but clinched his knife with a firmer hold, which plainly indicated his decision. As he advanced the hunter slowly retreated; the Indian circled round as if ready to spring, but the other saw his opportunity, and was about to strike, when he found Manulito in his presence unarmed, for as he rushed forward, the Indian, with a quick flirt, threw his knife into the woods, and stood before him with bared breast and folded arms. The hunter's uplifted arm quivered and fell powerless at his side, for he could not strike a cowardly blow on this defenceless man, and stepping back, he said in surprise,—

"Did not Manulito want to fight with knives?"

The Indian replied, "My tribe is gone, Manulito is alone, and the only friend he ever had among the whites stands before him. Yesterday, when at the village, he drank fire-water until the sky and

c

trees danced before his eyes. The village boys
said he was a squaw, he could not shoot, he could
not hunt because his footsteps were heavy and
he frightened the deer. Gray Eagle is a mighty
hunter, said they, and kills all the deer. They
laughed at Manulito, and stoned his dog. Bitter
were his thoughts, and murder was in his heart.
He fled from the village, his sight was blinded, his
heart called for revenge, and the fire-water burned
his body and set fire to his brain. The Evil Spirit
whispered in his ear, ' The Gray Eagle ! the Gray
Eagle ! *He* is the one who has caused all this !'
And while the heart of Manulito was filled with
anger, and he walked almost like a blind man
through the woods, he saw his friend, and prompted
by the Evil Spirit, raised his gun and fired. Then
he fled, for he realized his cowardly and jealous
act, and that night when the Gray Eagle returned
to his lodge, and Manulito saw he was unhurt, he
thanked the Great Manitou for saving him, for the
Evil Spirit had fled, and again Manulito loved the
Gray Eagle better than his life. When my white
brother spoke and told his story, the story of the
stormy night, it burned into the heart of Manulito
like the molten lead when the bullets are cast.
The laws of his tribe demand that an attempted
crime on a brother must be punished with death.
His life was offered you last night, but you refused
to take it. To-day it is yours, but not one hair of
your head would Manulito injure. He is ready to

die, for he has told all to his brother, and the trail to the Happy Hunting-Grounds is broad and open. When the summer days of the white chief are passed, and the frosts of old age have whitened his head, he too must die, but in the arms of his friends, and long after his silver tongue has moved to anger or melted to tears the tribes of his nation. Manulito is ready to die."

The hunter was deeply touched at this recital, for he saw now that it was only because he was insane with jealousy and crazed with liquor that the Indian had attempted his life. He took him gently by the hand, bade him be seated on the grass, and said,—

"I, too, have been hasty, and sought to enter into a conflict with you to-day that meant death to one or both of us. You were too brave, too proud, to explain last night, but deliberately met me here, intending to cast your life away and die by my hand, leading me to think it was a contest, and not a murder on my part. We have both been wrong, and here in your presence, I say, I forgive you freely and fully, as freely and unconditionally as I hope my sins will be forgiven in the world to come. A wound does not quickly heal by being torn apart, but the salve must do its work, and with us, we will forgive and try to forget. What has happened, —let it be between you and me. It does not concern the world, and no man shall know of it during your life. And now, Manulito," said he, as he looked tenderly into his face, "while I live my home shall be open to you. In the lodge of the Gray Eagle there will always be food and blankets for his friend, and I will be your brother, and we will hunt and fish together as we have for years. Then should you be called to the Happy Hunting-Grounds first, at your grave will I stand and mourn for my red brother. Perhaps,"—and his eyes assumed a far-away, thoughtful expression,—"perhaps, with your spirit in the land of your God, you can look down and see me weep for you, for I have sometimes wondered if those in heaven could not look down on earth and see us weeping over the grave of some dear, dead friend."

As he finished, he slipped into the Indian's hand the marked bullet. Manulito proudly raised his head, and laying his hand gently in the hand of the hunter, said,—

"The south wind in the spring-time breathes new life into the departed year, and sweeter than the songs of the thrush or the perfume of the lily are the words of his brother to Manulito. Like the voices of his father and brothers who will greet him on the prairies of the Happy Hunting-Grounds, and bid him enter and hunt for evermore, so are the words of friendship and forgiveness that my brother gives to me. From this day, whether Manulito is on the prairie, or in the village, or sick in the medicine lodge, no fire-water shall ever again pass between his lips, and Manulito hopes that in years to come, some time, the Great Spirit will let him save the life he sought to take."

At this moment a gray form shot through an opening, and in an instant Hector bounded before his master, and joyfully licked his hand as he lay down and whined at the hunter's feet.

From the farm-house to the village the hunter had moved, and with him his Indian friend. One day the hunter's wife said to her husband,—

"For more than a year I have noticed such a change in Manulito. He idolizes you, and to me and the babies he is as affectionate as a woman. He takes advantage of every opportunity to do some little act that will show his love for us, and often when you go in pursuit of deer he steals silently from the house, and at times I think he follows you lest, if an accident should befall you, he might not be near to render you aid. I sometimes wish you would quit hunting, for since the sad death of poor brother Harry I cannot look at a rifle without thinking of him. To be sure, he was thoughtless in sounding the ice with the butt of his gun, but maybe all hunters at times do thoughtless things, and when no accident occurs, think nothing of it."

"Why, bless your sweet heart!" exclaimed Wellington,—for he will hereafter be known by this name,—"borrowing trouble? One-half of all the ills flesh is heir to are imaginary. You know I

4

am careful, and what would our good people do if
I did not hunt? Why, last winter I know that
half the fresh meat brought to this village fell to
my gun. And now," said he, and his handsome
face brightened with a smile, " they say I hunt for
a living and practise law for fun. Well, I don't
know which I enjoy more, but I believe I like them
both so well that—well, I will stick to my books."

" Unless," she said, " some person enters your
office and tells some wild story of seeing the track
of the much-hunted but never-captured big buck."

He laughed and said, " I won't discuss the matter
with you, for you know my weakness, and it would
be foolish for me to provoke a discussion, or say
anything of which my past life would be a denial.
But," continued he, " it does seem strange that
with all the hunting I have done, and all the experience I have had, I have never seen and can
never strike the trail of this much-coveted big
buck. I have hunted every foot of ground within
a hundred miles of here, in all directions, and have
gone to places where he has been seen, but to me
he is an *ignis fatuus.*"

" A charmed beast," jokingly responded his wife;
" but possibly, some day when least expected, he
will appear to you, and if he does," and she looked
at him with confident affection, " I am afraid it will
be his last day in the woods."

The next morning Wellington was up bright
and early, and before many of the villagers were

astir was at his office. It was the day before Christmas, and as he walked briskly along, the perfect morning filled his soul with delight. It hardly seemed the month of December, for the autumn had been so pleasant, and winter had hesitated so long in his coming, that it seemed more like early November. The sun had not yet risen, and the quiet village was scarcely astir. The noisy dogs barked at intervals, and the white smoke lazily ascended from a few chimneys. Not the slightest wind prevailed. There was no snow on the ground, and as Wellington walked along, his footsteps left a perfect impress in the flaky frost which had covered the ground.

By this time the sun rose as if from the long grass, and a flock of prairie-chickens sailed gracefully over the village in their morning flight.

He was soon in his office and had a roaring fire in the old-fashioned fireplace, which seemed almost as wide as the room. The furniture was rather primitive in design and construction. There were a few chairs, carved and scarred by the knives of thoughtless callers or clients, and a table of pine, made by Wellington himself. His pens and holders were from the quills of the wild goose. His library, however, was quite complete, with Blackstone, Chitty, and the English Reports. As he searched these authorities, making a brief on some case, his pen glided easily over the foolscap, jotting down his points and making that peculiar sound which, once heard, can never be forgotten.

He sat back in his chair, put his feet on the table, and dived deep into the contents of the dingy yellow volumes. Soon the door quietly opened, and in stalked Manulito, who gruffly bowed, seated himself before the fire, and drew his blanket over his shoulders. The lawyer studied and the Indian stared into the fire, each apparently oblivious of the presence of the other. Their dogs were more companionable, however, for they wagged their greeting and occasionally beat a tattoo of welcome with their tails on the bare floor. The silence was broken by a familiar voice from without. The Indian looked up in disgust and drew his blanket more closely over his shoulders, while the lawyer smiled and laid down his book.

"Whoa! Consarn ye! Whoa! Consarn ye! Can't ye stand still, ye tarnal critters? Say, Bill, why don't ye come out an' help a feller?"

The lawyer was about to comply when the door opened and in walked the questioner. He was a man short of stature, with a grizzly, stubby beard, whose whiteness was sadly discolored by tobacco juice. He wore a cap made of coon-skins, a faded yellowish-brown overcoat, belted round the waist with a leather strap, shoes of buffalo-skin, and in his hand held a whip with a short handle and a long lash.

As he entered the door he greeted the lawyer

uproariously, and continued to laugh as if at something irresistibly funny.

" Oh, Bill !" said he, " you would have hurt yourself if you had seen the fun me an' thet steer had."
And then he laughed again and slapped his knee in
his merriment. " Why, the confounded critter was
goin' ter foller me plumb into your offis. You see,
he ain't never been ter town afore, an' he's jes' as
green as grass an' don't know nothin'. I allus
liked the critter, an' this mornin' I says ter the ole
woman, ' Mother, I b'lieve I'll go ter town an' take
Wellington a load of wood.' ' Do, Kirtley,' says
she, ' an' hitch Rube'—Rube is this green ox—
' long-side of ole Jerry. He's kinder fond of you,
an' 'sides you can break him in ter yoke.' So I
loads up the wood an' hitches up the oxen, an'
here I be. Well, thet tarnal critter was jes' like
a green country boy, an' ev'rything was new ter
him. I didn't hev no trouble with him, 'cause when
he kinder hes'tated-like, ole Jerry jes' snatched him
right along. Well, when I arrove in front your
offis an' started in, I'm blowed if Rube didn't try
ter follow me in, wagon an' all." Then, at the
thought of it, the old man laughed immoderately.
" Say, Bill, I ought ter hev paid yer some money
afore this, but times is dull an' my corn didn't pan
out well, the hogs got the cholera, two of the cows
went dry, an' it made me an' the ole woman
kinder hard up for cash, but you can burn wood,
Bill, an' I bro't you as nice a load as ever was

chopped,—hick'ry an' white oak,—an', Bill, I hope
afore long ter squar' up with you complete."

They were on the most familiar terms, these two
men, lawyer and client, for while Kirtley was not
exactly quarrelsome, still a lawsuit lacked its flavor
in this settlement if he was not either plaintiff or
defendant.

The old man seated himself at the table opposite
the lawyer, and, slyly curving his thumb over his
shoulder at the listless Indian, said,—

"Don't you sometimes feel, Bill, that two is
company an' three's a crowd?"

"Never mind," said Wellington; "Manulito don't
care for our talk. Besides, he can keep a secret."

"Mebbe so, mebbe so," said his visitor; "but,
Bill, you an' me is different. I've lived in these
parts many years,—yes, years afore you come West,
—an' I ain't yet seen no good comin' of an Injun.
An Injun is an Injun an' allus will be. I won't
say they will allus steal, 'cause they don't allus get
the chance. But when I sees one loafin' round my
cl'arin', I can't help but feel that my chickens ought
ter roost high."

"The trouble is, Kirtley, you are prejudiced, and
can see nothing good in an Indian. You can feel
free to slander the Indians in the presence of Manulito, for he respects your age and will not resent
it."

Manulito looked up and said, "The words of the
gray head are like the rain-drops on the lodge of

the warrior,—they make much noise but do no harm. The gray head is like a squaw; he likes to talk, for it does him much good and injures no one."

"Bah! on your smooth words," said Kirtley, turning from the Indian in disgust. "A smooth-tongued Fox once stopped at my house and got on the good side of the ole woman with his fine speech. She thought him *such* a nice Injun. He *was* a good judge of hoss-flesh, anyhow, for next mornin' he didn't come ter breakfus', an' he took with him the best pa'r of hosses thet ever forded the Wapsie. Wot's goin' on in town ter-morrer? Shootin'-match? I heerd tell, as I was waterin' the critters at the trough, thet thar was goin' ter be a shoot on Christmas, an' thet's ter-morrer; but thinks I to myself, if thar be a shoot ter-morrer, it will hev to go on without the best shot in these parts bein' thar. 'Cause why? 'Cause, Bill, you is goin' with me."

"Going with you?" asked Wellington, in astonishment.

"Yaas, goin' with me." And then he placed his hand to shield his voice from the Indian, leaned over the table, and cautiously said, "I hev seed him twic'd!"

"Seen him twice?" queried Wellington. "What do you mean?"

"I mean," said he, "that within the last two days I hev seed the big buck twic'd, an' both times at the same place."

CHAPTER IV.

OLD MAN KIRTLEY.

" Fields, woods, and streams,
Each tow'ring hill, each humble vale below,
Shall hear my cheering voice; my hounds shall wake
The lazy morn, and glad th' horizon round."

SOMERVILLE.

" I DON'T know what to think, Kirtley; but so many have told me of seeing this buck, which seems to bear a charmed life, that I always feel when I hope to find him that I will be doomed to disappointment. But tell us where you saw him."

The old man rested his arm on the table, bit off a big chunk of tobacco, and said,—

" The fust time was day afore yesterday. The hogs hed broke out, an', es the wolves air gettin' kind o' thick in the timber, I went ter look 'em up. I started airly in the mornin', an' tramped an' tramped till my old legs said ' Rest!' Yer know I'm bothered with the rheumatiz, an' can't tramp like I could onc't. My dog was with me, an' I tuk out my lunch an' sot down by a log thet was down by the south ford; yer both know the place, jes' whar the sand-bar is, whar the eddy is, whar I seed you two fishin' two years ago,—you know whar, jes' about ten rods above the cattle ford. All at

onc't the dog gave a low whine, then growled. I
looked up, but saw nothin'. Then I looked ag'in,
an', Lawd! Bill, if thar, right in gunshot, wasn't
the biggest buck I ever laid my eyes on, an' I hev
been here fur twenty years. Fust I thought it was
an elk, he looked so big. An' what do you think?
I'm blowed if I hed a gun! How I wished fur
you, 'cause I know'd your heart is sot on gettin'
him. Well, he didn't see me, but stood on the
bank an' looked up and down es if he hed lost
somethin', or was afeard some one was lookin' fur
him, then he waded inter the Wapsie, an' come
straight across at the foot of the bar. I jes' kep' still.
Gosh! but he was a big feller, an' his left horn was
broke off near the tip, an' his face an' head looked
kinder gray-like. He come straight on, an' waded
up, then climbed the bank within twenty feet of
me. I ain't no coward, but somehow I felt kind o'
scairt, fur the brute looked powerful ugly. The
dog got brave, an' I said 'Sick 'im!' Well, he
did 'sick 'im,' but thet buck jumped about four-
teen feet one side when he first saw the dog, then
the next thing I seed, the dog was about ten feet in
the air, an' the buck stood waitin' fur him ter come
down. When he did, he went up ag'in, then
landed in the river. I stepped out, an' when the
buck saw me his eyes looked es big es saucers, his
horns seemed ter kinder grow sharp, his hair riz, he
stamped and snorted es though he tho't I wanted
ter fight, an' thinks I ter myself, 'Kirtley, yer hevn't

got no gun, an' yer hev got a big family. Yer ain't lost no buck, you air lookin' fur your stray hogs.' So I jes' got behind a tree, an' the buck walked away, all the time. lookin' out the corner of his eye at me. Then he started inter a trot, an' I waved my hat at him an' hoped ter meet him ag'in when I hed a rifle, an axe, a Bowie-knife, an' you an' the Injun with me."

Wellington laughed as he thought of his friend's plight, but Manulito drew his chair nearer and let not a word escape him.

"That was the fust time," continued Kirtley. "The second time was yesterday. I got my gun in the mornin' an' tho't I would lay for his buckship, an' I felt kinder proud ter think that I was goin' ter be the one ter kill the buck, an' I pictered in my mind how cheap you an' the Injun would feel ter hev me come ter town with the animile, an' hev all the boys crowd 'round an' congratulate me, an' shake hands with me, an' thet sorter thing. But, drat the luck! When I come ter start thar wasn't a bullet in the house, an' I couldn't find the moulds. Now, I *was* mad; but I was ready ter go, an' go it was. I didn't hide in jes' the same place, but I got where the buck couldn't scent me, an' then hid. He didn't come on time ter the ford, but come he did at last, an' acted kinder timid-like. He looked, an' sniffed, an' acted mighty cautious, then hurried across, an' soon es he struck the bank trotted off. I didn't make any noise, so he didn't

know I seed him. Arter he was gone, I went ter
the bank an' looked at his tracks. Big? They
were es big es a cow's an' lots of 'em. I jes'
quietly come home, said nothin' ter nobody, an'
bro't this load of wood es a blind. Now, I hev
told yer whar the brute is hidin', an' if yer don't
want ter go, I'll try him myself."

"Go! said Wellington. "I wouldn't miss the
chance for a farm. You have struck his runway,
and he will show up again. If I am alive and well
I will be at your house to-morrow morning before
daybreak, but not alone, for Manulito will go with
me."

"The Gray Eagle needs no help to kill the buck,"
replied the Indian. "His footsteps are light, his
aim sure."

"But perhaps you will be favored with a shot,"
replied Wellington. "Have you ever seen this
buck, or struck his trail?"

"Ugh! two years ago, at the mouth of the Elk
River, when Manulito was on the trail of another
deer, he saw, away up the stream, this big buck,—
too far to shoot. He followed the trail three days,
sleeping at night wherever the darkness overtook
him,—through the bottom-land, over the bluffs, to
the mouth of the Maquoketa, then through the
timber until he reached the land of the Lost Nation, but did not get a shot. Another time he saw
the big footprints on the sand at the mouth of the
Meredosia, and followed the trail along the river as

far as the Rock River, then across the Meredosia
to the Mississippi, and struck its trail in the land
of the Iowas, but lost it again on the Wapsie bottoms."

As the Indian finished, Wellington said,—

"Let us hope that to-morrow we will be more
fortunate, and capture this charmed buck. But
one thing I regret, that Hector cannot go with me.
He is too lame, and his shoulder hasn't healed from
the cut he received in his last fight with that four-
pronged buck. But Ben can go; he is young but
courageous, and will be all right."

Kirtley arose to depart, saying, "Airly in the
mornin', Bill, we'll look fur yer at my cabin. The
ole woman thinks es much of you es she does of
her own boys, an' yer will find suthin' hot ter drink
an' suthin' good ter eat waitin' fur yer at the
clearin'."

As he left the door, he turned again and said,
"Don't furgit ter come airly, Bill, fur me an' the
ole woman will be a-waitin' an' a-watchin' fur ye."

Wellington tried to induce the Indian to go with
him, but he replied,—

"Twice has Manulito been on the trail, but lost
it. Let the Eagle try."

Next morning, long before the break of day, the
hunter was prepared to start. It was a tramp of
four miles to Kirtley's home, and as he bade his
wife good-by she tenderly clung to him, loath to
have him go, and said,—

"Last night, Will, I dreamed of brother Harry, and saw him just as I see you now, light-hearted, active, and merry. It was a happy dream, for the past was hidden from me. I awoke, and—and—oh, Will! I could not help feeling, although I fought against it, that some evil would befall you to-day. Don't think me foolish, but I have had one dear one accidentally killed while hunting, and I cannot bear to think of harm to you."

"Why, darling," said he, "dreams always go by contraries. To dream of evil to me means I will have good luck, and so I believe I will. Dry your tears, and, if weep you must, then wait until I return, and let them be tears of joy."

He kissed her good-by and stepped out into the frosty air, while the twinkling stars feebly lit his pathway. Before the break of day he, with Ben at his side, stood at the door of Kirtley's dwelling in the clearing. He received a hearty welcome from the master of the house, while the good woman shook both hands, gazed at him fondly, and cried,—

"Oh, *but* I be glad ter see you, Will! You don't *know* how glad I be. You jes' ought ter be 'shamed of yourself not ter drap in on us oftener. But I s'pose," and she drew herself up with assumed dignity, "thet sence they is goin' ter make you jedge you hev kinder forgit your ole frien's; but we ain't goin' ter allow you ter forgit us, be we, pap?" And she looked to Kirtley for an answer.

"Not by a jug-full," replied that worthy. "Bill an' me understan's one 'nother. Bill knows we ain't much fur style, but our hairts is right, eh, Bill?"

Wellington laid his hand tenderly on the good woman's arm, and said,—

"Mother, you have known me too long to think that any honors I might receive would lessen my love for you and my dear old friend beside me. Don't think of that, but remember, whatever I may be, to me you will ever be *Mother Kirtley*, and to you," said he, turning to Kirtley, "I will always be——"

"Bill!" said the old man, as he struck his fist on the table.

As the sun rose and the leaden sky turned to a golden yellow in the east, Wellington and Kirtley left the house. The reflection of the sky on the water in a pond near the house attracted the hunter's attention, and he said,—

"See, Kirtley, how beautiful the water is. It looks like a mirror, and draws from the sky its beautiful colors of gold and crimson and blue, and out there at the northern edge it merges into a rich carmine, a rosy red."

"Yaas, Bill," replied his companion, "them colors is all right, an' the pond looks purty, es yer say, but jes' es yer spoke I wasn't ezzactly thinkin' of thet, but I was thinkin' w'at a good place it would be fur the hogs ter waller in, or the critters ter stan' in an' fight flies next summer."

Wellington laughed, and said, "If I am poetical, you are certainly practical, Kirtley."

A short walk brought them to the banks of the Wapsie, a crooked, meandering stream, which flowed in uncertain directions its entire length. The river was low, and the current passed along this quiet morning in sleepy languor. During the rainy season, or when the snow melted at the breaking up of winter, it soon overflowed its confined banks, and spread, like a pestilence, no one knew to what limits. But the spring-time had departed, and with it the high water. The autumn had been dry, and the crooked stream with its stranded logs, its drooping trees with roots clinging to the banks, and its great sand-bars, seemed stripped of its power, and caused the beholder to look on its bed with indifference.

As Wellington and his companion walked speedily along, the latter said,—

"Be yer goin' down ter the ford fust thing? If so, it ain't more nor three miles, takin' a straight cut."

"Yes," replied Wellington, "we will go the shortest route; and"—he stopped and faced his companion—"remember that silence in the woods is the only true way to success in hunting. Anything you have to say, first touch my arm, then whisper it to me. Another thing: follow in my footsteps and avoid treading on dry sticks."

They had gone but a short distance when Kirtley

touched his companion, and, standing on tiptoe, whispered to him,—

" Say, Bill, can't talk much ?"

The hunter smiled and shook his head.

" Then yer must ease up your long legs, fur when I try ter foller in your steps I kinder strain my trousers, an' I feel the rheumatiz in my side."

Wellington laughed, and walked slower and with shorter step, while the old man tried to step in his footprints. At times they penetrated the deepest thickets, then came again and again in sight of the river, but they knew the lay of the land, and went silently on. Game was plenty, and quail, grouse, and turkeys were at times seen, oftener heard, in the bottoms. As they stepped into an opening where the tall grass met the young willows on the water's edge, Wellington peered down the river, looking intently at a point below.

" Yaas, thet's the p'int," whispered his companion, " 'way down thar whar the big sand-bar runs inter the river."

They stepped quietly back, and proceeding with caution walked stealthily along. As they neared the bend Kirtley touched his companion, then whispered,—

" We're here, Bill; this is the spot, an' jes' 'cross the river, by thet tall elm, is whar I fust seed the big buck."

Placing his finger to his lips to indicate the necessity of caution and silence, the hunter, his companion, and the dog stepped into a thicket of willows, where they had an open view up and down the stream.

As they sat in their blind, Wellington, with a true hunter's instinct, looked inquiringly in all directions and studied the situation. Up-stream the winding river curved and was lost behind the projecting banks, while below it wound around and turned in again, leaving the hunter and his companion hidden on an out-jutting point. On the opposite shore, the place where at each previous time the buck had made his appearance, the bank stood up in tiny bluffs, cut sharp by the flowing river, or receded gradually from its bed. The tall slough-grass shone pale-yellow in the sunlight, while here and there the darkness of the deep forest was relieved by the whitened trunk of some birch-tree. In spots little willow patches extended into the stream, showing their green withes strongly in contrast with the grayish-brown of the huge elms which seemed to preponderate in the woods. In front of them a great sand-bar filled half the river width and raised its huge back three or four feet above the water's level.

Wellington and his companion had been seated for fully half an hour, and there were still no signs of the deer. Kirtley, who was unused to such long-continued silence, occasionally shook his head at Wellington, and at last whispered,—

"I hope yer hev'n't doubted me, Bill, 'cause

5*

what I told yer 'bout seein' the buck was the Lawd's truth."

Wellington did not doubt him, but thought perhaps it was his ill luck not to be able to get a shot. Ducks and geese were plentiful, and, hearing the swishing of wings, he turned his head in anticipation, when he saw a flock of Canada geese coming with set wings close down to the water's edge. Their great speed carried them beyond the bar, when they turned, swung over the blind, and settled on the sand. Kirtley touched Wellington's arm, and whispered,—

"Gall, Bill, gall! Did ye ever see sech imperdence? Why, when they sailed over us thet old gander kinder looked down at us es much es ter say, 'Hello, boys! What are ye doin' thar?'"

Wellington pressed his companion's arm and motioned with his head to the river. As he did so a flock of fully twenty mallards dropped softly into the stream and drifted lazily with the current within thirty yards of their blind. The ducks chatted, while an old drake uttered with musical vibration a mellow "M'amph" which words cannot describe. The sunlight playing on them produced a most pleasing picture of glowing colors. Wellington was a great lover of nature, and he was silently admiring the beauty of the scene when his arm was touched, and, much to his surprise, his companion whispered,—

"Thar, Bill, thar's what I call a purty sight.

In my 'pinion
iem birds. I
ly handsome,
p like bright
enin' himself,
ider stan's on
d! An' talk
on his head?
l. Then see
d his neck is
l water is all
:he sky, but I
ches'nut, an'
a maple-leaf
our colors in

ducks slowly
. As he fin-
nd was about
the opposite

don't move!
w flash at the
your head!

To the ordinary observer nothing would have
been visible, but Wellington had discovered something which made his heart bound, for above the
tops of the willow-twigs he saw a pair of wide-
spreading antlers, white and branched like a scraggy
burr-oak. He knew they must belong to an animal

what I told
Lawd's truth.
Wellington
haps it was hi
Ducks and g
swishing of w
tion, when he
with set win
Their great e
when they tur
on the sand.
and whispered
"Gall, Bill,
dence? Why
gander kinde
say, 'Hello, b
Wellington
motioned with
a flock of full
the stream and
thirty yards c
while an old
a mellow "M'
The sunlight
pleasing pictur
a great lover of nature, and he was silently admiring the beauty of the scene when his arm was
touched, and, much to his surprise, his companion
whispered,—
"Thar, Bill, thar's what I call a purty sight.

Talk about reflections on the water! In my 'pinion it ain't nowhar ter be compared ter them birds. I can't say es them ducks is partickerly handsome, 'cause yaller and brown don't show up like bright colors, but jes' look at thet drake preenin' himself, an' see how he flips his wings an' kinder stan's on the water. Look at him juke his head! An' talk 'bout colors! How's thet fur green on his head? Greener nor eny grass ye ever seed. Then see how it shines! An' thet white 'round his neck is whiter nor a parson's tie. Your still water is all right, Bill, reflectin' the colors from the sky, but I calkilate thet the green, an' white, an' ches'nut, an' purple, an' gray, an' the colors like a maple-leaf after the frost has teched it, beats your colors in the pond all holler."

While Kirtley was talking the ducks slowly drifted out of sight around the bend. As he finished his speech Wellington smiled, and was about to reply, when he gazed intently at the opposite shore, then hissed,—

"Silence, Kirtley! Don't speak! don't move! but look across the river in that willow flash at the foot of the bar. Careful; don't raise your head!

To the ordinary observer nothing would have been visible, but Wellington had discovered something which made his heart bound, for above the tops of the willow-twigs he saw a pair of wide-spreading antlers, white and branched like a scraggy burr-oak. He knew they must belong to an animal of immense size, and yet their owner did not move them, but, standing with body concealed, apparently thought he was fully hid from view. Wellington's finger was on the trigger-guard, and he waited and watched, as cool and as calm as if nothing were in sight or expectancy. Suddenly and quietly the willows parted, and the nose, then the head and antlers, of an enormous buck appeared. He was as shy as a wild turkey, and as timid as a maiden taking her first ocean bath. As his head and shoulders moved into sight he looked up, down, and across the river as if in expectation of danger, then, after becoming satisfied that there was nothing to be feared, he moved to the water's edge as if to cross. He stepped cautiously into the clear stream, bowed his long neck, daintily sipped the water, then, like a connoisseur tasting wine of ancient vintage, raised his head and thoughtfully swallowed it, as if inwardly passing on its merits.

Kirtley sat in joyous anticipation, for he felt certain Wellington would get a shot; the dog saw the deer, and his teeth chattered with excitement. The buck stopped and listened, as if he heard some sound, but nothing was audible except the rustle of the dry leaves as they fell to the earth, or the swishing of the water against an overhanging limb as the current moved it up and down.

Wellington now had a good chance to shoot, for the deer was in the water, and he saw that the course it was taking would bring it into an opening within fifty yards of him. As the buck reached the shore he was temporarily concealed behind a fallen tree, and as he walked into view his back was towards the hunters. Wellington, with rifle levelled, waited for him to turn his body or head, but fortune seemed to favor the deer, for he walked swiftly away, giving no chance to secure a side or head shot. Wellington whistled slightly to secure the animal's attention, but he only hastened his gait. Despairing of getting a better shot, he aimed at the head just below the butt of the horns and fired ; as the rifle cracked the buck dropped in his tracks, and Kirtley yelled and danced like an Indian, but Wellington sprang towards the deer, drew his knife, and touched its point to the animal's throat. The effect was electrical, and the buck sprang to his feet, transformed into a beast of the most deadly character. His nostrils dilated, and there issued from them blasts of defiance and anger. His hair was reversed and stood up like the bristles on a hog. His eyes flashed with a deadly light and seemed twice their natural size, while they changed rapidly to red and green.

Wellington recognized his danger. The dog, young but brave, seized the animal by the throat; but the enraged buck seemed to see in the hunter his natural enemy, and before Wellington could get to a sheltering tree sprang with lowered antlers towards him, and the impetuosity of the charge carried hunter, dog, and deer into the stream. As they struck the water the dog loosened his hold, then swam to the attack again. The water was shallow, perhaps four feet deep, which gave the buck a chance to exercise most, if not all, of his strength. As the dog neared the buck, the enraged animal stood on his hind legs, raised his forefeet, and with a sickening crash his sharp hoofs, with scarce a second's variation, clattered upon the noble animal's head, and with a low moan the faithful brute sank lifeless beneath the water.

While this was going on Wellington had seized a log, whose end had drifted on the shore, and pulled it in front of him. He was none too quick, for now the maddened brute started towards him. It was the first time this king of the forest had been brought to bay, and all the animosity and fearlessness which had been concentrated in him for years suddenly broke forth. He surged the water before him, then, as if on land, he beat it in his pawing till it frothed and foamed with the whiteness of snow. His eyes were now a greenish-red and blazed with anger, while there was inter-mittently ejected from his nostrils a " p-shew" like steam escaping from a leaking valve.

Wellington had been in close quarters before, and waited coolly for the attack, intending to keep the log between him and his enemy. The buck attempted to climb over this barrier, and as he did Wellington struck at his throat with his knife, making a deep incision on the animal's neck, which only increased its anger. It then tried to jump over the log, but the water held it back; again it attempted to climb over, and as it did Wellington seized it by its antlers, pulled its nose beneath the surface and tried to drown it, but the animal seemed possessed of endless strength, for it raised its head and shook him off. Again it tried to get at him over the log, and, infuriated himself, he struck at it again and again with his knife, but the buck seemed to bear a charmed life. Determined to end the contest, Wellington advanced. The buck sprang at him, and as he tried to avoid the plunge of its horns its sharp hoof struck his hand, cutting it to the bone, and his knife flew spinning from him and fell, yards away, into the river. A dull feeling of despair came over Wellington.

-

CHAPTER V.

THE BATTLE IN THE RIVER.

" Hand
Grasps hand, eye lights eye in good friendship,
And great hearts expand,
And grow one in the sense of this world's life."
                                ROBERT BROWNING.

KIRTLEY saw what had happened, and shouted
to him to keep his courage up.

" Shoot him !" cried Wellington.

Kirtley seized his rifle, levelled it, and the ham-
mer fell with a dull snap.

" Load it quick, for heaven's sake !" cried Wellington.   But his heart sank within him as Kirtley
replied,—

" Can't do it, Bill, 'cause you hev the powder-
horn 'round your neck."

At these words Wellington knew that unless he
could drown the buck or tire him out he must lose
his own life.   The great animal was becoming exhausted, but the cold had chilled Wellington until
he had lost half his strength.   Time and again he
tried to keep the brute's nose beneath the water,
but each time was shaken of.   He knew the battle
must be decided soon, or, chilled and enfeebled as

he was by his long fight and by the cold water, he would be at the mercy of the mad beast. As the buck tried again to clamber over the log, Wellington threw his whole weight onto its antlers. Man and beast struggled and fought, now up, now down. The log floated from them. Still they fought on. At last, with an awful shriek, the buck tore from the grasp of the hunter, and both man and beast saw there was no barrier between them. Breathless, and scarcely able to stand, Wellington knew his time had come. Swifter than a thousand visions his past life flew before him, but above all was the thought of his wife and helpless babes. The buck jumped towards him, with bloody froth dripping from its mouth; his cruel hoofs were raised to strike. Wellington feebly raised his hands above his head to protect it and closed his eyes, but at that moment a quick report of a rifle broke from the opposite shore,—the buck swayed, his head drooped to one side, and fell with a heavy splash. Wellington feebly staggered backward, then, with a last effort to catch himself, fell forward fainting, with his arms across the body of the dead buck, his face as white as snow in the shining sun. A dark form shot with incredible speed from the shore, and the apparently lifeless hunter was tenderly lifted in the arms of Manulito.

During the final struggle Kirtley ran up and down the bank like a wild man, wringing his hands, crying, swearing, and praying, and when

6

he saw Manulito raise the head of Wellington from the carcass of the buck, he waved his hand and danced and yelled with joy.

"Make fire quick," cried Manulito, and never was a fire started sooner.

As the Indian came ashore, towing the inanimate form of the hunter and the dead deer, Kirtley ran to meet him. "Is he dead?" he asked, sorrowfully.

"No; only fainted and very weak," replied the Indian.

At this Kirtley laughed and cried alternately, "Oh, Manulito, you are an angel,—a brick,—a warrior,—a cuss! Lawd, but I'll never furgit this act yer done ter-day."

The Indian simply replied, "More fire; give Manulito fire-water."

As he received it from Kirtley, he poured a few drops into Wellington's mouth. The effect was quickly apparent, for the unconscious man stirred, opened his eyes momentarily in doubt, then, as if understanding all, threw a soul of love into one look which he gave Manulito, and then closed his eyes again. They built a wall of brush around the fire except at his feet. Kirtley gave him his heavy coat, they rubbed him, and in a short time he looked at them both with that fond look they knew so well.

"Where is the buck?" said he.

Manulito replied, "My brother shall see him."

Saying this they dragged the huge beast to his feet.

"Let me open him up," said Kirtley. "I hev an ole grudge ag'in' him, an' it'll be heap o' satisfaction to git partly even with him in thet way."

He deftly took out the inwards, and as he did so something hard dropped into his hand. He looked at it, then handed it to the Indian, saying,—

"Here, Manulito, is your bullet thet sped true to the heart an' saved your best friend."

As Kirtley said this, the Indian took the misshapen bullet and handed it to Wellington, saying,—

"See! my brother, see!"

As Wellington looked his eyes filled with tears, for there, plainly to be seen, was the "W" he had marked. It was the bullet he had dug from the tree and had given to Manulito in the forest. He put it in his hunting-shirt, while the Indian said,—

"When the ground is ploughed in the spring-time and the seed sown, the warm sun makes it grow to ripened grain; so evil deeds, when forgiven in a brother's heart, are things the Great Manitou does not overlook. When the Gray Eagle left his cabin this morning Manulito did not intend to hunt this day, but as the sun rose in the heavens and he saw how beautiful was the morning, his heart longed for the stillness of the woods, and he struck the trail which leads to the Wapsie far below the ford. His footsteps were aimless; his heart was light, his head clear; and the birds seemed never

to have sung so sweetly or the winds to have blown
so musically as to-day. At one time he leaned
against a tree while he looked on the smooth
waters, and in fancy he saw himself a pappoose
again, and lived among the birds and flowers as he
did when a child in years gone by. Then in the
waters he read, as if written in a book, his whole
life, and he saw the fate of his people. He wandered through the bottom-land down to the mouth
of Silver Creek, and as he did, a buzzard sailed
high in air, but fell dead at the report of his rifle.
Then he loaded his gun, and, when too late, for he
intended always to keep it, he saw that he had
placed in the muzzle the marked bullet. He could
not withdraw it, and so forced it down. It seemed
at this time as if the day was growing chill, for the
blood in the veins of Manulito was cold. The sun
was bright, the air warm, and he could not understand. A crow flew over his head, crying, ' Caw,
caw!' and its cry grated on the ears of Manulito,
for it sounded to him like the voices of the children
in the village the day they stoned his dog. It
seemed as if some great danger lurked in the
woods, and the wind through the tree-tops was like
the lonesome wailing of the squaw when her warrior has been brought to her, dead. Manulito
looked around, but saw and heard nothing. Then,
as he stood still and hearkened so silently that he
ceased to breathe and his heart almost stopped beat-
ing, a faint sound reached his ears, and in spite

of the noise of the chattering birds, he knew it was a human voice. The blood rushed like fire through his veins, and the winds shrieked to him, 'The Gray Eagle! The Gray Eagle! To the ford! To the ford!' Swifter than the hawk darts after its prey, swifter than the tiger rushes to defend her young, swifter than the antelope bounds over the plain, Manulito sprang forward. At other times he would have thought this speed faster than the wind, but now it seemed as if he could not run, yet so swiftly he flew that trees and bushes fled from him and went backward, and he seemed to be standing still. He ran through thickets, through the tangled grass, through the water in the bayous, leaped over fallen trees, ran thus for miles, but never grew tired, for ever behind him and spurring him on was the voice of the Good Spirit in his ears, saying, 'To the ford! To the ford! To save your brother!' Then as he neared the ford he heard the voice of the Gray-beard, and swift as the frightened deer he hurried on, when in the bend he saw his brother in the water. Like the beast maddened when she finds her cub in danger, Manulito seemed not to touch the ground, and when the buck thought he had the Gray Eagle in his power the rifle of Manulito belched forth, and the bullet, guided by the good Manitou, sank deep into the heart of the big buck, and the prayer of Manulito was answered, for *this day* he has in part paid the debt he owes his white brother."

"Paid in part!" yelled Kirtley to the Indian.
"Why, consarn it, what yer've done for Bill ought
ter pay him all yer owe him, an' I know Bill well
'nough ter know thet arter this day's work, an' the
way yer saved his life, he will give yer a receipt in
full fur ev'rything yer owe him.   Ef he don't,
why, I'll be durned ef I won't pay the balance
myself. 'Nother thing, Manulito: now, yer know I
ain't got any love fur an Injun, nor never had, but
no white man could hev done hisself prouder than
yer did yourself ter-day. An' when the time comes
when you air goin' ter be tried fur murder, or
what's wuss, hoss-stealin', ef Bill don't defend yer
free gratis fur nothin', an' get yer clar, an' save your
good character,—don't make no difference whether
yer be guilty or not,—he ain't the man an' lawyer
thet I know he is."

Wellington replied, "Any obligations Manulito
owed me are more than cancelled; he knows it,—
you know it.   There are times," he said, as his
voice grew husky with emotion, "when words fail
to express a man's feelings, and the heart leaves its
hiding and fills his throat so that he cannot speak.
I do not know that life is any sweeter to me than
to any one else,—indeed, I did not know how sweet
it was until now that I have so nearly lost it.
Manulito has renewed it for me, restored it to my
wife and children, and here, Kirtley, in your presence, in the presence of my *true friend*, Manulito,
and in the presence of the ever-living God," and

he raised his eyes reverently to the vault of heaven, " I promise this day will never be forgotten."

For a few moments each gazed intently into the fire in deep thought. The Indian was first to speak, and said,—

" The sun is weary of the day and will hide from it. See! he will soon sink behind the great elm-trees. The birds rise in their evening flight, and we must start for the home of my brother."

They hung the huge animal to a tree to keep the wolves from it, and, arranging that Kirtley should go after it on the morrow, they started on their homeward trip.

As the twilight deepened, they bade " Good-night" to Mrs. Kirtley, after they had partaken of the generous meal which she had offered them. When they parted at the door the moon had risen and was shedding the softest light on all the surroundings. Kirtley followed them to the wagon-road. He had left his hat at the house, and his gray hair shone like frosted silver in the mellow light. As they parted, he took Wellington's hand in both of his, and said,—

" Lawd, Bill, but I'm glad it came out right, an' ter-morrer yer'll see me in the village in the mornin'. Watch fur us,—me an' the oxen an' the buck! I would bring the ole woman too, but yer know how 'tis, wimmen hes their places, an' a woman hes no business 'round when her husband is celebratin'. Celebratin'?" said he, as he roared and slapped his leg at the thought of it. "Why, boys, the *whole village* ain't goin' ter be none too big fur me when me an' the big buck comes ter town."

The moon had ascended high into the dome of the sky, and the two hunters were walking side by side. At first, as was his wont, the Indian led, Wellington following in his trail, but soon they walked together. The night was clear; the stars shone feebly, paled by the brighter moon, and the frost glittered on the bushes and blades of grass. A contented silence fell on both men as they thought over the events of the departed day.

As they walked along in close proximity, Wellington's hand dropped to his side, and as it did, it touched his companion's. They spoke not, but a gentle pressure, such as a woman confidingly gives to the man she loves, passed between them, and as they looked in one another's faces their eyes shone with a love more than fraternal, and the silent moon brightened the scene and witnessed their secret pledge of life-long friendship.

Next morning, before break of day, Kirtley was astir; and, having breakfasted and fed his oxen, he pulled his coon-skin cap well over his ears, drew tighter the belt which encircled his waist, yoked his oxen to the wagon, and started for the settlement.

The stars were glittering and the day seemed far off, but the still, frosty air of the morning carried for miles the " creak, creak" of the wagon and the cheery tones of Kirtley as he encouraged the team. Now and then he glanced into the wagon where the huge buck lay quiet in death, and then he would break out into spasmodic speeches, exclaiming,—

"Well, I declar' ter goodness, but thet wuz a close shave fur Bill! An' ef it hadn't ben fur me an' the Injun, there's no tellin' whar Bill wud be now,—perhaps tryin' lawsuits in the lan' of Canaan or sum other furrin country.

"Cours', cours'," he continued, "I didn't do ez much ez the Injun in one sense; but at the same time, ef the praayers uv an old sinner 'mounted to much, then I did a heap o' good, fur, stretch my gallus ef I didn't pray powerful hard thet the Lawd or sum un wud step in an' help Bill outen thet scrape. Cours', I wuz kinder mix-cumfuddled an' sufferin' with nervous prostrashun, an' didn't know jes' wot ter say, or how ter go at it ter make a praayer, seein' ez how I hevn't sed enny fur a long time, so I sed 'Now I lay me down——.' Then I kinder cum ter myself an' tho't wot a fool I wuz to think o' layin' down fur a minnit when the buck wuz arter Bill. So I kinder shrugged my shoulders, an' sed, fast an' loud, 'O Lawd, we thank thee for the food——.'. Then I cum ter myself an' tho't wot a fool I wuz ter be thankful fur food, when the food wuz havin' the bulge on my best frien', an' wuz liable ter make *him* food fur fishes, mud-turtles, and sech-like reptiles. Talk 'bout a man, when he's drownin', thinkin' over all his sins in a minnit! Why, I tho't uv mine in half thet time, an' I wuz jes' goin' ter try 'nother praayer w'en the Injun fired an' sprung inter the water ter save Bill. Then I jes' drapped onter my marrers, clasped my han's together, jes' ez yer see innercent babies in the picters, an' sed, ' Thank the Lawd! thank the Lawd!'

"I'll tell yer what, Jerry," continued he, addressing his conversation to the ox nearest him, " yer ain't human, yer can't talk,—leastwise in our language,—but, et ther same time, yer all right, an' I ain't afeerd ter trust yer, cause ef yer don't agree with me, at any rate yer won't mix-cumfuddle me with dictionary wuds like sum uv 'em does in the settlement. An' wot I·wuz goin' ter say wuz this: thet fine wuds be all right, butiful praayers in the churches, but w'en a man wants the Lawd's help in downright airnest, wuds fail ter cum, an' he sez, ' Lawd, save me!' An' ef the Lawd concludes to enter inter the contrac' the man is saved, an' his thanks is given in mighty few wuds. Now, in cours', ef I hed ben eddicated like Bill or the parsin at the settlement, I wud hev given thanks in meny butiful wuds; but, doncher know, Jerry, thet I thinks the Lawd jedges by the man's heart, an' whether he means wot he sez. Ef he does mean it, purty language don't count. An' I feel sure my thanks wuz ez 'ceptable ez if I hed sed 'em in the butifulest wuds."

The day had commenced to break, and the gray in the east was tinged here and there by the reflection from the rising sun. Kirtley seemed in a talkative mood, and, as the faithful oxen trudged along, the old man patted his patient listener on the shoulders, and continued:

" Yes, Jerry, fine wuds air nice to keep in stock; they air like fresh goods at the store : they air allus pushed out whar they'll do most good; but good, plain wuds is wot I like. In cours', ez yer know, I use thet kind. I admit, sometimes w'en I want ter be pertick'ly 'mpressive, I use cuss wuds. But then I'm used ter it, an' it don't do enny harm, an' ter me it surely does a heap uv good, fur it makes the wuds before an' arter the cuss wud pecoolarly strong an' 'mphatic. In cours', ef I was eddicated, I don't s'pose I wud swar, fur then I wud hev wuds enough without rizzortin' to perfanity.

" Bill sez I wud a make a good lawyer. Now, Bill is a good frien' uv mine, an' he wudn't 'tentially deceive me; but fur me ter be a lawyer? No, thanks, Jerry. As they say in the settlement, ' I 'preciate yer kind invertation, but pleas' 'cept my regrets.' I've seed a good deal o' law, an' Bill will tell yer thet thar's hardly ever a lawsuit tried 'less I am on hand, either as plaintiff or defendant; an' ef thar is no chance fur me ez either, then I make a mighty good juror. I tell you, Jerry, what I've seed in courts wud make a book, a whole book with a supplement throwed in. Don't yer remember wot Sampson said ter the Philistines? Cours' you don't. Well, he said, 'Truth is mighty and will pervail.' Now, Jerry, 'tween you an' me, Sampson wuz off,—clear off,—though I want ter give him the benefit of ther doubt, an', ez the lawyers sez, 'Will admit, fur the sake of ther argoo-ment, thet wot the sed Sampson sed wuz true.' But I hev seed too much uv law ter be han-swaggled inter believin' that truth is mighty an' will pervail. It depen's. It depen's on the lawyer an' the jury. Give me a good lawyer an' a fat pocket-book, an' a day ter git 'quainted with the jury, an' I'm bettin' thet ther man thet sues me fur damages will hev the costs ter pay. Perhaps I wud make a good lawyer, Jerry," continued the old man, "an' Bill sez thet my eloquence wud carry me through the jury. It may be so! it may be so! Et the same time, I wud rather be plaintiff or defendant, an' let the *jury* carry me through."

As the old man rounded the bend, within a mile of the village, he looked at the surrounding coun-try as if anticipating the approach of some one, and, seeing no one, came to a halt,—a proceeding which was most acceptable to the patient oxen.

CHAPTER VI.

UNCLE RASTUS.

" There is in souls a sympathy with sounds,
And as the mind is pitch'd, the ear is pleas'd
With melting airs or martial, brisk or grave;
Some chord in unison with what we hear
Is touch'd within us, and the heart replies."

COWPER.

" FUNNY !" exclaimed the old man. " Funny thet ole Uncle Rastus don't show up. He surely got my message ter meet me here, et ther curve in the road, et sunrise, an' bring with him Sweet Marjorum, the sorrel hoss thet I bought in Lexin'ton nigh onter six months sence."

Then the old man chuckled, and took a fresh chew of tobacco, as he muttered to himself,—

" An' won't they be supprised ! Sent the ole man home broke, las' summer, did they ? Well, I'm thinkin' thet this day the tables will be turned, an' when the gentlemen from on the Mississipp' look fur Kirtley, they'll find him. Find him !" he ejaculated. " An' w'en they do, the ole man will be on top. I ain't got much ter bet, I ain't got much ter bet," said Kirtley, as he laughingly patted his pockets and exposed a belt which seemed filled

D   7

with coin. "Oh, no, I ain't got much ter bet. I'll make it interestin' fur some of 'em."

At this moment there trembled on the still, calm air the mellow piping of the quail. The old man answered the call, when, a short distance from him, a rustle was heard in the dense hazel brush. As the bushes parted, there was exposed a face so jolly and so indicative of good nature that no one ever gazed on it without being insensibly drawn towards its owner. The face was black, with a fringe of grizzly whiskers. A pair of spectacles resting on the owner's nose seemed more for ornament than for use, as he continually looked over their rim. The head was covered with a hat of ancient origin, which constant use had changed from a genteel slouch to a cone-shape,—one which successive seasons of constant wear had converted to its present shape. Such was the first appearance of Uncle Rastus, a negro universally beloved and respected. As he saw Kirtley, his mouth opened, and while the woods echoed with the melody of his laughter, he exclaimed,—

"Heigh-ho! Brer Kirtley!" Then bowing and touching his hat with genteel chivalry, he continued; "How yo' is? Whar yo' ben dis long come back? Ah was heah sum time 'go, an' 'lowed yo'd cum et sun-up. Den, Ah 'lowed dis niggah bettah get little res', an' w'en Ah braced a saplin' wid m' back en' tuk one little snooze, Ah luked up, en' dar war de oxen, en', sho' nuff, dar yo' is too. Ah's mighty glad ter see yo', Brer Kirtley, en' hopes yo' en' de missus am well."

"Come out, Rastus! Come out!" exclaimed Kirtley, "an' bring the hoss. 'Scuse me, Rastus, fur quotin' Spokeshare, but I'm feelin' pertickly good this mornin', an' ef yer don't objec', I'll jes' say, as I've heard Bill say, 'My hoss! My hoss! My kingdom fur a hoss!'"

At this the old man laughed immoderately, as if it brought back pleasant recollections; while Uncle Rastus broke into an explosive guffaw that would have set a crowd of boys wild with laughter.

"Heah yo' is, boss! Heah yo' is!" he exclaimed, as he placed the halter-strap into the hands of Kirtley. "Heah is yo' hoss, an' a bettah hoss nevah looked troo a bridle. Yo' say, Brer Kirtley, yo' gibs yo' kingdom fo' a hoss. Don' yo' do it, 'caus' yo' don' hab ter. Dis yer animile, dis yer Sweet Mahjorum dat yo' has in yo' possess'n, can't be beat. Ah tole yo'," continued Uncle Rastus, "dat f'um de fust time Ah sot eyes on 'im 'e won dis yer ole h'aht ob mine. He knows so much,—no nonsense 'bout 'im! No rambunksh'-ness! Jus' ez gentle ez a lam', jus' like a kitten. 'Sides, Brer Kirtley, Ah's 'customed ter talk ter 'im jus' like 'e one ob de chillun, en' 'e do what Ah spec's ob him. Dat little pick'ninny mine, dat Eph, 'e en' Sweet Mahjorum great frien's. Ebery mawnin' w'en Eph go out en' ride 'im, 'e talk ter 'im jus' like 'e talk ter w'ite folks, 'tel de hoss unde'stan'

all 'e say. Yest'd'y mawnin' Ah tho't bes' ter speed
de hoss,—'e is nevah hit wid a gad, needah does we
use spuhs,—en' Eph, he ride 'im. W'en de hoss
cum nigh me, hit 'peared ter me ez ef hit wa'n't no
hoss, but jus' a sorrel ghost dat wuz goin' lighter
an' faster dan de win'. W'en 'e pass me, Ah says
ter Eph, 'Hi, dah! Let 'im out!' At dat, Eph
ben's ober 'is neck, en' de hoss go so fas' Ah tink
sho' 'im no hoss, jus' shadder. Den, a'terwuds, Ah
asks Eph, ' Wha dat hoss go so fas' pas' me ?' Him
say, ' Sweet Mahjorum like sugah, an' w'en we pass
you, Eph whispah in eah, Run, Sweet Mahjorum,
run! Hay in de mangah—sugah on hay—waitin'
fo' you.' Den hoss run so fas' dat Eph ha'dly
keep in saddle."

Uncle Rastus was very demonstrative in his
manner, and added to it by frequent gesticulation;
but Kirtley was a keen observer, and noticed with
pleasure the favorable reports as to the speed and
condition of his horse. The previous summer
Kirtley had been taken in by some professional
horsemen, and knowing that the same parties would
be present to-day and would try to repeat their
former successes, he had anticipated their coming,
and was prepared to entertain them. The fact of
his having this horse was kept secret, and only he,
Uncle Rastus, and the latter's son knew of its
presence.

Kirtley hitched the horse to the wagon, and
cautioning ·Uncle Rastus as to what part he was

to take, bade him good-by for the time, telling him to be on hand without fail at the hour agreed on for the races. The speed of the horse was well known to Kirtley, for he had seen it in many private trials, but Uncle Rastus wanted to impress on the owner's mind that *he* had developed the speed, and that he could vouch for the horse's ability to win.

As Kirtley started down the road, Uncle Rastus took a northeasterly direction towards his home.

Uncle Rastus was a character, and he was of such a disposition that the whole world was to him one eternal source of enjoyment. The disappointments that are constantly met with in life were lessons which taught him, by contrast, to be thankful for the benefits he enjoyed. When death overtook some one he loved, his grief was of that explosive kind which threatened to result fatally; but after abundant wringing of hands, copious shedding of tears, and violent outbursts of sorrow, he always returned to his normal state, which was one of sweet contentment with his condition in life. As he often said,—

" Wha' fo', chillun, sh'd yo' cry wid grief 'caus' de Lawd punishes yo'? Yo' can't allus 'spec ter eat widout de cook sometimes spilin' de meat. Don' complain 'caus' yo' gits too much salt in yo' broth, but be t'ankful dat de Lawd 'mits de bees ter make honey, and yo' knows whar de bee-tree am."

7*

His mind was full of odd sayings. He was always ready to extend rough but touching words of sympathy to the afflicted, and never at a loss for wit when repartee was essential to defend himself; and the native humor with which he was known to be always supplied warned his disputant that a prompt reply would be forthcoming.

He was short and very stout, and he often remarked that "if de Lawd had made him a little biggah roun' en' a little sho'tah, he would be no good nohow." Then he would continue:

"But Ah's got no complaint comin', fo' de wintah has done got ter be ver' cold w'en mah ole bones suffah."

He was often asked where he came from, but his answer was always evasive.

"Wha' fo' yer wan's ter know dat, honey? Ah 'low Ah's heah, en' cum ter stay. De woodchuck, en' de 'possum, en' de 'coon am in de woods. Wha' makes de diff'unce whar dey cum f'um? G'long, now, don' yo' boddah yo' noggin 'bout me. Ax no quest'ns en' I'll tole yo' no lies."

Then, seeing he had the best of his inquisitor, he would break into a hearty "Yah! yah!" which would end in a sizzle between his teeth.

When he first came to the settlement his worldly possessions consisted of a pack on his back and his clothes tied inside a huge red bandanna, while his boy trudged at his heels.

He was constantly advising this boy about the

evils of the world, and especially those to be found
at the settlement. Wellington had taken a fancy
to him, and had permitted him to erect a cabin on
a corner of the farm for himself and boy. Uncle
Rastus was a frequent visitor, in fact a daily one, at
the farm-house; and he loved Mrs. Wellington and
her two children with a devotion which was almost
idolatry.

He did not know his age, and when asked would
reply,—

" Wha, bress yo', honey, Ah can't confo'm eny
def'nit' idee. Ah 'specs hit wuz a long time 'go
Ah wuz bawn, but Ah disremembah de time. But
Ah 'membah hit wuz a'ter de Rev'lutiona'y wah.
Fac', mus' ben a'ter dat, 'caus' Ah 'membah w'en
jus' big 'nuff ter fight flies in m'lasses bar'l, mah
mammy useter talk 'bout Washin'ton en' dose oder
ginerals w'ich fit fo' dis kentry."

Like all darkeys, he was passionately fond of
music, and scarcely a night passed that he and his
son, isolated in the little cabin, did not, with violin
and banjo, while the happy hours away. Uncle
Rastus had a voice which blended the flute-toned
harmony of the tenor with the mellowness of the
alto, while his boy inherited his mother's voice,—a
voice of such singular purity and sweetness that it
thrilled through the listener, and when, moved as
if by inspiration, he raised his voice to the full
measure of its strength, the birds in the forest
caught its tones and softly twittered, as·if fearing

to lose the notes of a voice far sweeter than their own.

The boy did not realize his great gift. He loved to sing, but he did not know the surpassing sweetness of his own music. As yet, his voice had not changed, and was a perfect soprano. His father forbade his singing for the men at the village, and when any one remonstrated, saying that the boy might earn pennies by his singing, the old man would reply,—

"Dis yer pick'ninny 'longs ter me. Ah see 'im git clo'es ter weah; de Lawd en' Mars' Wellin'ton fu'nish de meat, en' de yarth fu'nish de bread. Ah 'low we git 'long all right widout mah boy singin' fe' men who don' 'preciate. 'Sides," continued Uncle Rastus, " w'en yo'-uns is sick, or yo'-uns's frien's, or et de chu'ch on Sunday, den yo' heahs mah boy."

The night before the day of the races, Uncle Rastus and his boy had finished supper, the dishes were washed, and the old man sat in the gloaming smoking his pipe. The little log cabin presented a weird aspect. It seemed almost devoid of furniture, there being only a bedstead, two chairs, and a rough pine table. The fire in the fireplace had died down to steady coals. The old man was in deep thought. Suddenly he raised his head, and, turning to the boy, said,—

"Honey, Ah 'low dat fiah am gittin' low. Put on some dem hick'ry knots en' punch dem coals mo'."

The boy did as requested, then picked up a book and began reading by the bright light of the fire. Uncle Rastus watched him with pleased intentness for a few moments, then said,—

"Strikes me, honey, yo' is consid'ably abstracted in de p'rusal ob dat book. Am jus' cu'us 'nuff ter ax yo' wot am de subjec' w'ich 'peahs to prognosticate yo' 'tention."

The boy closed the book, and said,—

"Robinson Crusoe."

"Golly!" ejaculated the old man. "Dat am a great book, sho' 'nuff. Missus read dat book ter me yeahs en' yeahs ago, 'fo' yo' wuz bawned. Ah tink dat Cruiser great man. He kin' ob a harmit; but de Lawd wuz wid 'im, honey, de Lawd wuz wid 'im, en' in all 'is trials en' tribullations de Lawd didn't go back on 'im, but 'bided wid 'im. We kinder Cruisers, don' yo' t'ink so, Eph? Only but our dog en' our cat done gone en' died. But, honey," continued the old man, as he laid his hands affectionately on the boy's head, "Ah bress de good Lawd dat yo' is spa'ed ter me, fo' ef de Lawd done gone en' tuk yo' f'um me, sho' as dere is 'gaito's in de Alabam', Ah would pray ev'y day dat Gabr'l would blow his hawn, fo', sho' 'nuff, Ah wouldn't wanter lib no mo'. But, Eph, Ah feel kind o' lonesome dis ebenin'; don' offun feel dat way, leastwise don' show it. An' dat's wot yo' will fin' ez yo' grow oldah, dat de man who is allus tellin' how bad 'e feels w'en 'e loses 'is wife, isn't

f

de man who suffahs de mos'. Shaller watah make
big noise, but de deep watah, 'e keep quiet. S'pose
yo' git out de fiddle en' yo' banjo, en' let's hav'
some music."

Eph did as he was told, but the melancholy feeling which seemed to have control of Uncle Rastus
had not touched the boy, for he gave a peculiar
sliding motion, which ended in the merriest kind
of a jig. He looked knowingly and pleadingly
at the old man, begging with his eyes for what
he wanted,—viz., an accompaniment with clapped
hands and a perfect beat of the foot. Uncle Rastus shook his head sorrowfully, and said,—

"No! no! honey! Yo' is 'titled ter hit, sho', but
mah h'aht don' crave fo' dat kin' ob music ter-
night, en' Ah don' want ter do wot mah h'aht
don' 'gree ter."

As the boy seated himself, he handed the violin
to his father, and continued to tinkle on the banjo,
humming a jig to himself. Uncle Rastus, by reason
of the discord of the sounds, was unable to tune his
instrument; and at last, out of patience, he laid the
violin across his knee and looked at the boy in disgust. Eph saw his error, and made haste to apologize, but he was speedily interrupted by the old
man, who said,—

"Yo', dar, Ephrum! Wha yo' done gone en'
chuned yo' banjo all de time w'en Ah wuz tryin'
ter make de connection 'tween mah A en' E string.
Yo' knows f'um prev'us 'xperiunce dat dar is

nothin' wot miscomposes me mo' den dat same
t'ing. Now, ef yo' t'ink Ah'm bleeged ter s'bmit
ter dis 'novation ter de rules ob dis house, Ah stan'
c'rect'd."

The boy showed his repentance in his looks. He
also saw the forgiveness accorded him, for his
father gave him the fond smile he anticipated and
loved so well. They played together, the father
leading, the son sustaining him with a brilliant
accompaniment; but tiring of instrumental music,
Uncle Rastus nodded to Eph, and they sang, their
voices blending with the harmony derived from
practice and natural sweetness,—

"Oh, whar sh'll we go w'en de great day comes,
  Wid de blowin' ob de trumpets en' de bangin' ob de drums?
  How many po' sinners 'll be kotched out late,
  En' fin' no latch ter de golden gate?

"No use fo' ter wait twel ter-morrer!
  De sun mus'n't set on yer sorrer,
  Sins ez sharp ez a bamboo-brier.
  Oh, Lawd! fetch de mo'ners up higher."

"Dat's true, Eph! Dat's true!" exclaimed
Uncle Rastus, "De great ques'n ob de day am,
'Whar shall we go w'en de great day cums?' Ah
'low whar we go depen's on wot we do yer, an'
Ah want yo' not ter 'sociate wid po' w'ite trash,
fo' now dat Ah toles yo' ob de or'gin ob de cullud
race, yo' 'll bress de Lawd dat yo' wuz bawned
black. Jus' lis'en en' Ah 'll tell yo' de story ob

de or'gin ob de cullud race. Yo' unnerstan', honey," continued Uncle Rastus, as he turned, sitting corner-wise on his chair, and throwing his left arm over the back of it for better support and to obtain a nonchalant position,—" yo' unnerstan's dat de story ob de or'gin ob de cullud race ain't ter be *foun'* in *books*, but hab cum down f'um gineration to gineration,—passin' f'um fadder ter son,— an' Ah gibs hit ter yo' ez hit wuz done tole me yaars en' yaars ergo. Dar am no disputin' de troof ob it, 'caus' Ah pussn'ly knowed er man mo'n er hundred yaars ole, who hed kep' trac' ob de cullud race, en' 'e wuz willin' ter swar ter hits troof.

"En' in ordah ter gib de whole story, Ah mus' ax yer 'tenshun, en' ax yer ter trabble back wif me ter de beginnin' ob de wuld, leastwise nigh onter hit. Ez yer will know, in dem times dere wuz a flood. Dis yer flood wuz bro't 'bout by de cussedness ob de peeple. De Lawd, he 'commodated dem in great meny ways, but dey didn't 'preciate hit, en' all wuz kinder coltish en' didn't seem ter t'ink dat sum day dey mout be punished. Co'se, dey wuz too big ter be whipped like chillun. 'Sides, de Lawd wuz busy 'rangin' t'ings so ez ter get de wuld runnin' smood en' right, en' a'ter dey hed run 'long, en' kep' gettin' sassier en' sassier, de Lawd done grown tired sech foolishness, en' he sen' fo' a gemmun by de name ob Noah. F'um wot Ah heah tell ob dis man Noah, de Lawd make good s'lection. So de Lawd say ter Noah, ' Noah, Ah's done been tired ob dis rambunksh'ness ob dese peeple. Dey is too big ter get a'ter wid a bar'l-stave, en' de co'se ob de law am too slow. Ah has 'cluded ter sen' a shower ter dis yarth, dat 'll 'stonish dem all. Yo' am all right; Ah got nuffin' gin yo'.' All dis time Noah ain't sayin' nuffin', jus' keep still an' lis'en. So de Lawd direc' Noah ter buil' er house, en' yo' knows, honey, de Bible sez hit wuz a yark. So de Lawd tol' Brer Noah wha' ter fin' de wood, who ter hire ter buil' de yark, en' gib 'im sp'ific d'recshuns, so dar can be no m'stake. But yo' knows, Ephrum, all 'bout dat, an' yo' hab read in yo' Bible Brer Noah wuz a little slow in buil'in' de yark. But de Lawd wuz pashun', en' sed, ' Peg 'long, Brer Noah! Peg 'long! Yo' is doin' all right. Ah 'low dere won't be eny rain twel yo' is reddy.' So las' de yark wuz done, en' Brer Noah announc' dat fac'. Now, lots ob dese yer smart fellers laff et Brer Noah, en' loaf 'roun' de yark en' made remarks. ' Hi dah! Brer Noah! Wot yo' goin' ter do wid dat big boat on dry lan'?' Brer Noah 'e ain't sayin' nuffin', jus' keep on en' min' 'is bizness. At las', on Chuseday, all wuz ready, Brer Noah hed eb'ry-t'ing in de yark, all de fambly, de fowls, de snakes, en' de animiles, jus' ez de Lawd d'rected. Den hit 'menced ter sprinkle. Hit hedn't rained fo' long time, so de peeple outside de yark—de onb'leebers —'menced ter laff en' say, ' Dis am de boss wedder!

8

jus' de t'ing fo' de cawn! But Brer Noah 'e in
yark, 'e ain't sayin' nuffin', but keep up big
t'inkin'."

At this time, the boy who had waited patiently
for some clue that would lead him to think that
his father was going to disclose what he had
promised, remarked,—

" 'Scuse me, daddy, but wot's dis ter do wid de
or'gin ob de cullud race?"

The old man straightened back in his chair, apparently much hurt at the interruption, and feelingly responded,—

" Pashuns am a jule, en' Ah's sorry dat a *son ob
mine* should interrup' 'is po' ole dad, w'en de dad
am relatin' an ebent w'ich is ob de greates' im-
portans. Ah's too ole ter talk nonsense, en' w'en
Ah talks ter yo', allus b'ar in min' dat de ole man
am all right, en' dat de ruffes' kernel kivers de
sweetes' meat ob de nut. Yo' knows, yo' does, dat
de harder 'tis fo' yo' ter get de sugah f'um de bar'l,
de sweeter 'tis fo' yo' w'en yo' does get it."

Then looking into the fire as if to collect his
scattered thoughts, he took his spectacles from his
nose, wiped them with his handkerchief, returned
them to their former position, and said, "Jee-
himiny! how hit did rain! Sho' nuff, honey, hit
cum down so fas' dat cawn crap all sp'ilt; eb'ry-
t'ing ruined, en' de yarth couldn't soak up all de
water. Whoo! what a lot ob water! Eb'rybody
drowned outside de yark. Noah den see 'im all

right. Hit rained fo'ty days en' fo'ty nights, in-
cludin' Fourt' ob July. Noah kinder hated dis,
'cause 'e wanted ter entertain de folks wid fiahwu'ks. Now!" exclaimed the old man,—" now,
yo' soon heah de or'gin ob de cullud race. Ter be
sho', fo'ty days en' fo'ty nights am a long time,
en' de folks in de yark got kinder lonesum'-like,—
dey didn't hev cards in dem days,—so de men
ha'dly knew wot ter do ebenin's, en' de ladies,
dey couldn't git out ter see de lates' styles, so dey
wuz handicapt on suthin' ter talk erbout. Co'se,
dey talked about de wedder, dar wuz plenty ob
dat, but ez Missus Noah sed ter her dawter, 'Dis
yer wedder is so hor'bly hor'ble dat Ah 'low we
bettah not mention hit.' Den de dawter she reply,
'Yes, ma, Ah t'ink hit miser'bly miser'ble, en' an
orful damp rain.' But one ebenin'—now, keep yo'
eyes en' years op'n, fo' wot Ah toles yo' will run yo'
bang up 'g'in' er big supprise,—one ebenin', w'en
dey wuz studyin' de al-manacks ter see w'en dere
would be a change in de wedder, dey heerd a
scratchin' at de fron' do', en' w'en Miss Noah ope'd
de do' in walked a 'Coon, jus' ez big ez life. 'E
didn't say nuffin', jus' looked roun' de room, den
seated hisse'f neah de fiah en' looked inter de blaze
kinder 'stracted-like, ez ef 'e had suthin' on 'is min'.
Reckon de dampness hed caused 'im ter ketch col',
'cause 'e sneezed; den 'e didn't say nuffin', but
looked kinder 'pology-like et de ladies, en' wiped
his mouf wid 'is tail. Dis yer proceedin' wuz

kep' up eb'ry ebenin', twel de ladies allus sent der
brudder Sam a'ter de 'Coon ef 'e didn't show up
eb'ry ebenin'. 'Dey all 'lowed dat 'Coon wuz de
smartes' animile dey eber seed, en' dey reckon'd
dey hed seed 'em all. Dey wuz great frien's, dem
ladies en' de 'Coon, en' de 'Coon got so familyus-
like, dat 'e don' make no hesitashun 'bout gettin'
on de ladies' laps en' lettin' dem pet 'im. De
ladies done grown ver' fon' ob 'im. Las', de rain
all quit, de dove sent out, en' de yark landed on
de mounting. Golly! but eb'rybody wuz glad ter
set foot ergin on de lan'. Po' chillun, dey housed
up so long dey almos' wild, en' run barefoot en'
holler like young Injuns.

"On de fourt' day, a'ter t'ings wuz kinder gettin'
strai't'n'd 'roun', a angel cum f'um de Lawd, en'
a'ter 'e sed 'Howdy!' ter Noah en' de res', he
axed Noah fo' a private confab. Noah wuzn't
'feared, 'cause 'e hedn't done gone done nuffin' ter
be 'feared ob. A'ter dey hed cum out, en' de angel
hed gone, de women-folks wuz cu'us, en' dey 'lowed
dey oughter know w'at dey wuz talkin' 'bout. But
Noah done sed nuffin' 'cept, 'Wait en' see! Wait
en' see! Ah has de powah.' Den de ladies wuz
mo' cu'us den befo'. But Noah, 'e felt sho' 'im
hed de powah. Sho' nuff 'e did, en' dat day, jus'
in de dusk ob de ebenin', w'en de screech-owls
wuz hootin' in de woods en' de flah-flies wuz
twinklin' in de lowlands, Noah called 'is family tergedder, en' all de peeples wot wuz saved, en' sed,—

"'My frien's, 'way off f'um heah dar is a lan' whar de sun allus shine wa'm. De Lawd wants ter pop'late dat lan'. We can't spah eny ob yo'-uns, but Ah has de powah ter transmoggerfy one ob dese animiles inter a pusson, an' am now goin' ter done gone en' do it. Ah ax yo' ter choose de animile.'

"Den dey choosed, sum de Elephantus, sum de Hippuspot'mus, sum de Girasticutus, w'ile one ob de ladies chose de Mouse; but Miss—Miss——" and the old man scratched his head and tried to recall the name,—"Miss—— Wall, Ah 'clar' t' goodness but dat name hab 'scaped de mashes ob mah mem'ry; but enyway, she wuz de fav'rit' dawter of Brer Noah, en' w'en hit cum her turn, she walk out en' say, sez she,—

"'Ah choose de 'Coon; de 'Coon am mah choice.'

"Den dere wuz a great clappin' ob han's, en' de young fellers dat wuz votin' fo' de Hippuspot'mus en de Girasticutus couldn't tumble over fas' 'nuff in changin' der votes. 'Cause yo' see dey wanted ter shine in de eyes ob Miss Noah, fo' her pa wuz de big man, en' dese young fellers wuz willin' ter stan' in wid 'im.

"En' now," exclaimed Uncle Rastus, "we cum ter de great 'xhib'shun ob de powah. Dey fo'med a circl', en' one ob de men 'e bro't de 'Coon, led 'im wid a chain. Dey took de chain off, but couldn't get de collah off, so Noah 'lowed hit wouldn't mak' eny diff'runce, en' de cer'mony

perceeded. Den sez Noah, sez he, 'Ah's goin'
ter transmoggerfy dis animile, dis yer 'Coon, inter
a man.' Whoo! Golly! Jus' 'magine how dey
took dat! De 'Coon, he don' unnerstan' dat big
wud,—'im don' say nuffin'.

"Den Brer Noah, he continue: 'W'en dis 'Coon
'cum a man, 'e be hones', full er fun, po' but allus
contented.' Den 'im say, 'Conten'men' better'n
great riches.' Reckon dat so, honey. Suthin' in
dat, sho'! Den de 'Coon 'e look at Brer Noah,
en' Brer Noah 'im look at de 'Coon; Den Brer
Noah, 'e rub 'is han's tergedder, pull up 'is sleebes,
don' say nuffin' but jus' mesm'rize de 'Coon.
Den de 'Coon lay down en' trem'l,—eb'rybody look
on in 'stonishmen'. Den de 'Coon move. Whoa,
dah! Jiminy! *Now* wuz de powah showed, fo'
de 'Coon changed, en' grew en' grew, twel 'Coon
all gone, en' dere stood big brack man. Den
eb'rybody hoorah. Jus' den Brer Noah say,—

"'Yo' mus' now go ter dat fa'-off lan' en' raise
cotton, cawn, en' watermillyuns. Yo'ah race sh'll
be bless'd, but yo' will allers hev ter wu'k ha'd.'

"Den dere wuz a whizzin' in de aih, en' two
hosses, w'ite ez snow, wid a kerridge ob gold, cum
f'um de sky; en' a'ter dis brack man hed shook
han's all 'roun' 'e jumped inter de kerridge, de
hosses sta'ted tru' de aih, w'ile de light dat followed
de man wuz jus' like sho'-nuff fiahwu'ks. De
hosses flew en' flew fo' t'ree days en' nights, en'
brack man sleep mos' de time. Las' 'e wake, en'

fin' hisse'f in de wa'm kentry, whar wuz dates, en' palms, en' b'nanas. He stay dere en' raise large fambly. Eb'ry yaar, w'en de watermillyuns wuz ripe, he wish ole man Noah en' his chillun 'd cum en' see 'im; but Ah s'pec's Noah wuz ver' busy, fo' he nebber cum ter see 'im.

"But," continued the old man, sorrowfully, "too bad! too bad! dat dey didn' git de collah off de 'Coon, fo' up ter dis time de po' man am strugglin' wid hit roun' 'is neck. But Ah b'leebe, honey, dat de day 'll cum w'en de yoke 'll be cas' off. De Lawd knows Ah prays fo' dat time ter cum. De po' w'ite trash hab heerd suthin' ob dis story, en' sometimes Ah'm 'bleeged ter t'ink dat is w'y dey calls us 'Coons."

The boy had listened intently until his father finished, then said,—

" Sho'ly yo' don' b'leeb all dat story?"

The old man looked thoughtfully at the fire, then replied,—

" Wha, honey, Ah'm 'bleeged ter b'leeb mos' ob hit, but, in co'se, de 'zact languidge Ah can't vouch fo', kase dis done happen long time ergo. 'Sides—— Law bress yo', honey, is yo' sleepy? Ter be sho' yo' is. Ah see dem blin's is droopin' ober de eyeballs, but hol' out li'l' long'r, honey, till we finish de music."

After Uncle Rastus had finished his story, he played " Money Musk," the " Arkansaw Traveller," and other familiar songs, but instrumental music did not touch a responsive chord in his heart. He tried to banish from his mind the melancholy which seemed to have control of him. He thought that bright, catchy music would cheer him up, but it was of no avail. Then he said to his boy,—

"Honey, mah life dis night is like de onwelcum cloud in de cl'ar sky; w'atsumever Ah does don' cheer me up, but Ah jus' kinder feel ez ef Ah would like ter be 'way down Souf dis night. Mah h'aht am dere, en' mah t'oughts am too. Get dat noo piece ob moosic dat Mars' Wellington bro't us f'om de city; mayhaps dat'll char me up."

The boy got the music, and they sang together,—

> "Way down upon de Swanee Ribber,
>   Far, far away,
> Dere's whar mah heart is turning ebber,
>   Dere's whar de ole folks stay.
> All up and down de whole creation
>   Sadly I roam,
> Still longing for de ole plantation
>   And for de ole folks at home.
>   All de world am sad an' dreary
>   Eb'rywhere I roam,
>   Oh! darkies, how my heart grows weary,
>   Far from de ole folks at home."

After they had repeated the chorus in subdued tones, Uncle Rastus exclaimed,—

"Oh, Ephrum! yo' sings de notes an' de wu'ds, but yo' young h'aht don' compr'hend de meanin' ob all dis. Ah hab been dere, en' now Ah knows de way back; mah h'aht tells me ter go. Ah knows wha, mah mudder, mah fadder, en' mah po' wife is buried, but Ah dassn't go back. Eb'ry night w'en de gloamin' comes on Ah 'magines Ah heah de mockin'-bu'd singin' en' de ole folks callin'. De Lawd knows, dat ef Ah is brack, Ah has senses, en' feelin's, en' a big h'aht dat sumtimes cums up in mah t'roat, but de tears cums an' sabes me f'um dyin' wid a broken h'aht. En' what de song say?— 'All de world am sad en' dreary eb'rywhere Ah roam.' Dat's jus' de way Ah feel, en' Ah is t'ank- fu' dat de cu'us can't tell f'um mah face de sorrer ob mah h'aht.'' And the old man wiped the tears from his eyes, and used his handkerchief vigorously, remarking, '' 'Pears ter me dat Ah done cotch col'.'' Continuing his conversation, he said, '' Le's sing de las' vuss; en' put yo' cap'dastrophe on yer banjo, en' Ah will put mah knife ober de bridge ob mah fiddle en' pick de strings. En' now sing de las' vuss sof' and low.''

They did so, this arrangement of their instru- ments subduing the tones and giving a tinkling melody that was peculiarly pleasant, and with their sympathetic accompaniment they sang,—

> '' One little hut among de bushes,
>   One dat I love,
> Still sadly to my mem'ry rushes,
>   No matter where I roam.
> When will I see de bees a-hummin'
>   All 'round de comb?
> When will I hear de banjo tummin'
>   Down in my good ole home?

All de world am sad an' dreary
　Eb'rywhere I roam,
Oh! darkies, how my heart grows weary,
　Far from de ole folks at home."

The boy sang with the sweetness he always commanded, but Uncle Rastus was affected to tears, for the words carried him back to scenes realistically sad. He longed for comfort, he craved for words of sympathy, and with trembling voice said to his boy,—

"No use, Eph! no use! The speerit don' move me, en' Ah can't half sing. Yo' sing su'thin', honey! Sing su'thin,—su'thin' yo' t'inks will cheer up yo' ole daddy."

The boy touched a few introductory chords, then his voice floated softly through the room and out into the still calm air. Each word and line added to the intensity of his feelings, and the sentiment of the artist within him took possession of his soul, and the mellow tones glided through the air chased by the trillings of his bird-like voice.

The old man laid aside his instrument and seated himself on the bed. The words of the song, descriptive of plantation life, picturing the negroes in the cotton-field, the shocking of the corn, the gala-day, the barbecue, the dance by moonlight at the river, the master's death,—all this recalled to Uncle Rastus his early life. The boy, as if entranced, heeded not the old man, who, carried back to those early times, ejaculated,—

"Yes, honey, dat so! Ah sees hit all ergin. Bress de Lawd fo' dis!" And sitting there on the bed, he clasped his hands and gazed upward.

The boy sang on, his accompaniment blending in perfect change and shading with his voice. The old man swayed to and fro. At last the boy sang with surpassing sweetness, in tones that seemed those of a voice from heaven,—

"Pity him, Lawd! a po' ole man!
Sustain him, Lawd! Oh, you can!
He's good en' kin'. So are yo'!
Cheer him, Lawd! Carry him t'ro'."

"Bress de Lawd!" cried the old man,—"bress de Lawd fo' leavin' me dis boy!"

Then Eph changed his theme, and softly sang of early days, when in the sunny South a dusky youth and maiden were wed. He described the rejoicing over the birth of a child, the long sickness of the mother, her death, the flight,—until to Uncle Rastus the voice seemed as the voice of his wife from heaven, and, burying his face in his hands, he fell back on the bed and sobbed, and, sobbing, fell asleep.

The boy kissed the old man's hand, and, gazing musingly into the fire, said,—

"Ah nevah seed mah muddah, but w'en Ah sang hit seemed ter me dat she wuz neah me, en' tole me wot ter say, en' Ah hopes she heerd me, fo' Ah done de bes' Ah could."

CHAPTER VII.

MR. THOMPSON AND HIS HORSE.

"If we do but watch the hour,
　There never yet was human power
　Which could evade, if unforgiven,
　The patient search and vigil long
　Of him who treasures up a wrong."
　　　　　　　　　　　　BYRON.

WHEN Kirtley left the old darky, he proceeded leisurely towards the village,—a mode of progress which was a necessity as well as a pleasure, for the oxen swung along in that slow, peculiar gait that is essentially of their kind. It fitted well the condition of Kirtley's mind, for he was in that state of contentment that made him not only satisfied with the present, but happy in the anticipation of the events which he knew would transpire during the day.

A village where the inhabitants have their own world, living, one might say, within themselves; where each knows the daily life of the other; where sectional jealousies do not exist; where secrets are almost an impossibility;—this was the kind of a place to which Kirtley was going,—a village where he knew personally every man, woman, and child.

This day he knew would be one of constant excitement and pleasure, the inhabitants vying one with the other to make fun follow fast on the heels of frolic; the men arranging the programme of sports, while the women supplied the inner man with both substantials and delicacies.

Surely the day was propitious, for as the sun rose the sky was not flecked or marred by a solitary cloud. As the day advanced the generous promises of the morning were more than fulfilled, for under the genial rays of the advancing sun the glittering frost disappeared and the air was as soft and balmy as in spring.

Kirtley appreciated the day, not in an idealistic way,—he was too practical for that,—but his admiration of its perfection was awakened because he saw in it an ideal occasion for the enjoyment of out-of-door sports.

The still morning air echoed again and again with the cracking of his whip. Kirtley was an expert in its use, and the long lash unfolded itself at frequent intervals over the heads of the oxen, then shot straight out, and a report followed like the explosion of a pistol. The oxen were accustomed to this diversion of their master, and, although they saw the lash circling and unwreathing itself above their heads, and heard the startling report which always followed, they never winced, but swung along in patient resignation. The horse, also, divined the intent of the driver, and after a

E   *g*   9

sudden start and spring at the first crack of the
whip, followed with the gentlest docility at the end
of the wagon.

As Kirtley tramped along, amusing himself by
swinging the long lash, then darting it out, snap-
ping off the tops of weeds with unerring precision,
he remarked,—

" Wall! wall! But this is a perfect day, an' ef
the boys et the village hev made up the right kind
ov a program, an' Bill an' the Injun shoot, ez I
knows they will, an' this hoss does wot I knows
he orter, an' the boys come from all 'round, ez
they allus does, an' they wind up with a dance at
the tavern, then"—and he nodded his head approvingly and tried to suppress a laugh, which
ended in a snort—" then I am inclined ter think
thet the sun never shined on a day whar they hed
ez much fun ter the squar' inch ez we will see ter-
day. But, Jerry,"—and he directed his attention to
his dumb listener,—" w'en we go home you'll be a
member of a surprise-party. I'll be thar, too, old
boy," and he looked around; then, as if satisfied
that there were no other listeners, continued, confi-
dentially, " the surprise be this,"—and he closed
his lips in firm determination,—" I'm not goin' ter
drink a drop ter-day. I know I hev promised this
same thing afore, an' you hev seed thet I got home
safe an' sound; but ter-day,"—and he slapped his
chest approvingly,—" ter-day strong drink an' I is
strangers. Licker is all right fur sprains, bruises,

an' rheumatiz', all right ter get up a man's courage
w'en he wants ter fight, but ter-day licker an' I
can't hitch. I jes' inten' keepin' away from him,
'cause we like one 'nother too well, an' we allus
agree too well,—so well thet I allus give in an' don't
remember jes' wot the argooment wuz 'bout 'til
the next day, w'en my head aches so I can't think,
an' the ole woman sez thet I hev been makin' a
fool ov myself, w'ich, knowin' she is a truthful
woman, I admit. No use 'sputin' with a woman,
Jerry, 'specially ef yer knows she is right. But
with the fellers thet I know will be at the village
I've an old score ter settle, an' I'm goin' ter do it,
else I'll be a mighty poor man w'en the sun goes
down ter-night. But——" and he stopped, as if
something of vital interest had suddenly confronted
him. Then, as if satisfied it could not be, he
snapped his fingers impatiently, and said,—

"No! no! I won't think it! I've no reason
ter think so. Uncle Rastus hes allus been true ter
me, so hes the boy, an' w'en they see how much
I am bettin' they won't go back on me. I would
swar by thet ole darky, an', sence the father is
squar', thet gives me a heap ov faith in the boy.
I'll hev a talk with them, then watch both, fur all
things is fair in love, war, an' a hoss-race."

By this time he had reached the outskirts of the
village, and the oxen swung slowly along the hard-
beaten road. It was early yet, and but few were
abroad. Kirtley watered his oxen at the old town

pump; he then led the horse to the trough, and, hearing light footsteps, turned and saw young Eph, the colored lad, who doffed his hat and stood grinning at him, saying,—

"Good-mo'nin', Brer Kirtley! Ah's been watchin' fo' yo' fo' sum time. De ole gem'man, my pa, said yo' would want ter see me, en' I was only too glad ter cum ter town dis day, 'caus' ob de cel'bration, 'specially de hoss-racin'. En' how is my pet?" said he, as he walked up to the horse and threw his arm over the arched neck that was bent over the trough.

The horse laid his ears back in playfulness, whinnied his greeting, then rubbed his head against the boy's shoulder, while Eph gently patted his neck and rubbed his nose with affection. Kirtley noted all this, saying,—

"Yer seem ter be very fond ov the hoss, Eph, an' he's a good friend of yourn, too. Do yer think he can win the race ter-day?"

"Yes!" exclaimed the boy, eagerly. "He can win, en' will win ef I has my way."

"Your way!" replied Kirtley, in astonishment. "An' wot in thunder do yer mean by that?"

"Ah mean," said the boy, "that yo' gib me cha'ge ob dis hoss ter-day, let me do wid 'im ez Ah t'inks bes',—me en' de ole gem'man,—Ah'll ride 'im." And the boy's eyes grew brighter as he continued: "En' w'en I am on 'is back de hoss don' lib dat ken beat 'im a mile."

Kirtley looked down at the ground, then steadily at the boy, and said,—

"Ephrum, I have in my pockets, an' whar I can lay my han's on it, clus' ter a thousand dollars, an' besides I'm goin' ter bet cattle, hosses, an' anything I have. I don't take no bluffs ter-day from no one. Knowin' thet I am goin' ter do this, air ye willin' ter undertake ter win fur me?"

The boy's eyes filled with tears, as he replied,—

"Brer Kirtley, dat hoss 'd fly ef Ah axed 'im ter. Ah lubs 'im, en' 'e lubs me. Ah don' want no spuhs, no gad,—jus' de op'chunity ter git on 'is back,—jus' de chance ter lean ober en' whisper in 'is years. Den, den——" and the youth excitedly finished, "Ah don' t'ink a teal duck or a sparrer-hawk c'd ketch us. Yo' can trus' me, Brer Kirtley, en' Ah feel sho' Ah can win."

"Wall!" replied Kirtley, "I'll think it over. You take the hoss now, an' don't 'low no man ter tech him er go near him, fur the gang that 'll be here ter-day 'll stan' watchin', an' I don't want ter give 'em a chance ter work any ov their tricks on me."

The boy looked his delight, and, seizing the horse's halter-strap, said,—

"T'ank yo', Brer Kirtley, yo' won' regret dis. Ah'll watch yo' hoss, en' no one sh'll tech 'im or go nigh 'im."

At this he led the horse away. The curious villagers by this time had surrounded the wagon,

and when they learned that the huge antlers belonged to the charmed buck which for years had
defied the skill of the most successful hunters,
their curiosity was still greater. But Kirtley had
covered the animal's body with blankets, and,
motioning them away, spoke in an authoritative
manner,—

"Stan' back, gentlemen! Stan' back! The
menag'rie ain't open yet. Wait till the proper
time comes an' ye sh'll see the buck in all his
dead glory."

With that he drove his team along, the crowd
moving aside to let them pass through, and when
he reached the stable belonging to the tavern he
placed the oxen in charge of the hostler, giving
him parting instructions not to let the deer be uncovered, for there would be a time and place for
that. Then he proceeded to the tavern, where he
was accorded a hearty welcome.

In another part of the village, Wellington and
Manulito were seated in the office of the former.
The huge fire was throwing out its warmth, penetrating every recess of the room. The occupants
had evidently been discussing some disputed question, for the Indian said,—

"I know, Gray Eagle, what you would say, and
how you feel; but last night was the happiest of
my life, for I lay awake for hours, then fell asleep
dreaming of the deed I had done; and I thanked
the Great Manitou that he had permitted me to

save the life of my brother, the man I love better than all the world besides."

" Yes," replied Wellington, " I can well imagine how you felt, although I have amply proved to you that I fully and freely forgave what happened months ago. Up to this time neither you nor I have ever mentioned what occurred then. I thought we never would, but what you did for me and mine yesterday permits me to speak freely, and seems to make more holy the promise I gave you that day in the woods,—to be always your brother. I always will be. I shall never forget that dreadful moment of suspense, when, utterly exhausted, I raised my hands over my head and closed my eyes, expecting to feel the sickening crash of the mad brute's hoofs through my head. Then I heard the report of your gun as if in a dream, a report way off down the stream, and then I sank into unconsciousness, for the next thing I knew I was on the bank and you were rubbing my hands and limbs. I opened my eyes once and saw it was you ; you did not see me, but tenderly kissed my hand."

At this the Indian started in surprise, as if to deny it, but Wellington softly laid his hand on his arm, and said,—

" No, Manulito! Do not be ashamed of that token of affection. A kiss from one as proud as you, and at such a time, was the imprint from the lips of one who possesses a soul second to no living man's. When I saw it was you I drifted gently into the sweetest sleep, and dreamed of you and me hunting together in the warm summer-time. How long I slept I do not know, but your voice and that of Kirtley awakened me, and I then realized all that had happened."

As Wellington finished the Indian dropped his blanket from his arms, exposing his broad shoulders, upon which the firelight flickered, and addressed his companion.

"The darkest clouds come before the day, and the days of greatest sorrow are followed by many happy ones. The Great Spirit does not intend that the life of man shall be always like a winter's day, cold and dreary, but strews the bright and pleasant ones along like flowers in the prairie-grass, so that at times we find them where we least expect them. For many moons the heart of Manulito has been sad, ever since the meeting in the forest. It seemed as if he were less a warrior to let his heart grow so heavy, and he tried in hunting and in other ways to throw this burden from him. At times he did so; it was but for a short time, however, for the old feeling came back. His heart was weary and there was something wanting; what, he did not know, but he felt sad, as he did when his mother died. Manulito knew the Gray Eagle had forgiven him,—that did not trouble him; but it must have been that the Great Spirit burned with fire the heart of Manulito until he knew the sin he had committed, for he could not free himself from

the remembrance of it. But when the Great Manitou directed the footsteps of Manulito to the ford,
and gave him the speed of the deer and the eye of
the eagle to save his brother, *then* Manulito felt that
his sin was forgiven and that he could once again be
a warrior and a man. Since that time his heart has
been glad, the sun shines more brightly and the
time passes more pleasantly, for he feels that the
Great Manitou has forgiven him for attempting to
take the life of his brother."

Wellington seized the Indian's hand, and, warmly
pressing it, said,—

".Let's drop the subject, Manulito, and talk of
what we are to do to-day. Shooters will be here
from the surrounding country, and our fame is
known. Nothing would afford these visitors greater
satisfaction than to outshoot you and me."

The Indian drew himself up proudly, and said,—

" When two men shoot better than the Gray
Eagle and Manulito it will be when our eyesight is
dimmed with age or we are in our graves."

" I am glad you feel that way," laughingly replied
Wellington, " for I am sure I never felt more like
shooting in my life. We ought to do well to-day,
for there isn't a particle of wind blowing. But
come, let's go out into the street. It is nine o'clock,
and some of the people will gather at the square
to hear the announcement of the programme for
the day."

As they stepped into the street they met a man

who was well known throughout the West,—a man who never denied his vocation when directly questioned, but one whose personal appearance did not indicate his calling. He was born and raised in Massachusetts. His early training and education were such as cultivated parents would give their children. His father was a man of brilliant attainments, who desired his son to follow mercantile pursuits; his mother was a woman of great refinement, noted for her charitable deeds and generosity. The son had every opportunity to make for himself a fortune and a name, but he was led away by evil companions until the straight path of honorable dealing was abandoned, and he followed the variable but fascinating life of a gambler. He was of such a disposition that, whether basking in the smiles of prosperity or laboring under the ban of evil luck, he was the same, always smiling, glad to see his friends, generous to all. He would take every advantage of a man when dealing with him, but afterwards he would willingly lend to his victim, without security, more than the amount won from him.

His favorite game was with cards, and whether playing poker or risking large sums in faro and roulette, or sitting beneath the shade of some large tree playing penny ante or seven-up for twenty-five cents a corner, he was equally happy. He never played for fun,—that is, a game for the purpose of idling away his time,—for when invited to join in a game of that kind, his invariable reply, accompanied with the blandest smile, was,—

"I know I would enjoy your company, gentlemen, but really I am such an indifferent player that I know my poor playing would result in a loss of interest in the game to the rest."

But his special hobby was fast horses. He did not care for trotters, believing that running was the natural gait of the horse. This theory he dearly loved to demonstrate, and at his breeding-farm he always had at command a choice lot of youngsters, or three- to five-year-olds. He was a great believer in blooded animals, and felt that speed could be attained only by the proper admixture of the purest blood.

In personal appearance he was fully six feet tall, with smoothly-shaven face; his eyes were dark gray, while his hair was jet-black and grew long and straight, spreading over his shoulders. The constant smile on his face was not repulsive, but it caused one to feel that it was a mask which concealed unexpressed thoughts, and that the man who confided in him would be deceived. Such was Thompson, whose presence Kirtley had anticipated, and as is usual with such a man, he was followed by numerous confederates or adherents.

Wellington had done considerable business for him from time to time, so that their meeting was cordial. Thompson knew the Indian, and seeing him in company with Wellington, gave him a

kindly nod of recognition, as he grasped the lawyer's hand, and exclaimed,—

"Well, Mr. Wellington, how are you, anyway?
Growing younger and handsomer every day, I see!"

"No, Ed, I can't say that," replied Wellington,
"but I have no especial cause for complaint; on
the contrary, if I am not growing younger, I am
growing stronger, for I never felt as well as I have
this winter."

"The fields and the forest, the prairies, the winding streams, and the open air,—it is to these he owes
his good health," responded Manulito.

"I don't doubt it," said Thompson, "for I lead
a roving, unsettled life, and I never enjoy as good
health as when I am knocking around, camping
out and making overland journeys. But there's
a crowd gathering out there on the common. Suppose we go out and see what's up. Probably they're
arranging for the day."

As they neared the spot, the crowd turned and
faced them. Then a great shout went up, and a
voice cried out,—

"Three cheers for Wellington!"

After these were given, the same voice yelled, —

"And three times three and a tiger for Manulito,
the Indian who saved his life!"

At these demonstrations Wellington blushed,
and glanced affectionately at Manulito, but the
Indian looked distressed, for he did not care for
such evidences of appreciation. His reward—the

saving of a life, that of his best friend—had been enough. Besides, his was a retiring disposition, and he avoided rather than courted notoriety. But the crowd cheered him again and again; and when he sought to get away, Wellington laughingly seized his blanket and said,—

"No, no, Manulito! You promised to stick by me to-day, and I won't let you go."

The Indian saw it was of no avail to attempt to escape, so trudged amidst the crowd in quiet resignation. Wellington knew that Kirtley had told of the previous day, and regretted exceedingly that he had not been a hidden listener to the tale that his friend had unfolded.

The crowd had placed boards across the wagon-box, and had then put the deer on top of them so that all could see it. The men and boys crowded around, admiring the great animal, especially its magnificent antlers, which hung over the wagon's sides in conspicuous prominence.

All, or nearly all, had tales to tell of this buck, the finest specimen of its race. A few had seen it in life; many had seen its imprints in the snow; while all knew of its ability to travel,—to be here one day, pursued by hounds, while on the following day it would be seen quietly browsing perhaps a hundred miles away. It was impossible to reckon its age, and now that it lay before them in the rigidity of death, insensible to its surroundings, more than one heart beat with pity at the recollec-

tion of the charmed life this beast had borne for
so many years. Indeed, the Indians believed it
was possessed of an evil spirit; that some one had
died steeped in sins and wickedness, and that the
Evil One had transferred the spirit of the deceased
to this deer.   While it lived, the dead person's soul
would be in direst distress, unable to obtain rest or
forgiveness.   This, they said, was why it could not
be killed or captured; many of them vowing that
they had shot it, only to have their bullets fall
harmless to the ground.   The dead deer disclosed
a history of a life,—a life spent in forest, prairie,
and dells.   The great body was scarred here and
there by traces of bullets which had reached their
mark but did not strike a vital part.   Here and
there on its head and on its limbs were white
seams, showing where hounds had bravely attacked
it, but in vain.   No wonder, then, that the villagers
flocked to see this king as he lay before them, for
they knew that the fact of his death and the names
of the successful hunters would be heralded far and
near.   Besides, they felt a justifiable pride in those
two hunters, and they believed that there did not
exist two men more skilful in the use of the rifle.

As they approached, Kirtley cried out,—

" Welcome, gentlemen ! Welcome ! I've jes'
b'en tellin', in my poor way, all 'bout the killin'
ov ther buck. 'Course, I couldn't tell it ez well
ez sum, f'rinstunce you, Mr. Wellin'ton, but they
got me up on the waggin, 'sisted I sh'd tell them

the hull story 'bout the shootin' ov the deer, an'
I don't know wot I sed, but I'm dinged ef I didn't
talk jes' like a Fourth o' July or'tor fur nigh a
half-hour."

"Hoop-la! Bully fur you, Kirtley! You sh'll
be our orator next Fourth!" exclaimed a voice from
the crowd.

At this Kirtley looked down, seemed confused,
and said,—

"Now, boys! Thet's hardly fa'r ter poke fun et
me. You know I hev'n't got ther gift ov gab, nor
the big wuds ter speak at sech a time, but ter-day
my speechifyin' wuz kinder spontan'us-like, an'
wot I sed I couldn't help, fur I sed it afore I
knowed it, an' didn't 'tend any ov the time ter
make a speech."

At this time, noticing Wellington nearing the
wagon, he cried out,—

"Here, Bill! Cum, git up here an' 'nounce the
program ov the day!"

Wellington came smilingly forward, bowed to
his friends as he passed through the crowd, and
climbed up on the wagon, where he could see and
be seen. As he appeared a great shout rent the
air, and several voices cried in unison,—

"A speech! A speech!"

But Wellington raised his hand to ask their
attention, and said,—

"Friends and Fellow-Citizens: I appreciate the
welcome you accord me. I appreciate the feeling

of friendship that I know dwells in your hearts. I appreciate the fact that you are not only willing but anxious that I should make a speech to you. But there is a time and place for everything, and you must agree with me that this is neither the time nor the place, because we have not met here to listen to an oration or the discussion of any subject, but solely to pass this day in such a manner that those who actively participate may feel they have been in the dwelling-place of hospitable citizens, and have been accorded a fair field for the exhibition of their special accomplishments in the way of skill; while the others, the larger class, who are here not as active participators but as spectators, will, when they leave this village to-night, depart with a sincere feeling of satisfaction,—a satisfaction derived from all they have seen and enjoyed,—so that they can say in their hearts that *this* day is one long to be remembered, and one of the pleasantest in their lives.

"As Chairman of the Committee on Entertainment, I desire to announce the programme of the day, which will be as follows:

"First, foot-races. After their conclusion, dinner. Then rifle-shooting for prizes, followed by fancy shooting by experts. And the day's sports to conclude with a grand sweepstake race, mile heat, best two in three.

"After this there will be a grand supper served by the ladies of the village, free to everybody; and at night we will conclude the day's sports with a dance over there at the new hotel.

" And now," he continued, " let every one seek enjoyment, for this day we are servants of the people, and bound by the sacred ties of hospitality to make your time pass gayly. No sighs nor tears to-day, but let everybody laugh and have a jolly time. Forget your troubles and your misfortunes! I wish to say here that we hope that you will all stay throughout the entire day, for the horse-race promises to be especially good, as Mr. Thompson is here from a distance, and has with him a very fleet horse, ' Imp o' Darkness,' which he has entered in the race. Mr. Kirtley has also entered a horse, ' Sweet Marjorum,' and there are several other entries. Thanking you for your attention, and asking you now to join us in the sports of the day, we will begin at once."

h   **10***

CHAPTER VIII.

A GALA DAY AT THE VILLAGE.

"If all the year were playing holidays,
  To sport would be as tedious as to work;
  But when they seldom come, they wished-for come,
  And nothing pleaseth but rare accidents."

SHAKESPEARE.

As Wellington jumped down from the wagon his hearers vigorously applauded him; then, as they wended their way to the grounds where the sports were to occur, all interest seemed to centre in the race, one saying to another,—

"Take my advice, don't you bet a cent on that hoss-race! 'Imp o' Darkness!' Why don't they call him by his right name? for he is the devil, sure enough, to run.

"Thompson is pretty cute to come strayin' in here. Probably thinks we don't know of this hoss. That's all right," continued the speaker, "but ef he's playin' me fur a sucker, he's goin' to get fooled, 'cause I know him an' all his hosses too well. He ain't comin' here fur his health."

"So Kirtley has a hoss," exclaimed his companion. "Wall, gener'ly speakin', Kirtley is up ter snuff, but I don't imagine he has any idee his hoss will win, but he jes' wants ter make some fun. He allus has some pretty fair hosses, but law! he ain't fool enough ter bet, leastwise I wouldn't think so. Thompson skinned him last year outen several hundred dollars, an' I guess he's had 'nough of Thompson an' his crowd. Et ther same time, Kirtley is gritty! His gizzard is full of sand, an' ef he gits 'bout two-thirds under sea,—licker makes him nervy,—he 'ill bet, an' keep bettin'. But there's no use foolin' with him, fur ef he takes a notion his hoss can run—let him go. No use interferin'! You can't stop him. It's the old story 'bout a fool an' his money."

Those in attendance were bent on amusement, and now that the exercises of the day were to begin, they surged forward, a jolly crowd, ready to shout and laugh on the least possible occasion.

When the names of the entries in the foot-race were called there was manifest surprise, for it was ascertained that Manulito was not among the number. His fame as a runner was well known, for he had participated in many races, and had never been defeated. The committee called on him and tried to induce him to reconsider his decision, but it was of no avail. He did not hesitate to give his reason, but said,—

"When Manulito fires his rifle, his aim must be true, his nerves steady, his blood cool. This cannot be if Manulito runs races."

As the crowd much preferred an exhibition of the Indian's shooting, they did not insist on his running. But there are always plenty to join in a foot-race at a country meet, and this was no exception. It was amusing to see the costumes in which some of them ran; several were in their stocking feet, and one fellow was barefooted; but the prevailing style was for the bareheaded runner to appear in his undershirt, trousers rolled up, stocking feet, and with a leather belt, drawn taut for the occasion, around his waist.

As they began disrobing for the race, Thompson stood near, and remarked,—

" Gentlemen, you are going to see a fine exhibition of speed; I know it from the active young men who will run. At the same time, it seems to me that more ought to engage, and if I were a young man I surely would. This young man at my side says he is a stranger here, but thinks he would like to try with the others."

" Good for him! The more the merrier!" exclaimed several.

Kirtley stood near, and quietly remarked,—

" Do yer think this young feller can run, Ed?"

" Why, Mr. Kirtley," replied Thompson, "I don't know, I'm sure. He says he is a stranger here; maybe he can run, maybe he can't. At the same time, while I don't often bet, I would be willing to wager ten dollars that he beats any one you say."

" Make it ten ag'in' the balance, an' I'll go ye."

" All right, I'll do it," responded Thompson.

The money was placed in a bystander's hands, and the young man leisurely walked out among the other racers. As he joined them, he was warned to get ready. At this he plunged down into his pocket, and produced a low pair of shoes, —light, but with corrugated soles to avoid slipping. He then divested himself of his outer clothing, and stood before them arrayed in flesh-colored tights.

The racers toed the scratch, their left feet and arms well forward, while their right arms were parallel with their bodies and their hands firmly clinched. After two or three false starts, they were off amid the shouts of the multitude. For the first seventy-five yards one of the resident runners seemed to have the best of it, but the stranger gained, passed first one, then another, until he was even with the leader at ninety yards; then with a spurt which could not be denied he bounded ahead and won by a few feet. As the result was announced there were not any cheers given, but many significant winks were passed, and some one quietly remarked,—

"Purty cute o' Thompson, wasn't it, ringin' in thet perfeshnal?"

His neighbor replied, "Sarved old Kirtley right to lose his ten. He oughter knowed better nor ter bet ag'in' Thompson. But you mark my word, he's begun bettin', an' he'll keep it up an' go home broke."

At this juncture the ringing of the town bell

announced to all that dinner was ready, and a temporary adjournment of the sports of the day was proposed. The crowd repaired to the tavern, well satisfied with what they had seen thus far, and feeling that the afternoon's events, the shooting and the horse-racing, would add still more to the enjoyment of the occasion.

When the majority reached the vicinity of the hotel, Kirtley slipped away and went to the stable where his horse was in possession of the colored lad. He thought his departure was unperceived, but, as he entered the door, a hand was laid on his shoulder, and, turning in surprise, he saw Manulito. He was impatient at the interruption, and said, sharply,—

"Wall?"

The Indian looked steadily at him, and said,—

"When the wolves are abroad the sheep need protection. Graybeard is not afraid of the wolves. In open battle he has no cause to be, but the one with the smooth tongue and mild looks is followed by a pack which wait for him to strike. Then they will snarl and rend the prey he has bitten."

"I onderstan', Manulito; yer want ter put me on my guard ag'in' Thompson an' his gang. I'm jes' as much 'bleeged ter yer, an' 'preciate yer good intentions, but I know wot I'm doin'."

The Indian persevered, and said,—

"When the cow beats the deer, when the sheep beats the antelope, then can the farmer's horse beat the thoroughbred."

"Oh, I see!" exclaimed Kirtley. "Yer think I've taken a hoss from haulin' wood, an' expect with it ter beat Imp o' Darkness. I've got a heap ov faith in yer, ef yer air an Injun; yer know I hev hed sence yer helped Bill outer thet scrape on the Waps', an' I want yer to step in here with me an' look at a *hoss*,—a hoss wot is a hoss. Yer a jedge, an' wot yer sees don't mention ter nobody, fur ther's goin' ter be a supprise this arternoon. I know I be old, but yer go down in yer pockets an' bet yer las' dollar on this hoss. I'm goin' ter, yer kin bet yer life on thet."

But the Indian felt that Kirtley was over-confident, and shook his head discouragingly. As they approached the stall where the horse stood, the negro lad stepped out and said,—

"Ah's heah, Brer Kirtley; Ah's been heah all de time. No one done tech dis hoss 'cept me an'——"

"Yes, sah, dat am true," responded another voice, and Uncle Rastus stepped out of another stall. "Yes, sah," said Rastus. "No one done tech dis hoss; but one dem gambler fellahs done kum 'roun' heah,—'e didn't see me,—an' 'e talked sweet ter Eph, den wanted ter look at de hoss's mout', jus' ter see how ole 'e am. Den w'en young Eph 'ject, den de gambler fellah sez, sez he, ' Am goin' ter see anyhow.' Yo' knows, Brer Kirtley, Ah was baun an' bred in de Souf, an' knows wot dis fellah am up ter,—ter dope de hoss. So Ah sez, 'Yo' want ter see, does yo'? Den Ah calls yo'.'

An' at dat Ah stahts fo' 'm, an' 'e stahts fo' de
do'; but, bress mah h'aht, ef dis foot ob mine didn't
ketch 'm, an' Ah spec's w'en 'e eats 's dinnah, 'e
won't ax fo' a cheer."

Kirtley saw his interests were being protected,
and thanked both father and son. The old darky
edged up to Kirtley, and said,—

" Is yo' goin' ter bet much, Brer Kirtley, on dis
hoss-race ?"

" Yaas," responded that worthy. " Yaas, I'm
goin' ter bet more'n I ever bet afore."

" Law me !" exclaimed Uncle Rastus, " dat's sand,
sho' 'nuff; but den, Ah don' b'leeb in hit, an' Ah
don' t'ink no good comes f'um money made in
bettin'."

" Oh, yes," says Kirtley. " You air mealy-
mouthed. Yer got r'ligion, that's wot's the trouble
with yer."

" Trouble wid me, Brer Kirtley? De Lawd
bress yo', Ah don' borrer no trouble 'cause Ah got
a little 'ligion." And he continued, feelingly : " Ah
wish yo' had it too. Hit would do yo' mo' good
dan anyt'ing yo' will git in dis wu'ld. Ah ain't
'shamed to 'knowledge it fo' man, an' Ah say right
heah, ef de Lawd dis minnit was ter send down
salvation ter yo', right smack t'roo de roof ob dis
stable, Ah don' keer how much de 'xpense am, po'
as Ah be, Ah would chee'fully pay de damages, jus'
ter see yo' git 'ligion."

Kirtley smiled and instructed the boy to lead out

the horse. When Eph did so, Manulito, who was an excellent judge of horses, loosened his blanket from his shoulders, throwing it carelessly around his waist,'and looked eagerly at Kirtley. Kirtley enjoyed the surprised look, and said,—

" Never mind me, Manulito ; I'm not goin' ter run ; it's the hoss thet's goin' ter do thet. Look at him an' let me know wot yer thinks."

The Indian gave one quick glance, which covered the animal, and said,—

" Horse born and bred where the summer-time lasts all winter ; horse's home same as the mocking-bird's."

At this Uncle Rastus broke into a loud " Yah ! yah ! Yo' can't fool 'im. Yo' didn't fool me, nuther. Dat hoss kum f'um Kaintuck."

While Manulito was admiring the horse, the animal stood as quietly as a lamb, except to occasionally rub his nose against young Eph, soliciting the caresses he knew he would receive. Manulito noted every point of his contour : the dark hazel eyes that looked so spirited, yet had the mildness of a gazelle, the small pointed ears, the transparent nostrils, the deep chest with the lung-power so well concealed, the strong forearms ; indeed, all the elements of speed essential to a racer were possessed to a marked degree. Sweet Marjorum was a dark sorrel horse, with a long, fine tail which nearly reached the ground, and his only conspicuous mark was a spot of white on the forehead.

When Manulito had feasted his eyes on this
equine wonder, he said,—

"'Twas such horse as this that, when Manulito
was a child, his father owned; gentle as a kitten,
obedient as a spaniel, brave as a lion, fleeter than
the wind. On the prairies no enemy could escape
my father—the great chief—when he rode his
horse. This one looks the same; nothing can beat
him."

"Bully fur you, Manulito! Bully fur you! Now
yer talkin' sense. I knowed yer wuz a good jedge
of a hoss, so I showed yer one."

As they finished their conversation, the young
colored lad approached Kirtley and said, impres-
sively,—

"Brer Kirtley, yo' promised me dat Ah sh'd hab
cha'ge ob dis hoss an' ride 'im. As de Lawd is
my jedge, Ah will do de bes' Ah can fo' yo'. But
Ah wants ter ride mah way, an', no mattah wot
'peahs ter happen ter de hoss, Ah want yo' ter keep
on bettin' till Ah tells yo' ter stop. De hoss an'
me on'erstan' one 'nudder, an' ef yo' *will bet*, den
Ah'll try an' make yo' a heap o' money."

Kirtley demurred to this, not being willing to
risk large sums of money on a boy's whim, but
Uncle Rastus felt that Eph would bring the horse
in a winner, and Manulito was so impressed with
the lad's sincerity that they prevailed on Kirtley to
consent to his demands. As Kirtley and the Indian
left the stable to go to dinner, Eph threw his arms

around the horse's neck and patted him affectionately, saying,—
" Honey, I knows we will win,—I knows it."

<hr />

CHAPTER IX.

THE HORSE-RACE.

" Round-hoof'd, short-jointed, fetlocks shag and long,
  Broad breast, full size, small head, and nostrils wide,
High crest, short ears, straight legs, and passing strong,
  Thin mane, thick tail, broad buttock, tender hide:
Look, what a horse should have, he did not lack,
Save a proud rider on so proud a back."

SHAKESPEARE.

IN those early days the principal resort for all
loungers—those who had leisure time and those
who wanted to hear the latest news—was the bar-
room of a tavern. It was not a drinking-resort, but
it had not gained the dignified name of office. It
was therefore to be expected that at the conclusion
of the dinner those interested in sports would find
themselves in this bar-room. The air was blue with
tobacco-smoke, and animated discussions were being
carried on in all parts of the room, the topics being
the rifle-shoot and the race. It was generally concluded that the prize for rifle-shooting would fall
either to Wellington or the Indian. But a few,

whose desires were probably father to the thought, said that the chances were strong that the prize would go to some outsider.

The trophy was on exhibition at the hotel, and as it was passed around, many were the expressions of admiration it elicited. The eyes of old hunters dwelt on it with eagerness, for to them, as with all excellent shots, it was not the intrinsic value of the article contended for, but the winning from those who were computed equal to themselves in skill, that afforded them the greatest pleasure and satisfaction. They were not to be blamed for looking with solicitous eyes on the prize. It was a handsome powder-horn, novel in design, and beautifully engraved. It was made from a cow's horn, but scraped to transparency, and polished to the highest degree. Its stopple was of silver, held securely from loss by a delicate yet strong gold chain. On the centre of the horn, where the bend was the fullest, a beautiful landscape was engraved, representing pastoral life. The base of the horn was of silver, having in relief figures of yellow gold and Etruscan bronze. These figures represented an Indian riding his pony in pursuit of a buffalo, and showed him just in the act of striking with his spear. The bronze had been so delicately shaded into a copper color that the Indian's limbs and shoulders seemed most lifelike.

Wellington's eyes sparkled with enthusiasm as he looked at the trophy, and said,—

" Perfectly beautiful, Manulito. How I hope that you or I may win it!"

The Indian gazed at it rapturously, handling it with affectionate interest, and said,—

" It shall remain at this village."

At this moment Thompson spied Kirtley, and called to him, saying,—

" What's this I hear about your having a new horse ?"

" Oh," responded the old man, " I allus hev a hoss ter enter in a race. Would be better off ef I didn't."

" No, I don't agree to that," said Thompson, " for you have a good farm, are a good judge of horse-flesh, and I don't see why you shouldn't have fast horses. But they tell me that you and I have scared the balance out. They have withdrawn and left us with our horses as the only entries. There is but one prize, the citizens' purse of fifty dollars, so I guess we are in for it."

" Wall," replied Kirtley, " I've entered my hoss, an' I ain't a-goin' ter back out. My hoss sh'll run."

" That's the stuff! That's the way to talk it! Good for you, old man!" were the outcries from those present. Kirtley was considered a resident of the village, and they took local pride in him, and while they thought it impossible that his horse could win, still they devoutly hoped he might.

" Wonder if we hadn't better sell some pools on the horses ?" said Thompson.

No one responded, and he mounted a chair and undertook to sell pools, but all were afraid. At last he appeared disgusted, and said,—

"I'll bet a hundred dollars that Imp o' Darkness wins the race."

Then, after waiting for a reply and receiving none, continued,—

"A hundred to ninety on the black horse." Still no reply. "A hundred to eighty," directing his attention to Kirtley, and saying, in a sneering tone,—

"It's very funny, gentlemen, how a man will enter a horse in a race, and then won't bet; afraid to back his judgment."

"Oh," responded Kirtley, "yer drivin' at me, air ye? Beg pardon, I was talkin' ter Mr. Wellin'ton, an' didn't hear ye; but I'll jes' take thet last bet."

At this the followers of the gambler held bank-bills aloft between their fingers, and cried to Kirtley,—

"A hundred to eighty on the black horse!"

"I'll take that,—an' that,—an' that,—an' that!" called out Kirtley, as they crowded around him.

Wellington thought the old man was wild, and tried to get him away. But he pulled back and said,—

"Let me go, Bill; these fellers can't bluff me." And, pulling coin from his pockets, covered all the bets offered him.

Wellington was made stake-holder, and by mutual consent was selected judge. He then announced that it was nearly two o'clock, the time appointed for the rifle-match, and requested them all to repair to the shooting-grounds, which the majority did. As they passed out the door, Thompson winked at one of his confederates, who whispered,—

" Just like finding it in the road."

The shooting-grounds were pleasantly situated, facing the northeast. Plenty of turkeys were on hand, and a Mr. Brown, an adept himself in shooting matters, was selected as referee. He announced, as he stepped forward, that the first match would be at one hundred and fifty yards range, the shooter to take any position he might select, and body shots to count. In fact, if blood was drawn as the result of a shot, it should be scored a hit, the prize to be the turkey hit.

As the shooters stepped forward from the crowd, there were ten of them. As the firing continued, it was evident that out of the ten there were but five that stood on an equality. These were Wellington, Manulito, a young hunter from the Wapsie by the name of Johnson, and two tall, raw-boned hunters, brothers, by the name of Smith, or, as they were known for a great distance; " the two Smiths, the Virginians." They brought with them rifles with extremely long barrels, and of forty-five calibre. These two brothers, shooting as a team, had never been defeated, and a turkey's body at one hundred and fifty yards was no test of their skill. After a few rounds were fired, the distance was shortened to seventy-five yards, the shooters to hit the turkey's head or neck. In doing this the turkeys were placed in a box, body concealed, with head and neck exposed to view. Three shots each were allowed. Johnson missed the first and scored the other two, while the two Smiths, Wellington, and Manulito made a clean score. As there were four ties for this prize,—ten dollars in gold,—it was agreed that the winner in the next match should take the money in this. As they prepared for the final test, the conditions of which they had not learned, the referee called them forward and said,—

"Gentlemen, your skilful shooting has pleased every one present, but it still remains undecided who is the best shot, and we are going to put you to the test. The winner of this beautiful prize, which I hold in my hand, may indeed cherish it, for the ownership implies a cool head, a clear eye, and a nerve of iron. I will place this card which you see, two inches in diameter, at fifty yards. With the edge of my knife I have marked both horizontally and perpendicularly a line almost indistinct; these lines cross in the exact centre of the target. You will be allowed three shots each, and the measurements are to be string measure from the point where the lines cross to the edge of the bullet-mark nearest the centre."

Johnson spoke, and said,—

" Mr. Referee, I object to the Smiths shooting, because of the way their sights are fixed."

The referee examined the rifles, and found they had been arranged to improve the sight by oval pieces of tin blackened and soldered over the front and rear sights for perhaps six inches. This made a telescope which unquestionably aided one's sight on a still, bright day like this was. But the referee decided the match was open to all rifles, and ordered them to proceed with the shooting.

By mutual consent a black spot, one-half inch in diameter, was pasted just above the crossed lines. This enabled the marksmen to note where the exact centre lines were.

Johnson was the first to shoot. As he stood ready to fire, his feet close together, his left elbow resting on his hip, while the fore-end of his rifle-barrel lay on the tips of the fingers of his left hand, he took deliberate aim, and, as the smoke rolled away, the marker announced, " Centre !" There was loud applause at the result.

Wellington was the next. His position was easy and graceful, the left foot slightly advanced, the left hand extended far along the barrel. His aim was quick, and at the report of the gun he turned and smiled, knowing, as if by intuition, where the bullet had gone, a feeling which a successful hunter often has, almost imagining he sees the bullet in its flight. He was right, for the marker called out, " Centre !"

i

As the elder Smith went to the score, his position was a peculiar one. He lay flat on the ground, and rested his rifle on a standard about twelve inches high and very solid. His aim was long and careful; his rifle was held as in a vise, and, as it belched forth, the marker ran forward and turned, calling, " Centre !"

The younger Smith was next. He took the same position, the same deliberate aim, with the same result. At this there was loud cheering, for the Smiths had many friends present.

Next, and last, came Manulito. As he stepped forward to shoot, he was greeted with loud cheers.

The Indian looked straight ahead, as cool and calm as if he were going to fire at random. His long piece rested in the crotch of his left arm; he shot with both eyes open; his rifle settled on his elbow as he glanced along the barrel, apparently not taking aim. Not so, however, for the marker threw up his hat and yelled, " Centre !"

Now the crowd could scarcely contain themselves. They slapped one another on the back, and exclaimed,—

" Hoop la ! Jes' think ov it ! Every one a clean score. Thet's wot I call shootin' !"

On the second round Johnson was a shade to the right. The marker produced his rule and announced, " Three-eighths !"

" Oh, that's too bad !" exclaimed a voice.

As Wellington fired, he again secured a centre.

The elder Smith did the same; but the younger Smith overheld a trifle, and the marker announced, " One-quarter over!" The Indian drove a centre again, in his quick, decisive manner.

The percentage was now in favor of the local shooters, but the match was unfinished, and the result could not be safely predicted. Johnson, attempting to benefit by his former miss, held too much to the left. As the marker cried, " One-half to the left!" Wellington stepped firmly forward and fired with perfect coolness. As he did, the marker hesitated for a second,—the crowd seemed breathless,—then, " A plumb centre!" rang out, and the crowd were wild with delight, for none could beat his score. The best they could do was to tie him.

The elder Smith seemed more deliberate than ever, but as he heard the result of his shot his heart was in his mouth, for the marker cried, " Three-sixteenths under on centre line!" The crowd were now more demonstrative than ever, for no one could tie Wellington except the Indian, and they did not especially care which one of them received the prize. In either case it would remain in the village. But they crowded forward, interfering with the shooters, and it was some time before order could be restored.

The younger Smith smiled and said,—

" No use shooting. I've missed the centre once. That lets me out."

But they cried, " Go on and shoot! Go on and shoot!" He did so, and made a centre.

As Manulito stepped forward for his last shot, Wellington said to him,—

"I want you to shoot as if I had not shot."

The Indian laid his hand on Wellington's arm, looked tenderly into his eyes, and walked to the score. He shot with the same celerity as before. The crowd were silent as death. His rifle cracked, and the target fluttered to the ground. As it did, the elder Smith said,—

" A perfect shot, and a generous act!" for his experienced eye told him that the Indian had not tried to hit the centre, but instead had driven the nail into the tree and released the target.

As Wellington saw this, his eyes grew moist. He seized the Indian's hand and said,—

" Oh, Manulito, that's not fair! You simply gave this beautiful trophy to me."

To which the Indian replied,—

" If the eye of Manulito has done it for you, it was only what his heart hoped he might be able to do. When the Gray Eagle looked so fondly at this horn, at the tavern, Manulito secretly asked the Manitou that his wish would be gratified. And the beautiful gift cannot make my brother any happier than is the heart of Manulito this day."

At this Kirtley cried out,—

" Look, Bill! Look over yer head."

As Wellington looked, he saw, almost directly over the crowd, a flock of Canada geese, in slow flight. Wellington raised his rifle and fired at the leader, fully two hundred yards above him. As he raised the piece, Manulito said,—

"Draw in ahead of him."

The rifle spoke out in its sharp tone, apparently without effect; the gander set its wings, sailed perhaps fifty yards, then tumbled to the earth, shot through the heart.

Those in attendance were in a jolly mood, and they prevailed on the Indian to give an exhibition of fancy shooting.

A card, the ace of hearts, was placed at fifty yards. Each time a shot was fired a new board was put behind it, showing three distinct centres were made, while the hole in the card looked as if but one shot had been fired.

A wooden ball was rolled on the ground. This ball was an inch and a half in diameter, and was about one hundred feet from the shooters. Wellington fired just under it. At the report of his rifle the ball bounded from the ground, and while it was in the air the Indian fired, completely shattering it. Silver-pieces were thrown up and invariably hit. Wellington stood thirty yards away, and threw towards the Indian an ounce bottle, which was smashed into thousands of pieces. Manulito then mounted his pony, and, while at full speed, broke small bottles thrown into the air.

12

As he finished his exhibition he was loudly cheered, and then the crowd started for the races.

The track, while decidedly primitive, was yet in perfect condition for speed. In early days a country town prided itself on its horses and its place for racing, and there was a smooth road near this town, which was straight and level for a mile, according to accurate measurements. The people—men, women, and children—were beginning to arrive, and gave a gala-day appearance to the scene.

The horses were on the grounds, heavily swathed in blankets and hoods, and were walked rapidly up and down to keep up their circulation. Imp o' Darkness was led by a stable-boy, while Sweet Marjorum was attended by Uncle Rastus and Eph.

As the time advanced, the horses were called up, and the owners instructed to get them ready for the race. So the riders mounted and gave them a preliminary canter. Both Kirtley and Thompson elected to remain at the starting-point, believing that a good start was a race half won. Many stayed at the score, while by far the majority went to the wire where the race was to end.

Kirtley was still confident that his horse would win, and large sums were wagered between him and Thompson and the latter's companions.

A flag was waved by Wellington, signifying that they were ready when the starters were. Time-keepers were with Wellington, while Manulito was to act as starter, dropping a flag when the horses were off. Thompson wanted a running start, to which Kirtley made no objection.

The horses were now stripped for the race in magnificent condition. Their hair was as glossy as silk, while their ribs wavered through their satin coats. As the jockey's saddle was being girded on the sorrel horse, he was as docile as if he did not understand what was to happen, and only occasionally laid back his delicate ears when an extra pull was made on the girth.

But the black horse was exceedingly restive, and was properly named, for it seemed as if he were possessed of the Evil One. In appearance he was a perfect beauty, black as jet, without a single white hair; his eyes had a wicked snap, while frequent racing and consequent rubbings had made him vicious to such an extent that he wore a muzzle to keep him from biting.

His rider was a man of uncertain age, smooth-faced, with a determined mouth and chin, and weighing less than one hundred pounds. Thompson removed the muzzle from his horse and seized the rings of the bit. The horse knew what was up, and reared and plunged, trying to get free in his anxiety to start, and at times fairly lifting Thompson off his feet.

Kirtley went to take his horse, but the boy said to him,—

"Nebber min', Brer Kirtley. Ah don' need yo'

'sistance. Ah'll staht de hoss, an' get none de wuss ob it."

"All right, Eph," replied Kirtley; "yer win this race and I'll give yer ther best colt I've got on the farm."

The young lad held back from the black horse, and as they wheeled and bounded over the score, the sorrel was slightly in the lead.

"Come back! Come back!" the starter shouted.

But the horses were on their mettle, and ran an eighth of a mile before they could be stopped. As they trotted back, Thompson cried out to Kirtley,—

"One hundred or two hundred dollars that the black horse wins!"

"Give me odds an' I'll take yer," said Kirtley.

"No, I'm done giving you odds. I won't do it."

"Won't yer?" said the old man, in sneering tones. "Then I'll *bet yer five hundred dollars even* thet my hoss wins!"

"What!" yelled Thompson.

"Thet's wot I said, an' here's the money."

As he produced it Thompson was temporarily taken aback, but recovered himself and said, with his serenest smile,—

"I am glad to see you possessed of so much sand, Mr. Kirtley, and we'll just accommodate you." And he and his companions put the money up in Mr. Brown's hands.

As the horses dashed forward the second time, the black had the lead; so much so that Thompson hung on the bit and did not release him. The horse was bound to go, and although Thompson must have weighed two hundred pounds, the horse dragged him along as he would a child.

On the third attempt the boy intended there should be a start, and as the horses swung around, they bounded forward with magnificent strides, neck and neck. The crowd saw it would be a start, and as they went over the line the flag dropped. The crowd cheered with delight, and the horses were off.

For the first quarter they ran like the wind, the black horse cutting out the pace, and his rider evidently trying to feel the speed of his antagonist, but the sorrel horse remained head and head with him. At the half the black horse gained a trifle, and its head showed just in front of the sorrel. When the flag dropped as they passed the half-mile post, the timer ejaculated in surprise,—

" Gracious! the fastest half ever run on this track! Look at 'em come !"

Down they came towards the three-quarters pole, their hoofs thundering their approach. The black horse was still in the lead and running like the wind, but seemingly unable to shake off his rival, who hung grimly a nose behind. The crowd was silent as death, too surprised and excited to shout, for they had never seen such running.

As the horses dashed into the home-stretch they seemed to realize it. The rider of Imp o' Darkness

now exerted every effort to rush him forward. He
dug his spurs into the horse, but he could not free
him from the clinging sorrel. However, the wire
was near, and, while the sorrel did not lose, neither
did he gain. So perfect their stride that many
said, mentally, "A dead heat!" But within twenty
feet of the wire, the black horse, ever vicious, and
distressed with his punishment, infuriated at his
antagonist, quickly turned and bit at the neck of
his opponent. Alas! a fatal move! For young
Eph saw his opportunity; he lifted the head of the
sorrel horse, and before the rider of the black could
straighten its head the nose of Sweet Marjorum
shot first over the wire and won the heat.

There was never a more demonstrative gathering. The time was not yet announced, but the
crowd knew it was better than they had ever seen
made, and they danced and whooped as only attendants at races can. Many who could not see the
outcome declared it a dead heat; others averred
that the black horse had won. But as Wellington
stood on a platform and asked their attention, there
was a perfect silence as he announced in a loud,
clear voice,—

"Sweet Marjorum wins the heat. Time 1.52."

At this the crowd yelled louder than ever, their
continuous cheering announcing to those at the
starting-point the result of the heat. To corrob-
orate this, a yellow flag was held aloft, denoting that
the sorrel horse won.

As they saw this, Thompson smiled and said,—
" A horse-race is never won until the last heat is
run."

Kirtley at first stood dazed; then, realizing what
had happened, threw his hat on the ground, and
executed a hornpipe in the most approved style,
humming his own accompaniment.

When it was ascertained that the heat was lost
by reason of the black horse attempting to bite the
sorrel, Thompson called his rider to him and asked
him how the heat was lost. The rider attributed
the blame to the ugly disposition of the animal, and
said,—

" I kin beat thet sorrel hoss every day in de
week! ˘ I played wid him most ov the time; jes'
feelin' ov him. He's a good hoss, but can't stay
wid de Imp!"

" Stay?" responded Thompson. " I should say
not! Now, Jimmie, next heat cut out the pace,
and run away from him until you get a lead so
you know you have him dead to rights, for the
Imp is lightning, double distilled, and nothing can
beat him."

Then, with some parting instructions, given in
cautious whispered tones, Thompson joined the
crowd.

The village residents were elated over the result
of the first heat. They were full of enthusiasm,
and any number of small bets were made between
them, mostly for new hats. Whenever their ardor

led them to a monetary consideration, Thompson
or his adherents stood ready and accommodated
them, for they considered the result of the first
heat an accident which could not occur the second
time.

Thompson felt supreme confidence in his horse's
ability to win notwithstanding he had lost the first
heat, and, approaching Kirtley, suggested that they
increase their wagers. Kirtley had bet all the
money he had, and told Thompson so; but that
worthy guyed him, and said,—

"Mr. Kirtley, when a man is willing to back his
horse he never can have too much money. If you
haven't the lucre yourself, circulate around among
your friends and let them make up a pool; surely
their local pride ought to induce them to come in.
Nothing ventured nothing gained, you know."

The old man looked fixedly at the ground for an
instant, closed his lips determinedly, and replied,—

"Ed, yer seed my team ov oxen this mornin',
didn't yer?"

Thompson nodded assent, and Kirtley continued,—

"Wall, they is wuth over a hundred dollars.
I'll jes' bet them oxen an' the wagon ag'in' a hundred dollars thet the sorrel wins."

Thompson put up the money in Mr. Brown's
hands, and that gentleman witnessed the bet.

Kirtley squeezed through the crowd, and found
Uncle Rastus exercising the horse, while Eph and

Manulito were quietly discussing the race. Kirtley seized the boy's hand, nearly crushing it, and said,— " Good boy, Eph! Good boy! Jes' keep it up an' the colt is yourn."

The boy smiled in confidence, and said,— " Brer Kirtley, de race am half won. Dat black hoss am a runner, sho' 'nuff! But afo' 'e git troo dis race him will hab ter show hit." And he grinned, showing a set of teeth of ivory whiteness.

The bell now rang for the second heat. The horses were divested of blankets, sponged, and brought to the starting-place. It was noticed that Thompson was over-cautious in this heat. No wonder; for, if he lost, he lost not only the race but thousands of dollars.

The colored lad watched every movement; nothing escaped him, and, not intending that there should be a false start, he urged his horse, and they bounded over the score together at the first attempt. The rider of the black horse rode him for all he was worth, and the speedy animal drew slowly away from the sorrel. As they reached the half, it was seen that they were going at a 1.48 pace. Never was such running seen in this section. The black horse was a full length in the lead, running like a scared deer, but the young darky sat his horse in easy confidence. At the three-quarters they were even again; but at the home-stretch with spurs and whip the black was plied, and, springing forward, he drew gradually away from his rival. Young Eph sat immovable upon his horse, but he seemed doomed to defeat, for Imp o' Darkness galloped in, a winner by three lengths.

As the black flag was held aloft there was but slight cheering, for the majority hoped that Kirtley's horse would win the heat, and consequently the race.

Thompson and his companions were supremely happy, yet quiet in showing it, as one of them remarked,—

"A mere scratch that the sorrel won the first heat. He will be distanced the next."

The crowd clamored for a change of riders for the sorrel, claiming he was not half ridden, and that the boy was bought up and did not try to win. Kirtley was distrustful, and looked for another rider. But the Indian had assumed charge of the horse, and said,—

"No! The negro boy shall ride!"

Kirtley sputtered around, and muttered,—

"Fool promise I made, an' now I'll have ter pay fur it!"

The colored lad stood silent, when Kirtley said to him,—

"Why in thunder don't yer say suthin'? Speak! Swear! Anything but standin' lookin' like an idgit!"

The boy looked calmly at him, dropped his glance, and said,—

"Dere's 'nudder heat ter run. Ah habn't tole yo' ter quit bettin'."

Kirtley drew back as if to hit the boy. Manulito, interpreting his thoughts, stepped between them, and said,—

"Manulito would as soon strike a woman, as soon a child, as an old man with gray hairs. But if the Gray Beard touches this boy, Manulito will strike him to the earth as if he were a dog."

"Very well," responded Kirtley. "I'm in fur it, an' if I'm beat I'll get even with yer two."

To which the Indian replied, "In every horse-race some one must lose."

Suddenly Eph darted towards his horse and led him from the crowd.

In the mean time, Thompson was looking for Kirtley, and accosting him, said,—

"Your horse has won one heat, mine the other. I should like to own your horse if he can beat mine, and if mine can't beat yours, I don't care to own him. You say you haven't any more money. I'll make you this proposition: I'll bet my horse against yours. If yours wins, you take both; if mine wins, I do the same. My horse cost me a heap of money, and I am giving you the best of the bargain."

The old man stood contemplatively, and muttered to himself,—

"He don't know wot I paid fur thet sorrel, or the expense ov the trip to Lexington."

Kirtley's friends told him he had bet enough, that he could not afford to take the chances, and insisted that he should not make this bet. But the old man was obstinate. The more they argued with him the more determined he seemed to have his own way, and, shaking them from him, said,—

"I'll do it! Hoss ag'in' hoss!"

He had no sooner made the agreement than a man rushed up to Thompson and whispered something to him which made him start and say,—

"Are you sure of it?"

To which the messenger replied, "Sure? Of course I am! I just left him."

At this Thompson smiled, took a pinch of snuff, and remarked to himself,—

"Well, the Lord does at times help a sinner."

The messenger's errand was soon known, for the word passed from mouth to mouth,—

"The sorrel horse has gone lame! The sorrel horse has gone lame!"

At this announcement a groan of lamentation issued from those present, for not only was the race settled, but Kirtley and many of them were going to be losers.

The crowd surged around the horse, trying to get near him, but were kept back by Uncle Rastus and Manulito. Eph had his fingers in the bridle-ring, and would allow no one to take his place.

Now it was clear to those present why the horse had not run better in the last heat, for they cried,—

" He is broken down ! Poor fellow! Will never run another race!" And innumerable expressions of sympathy and regret were heard on every side.

The lameness appeared to be either in the left fore-shoulder or left leg, it being impossible to locate it; but the poor animal limped, and seemed scarcely able to put his foot to the ground. All kinds of remedies were suggested. The shoe was examined, taken off, refitted and put on again, but all to no purpose. Uncle Rastus bound the leg firmly with a flannel bandage. It seemed to relieve the pain, but the relief was only temporary, and the horse limped as badly as before.

Kirtley was nearly wild, and was bitter in his denunciations of his evil luck. The race had to go on, he knew that. Two heats had been run, one won by each, and the third must be run also. If his horse could not race, then all bets must follow the winning horse, and all the black horse had to do to be a winner was to walk over the course. He now realized the enormity of his betting, for, like many others who could ill afford it, he had risked more than he was able to lose. He approached the horse, and the sympathetic crowd made an opening for him to get nearer, where he stood like one in a dream, not hearing the pitying remarks of his friends.

Young Eph and the Indian looked quietly determined. No one could read the pent-up feelings of the boy, while the Indian was a Stoic, and did not show his thoughts any more than he would have done were he made of marble.

When Kirtley approached, Uncle Rastus said to him,—

" Char up, Brer Kirtley! Char up! We will do de bes' we can fo' de hoss."

Kirtley neared them, and speaking in a low voice, just so the trio could hear, said,—

"I hev bet thousands ov dollars on this hoss! I've bet cattle, an' I've bet the hoss hisself——"

"Wot's dat yo' say, Brer Kirtley?" said Eph. " Yo' bet dis hoss too? An' ef I loses de race mus' dis hoss, mah Sweet Mahjorum, go 'way f'um heah ?"

"Yaas! If yer lose the race the hoss mus' go !"

At this the boy's eyes filled with tears, as he stroked the horse's head.

The flag now waved for them to get ready for the final heat. It seemed a cruelty to force this noble animal to run in his lame condition, and Kirtley was solicited to withdraw him and forfeit the race. But he declined, saying that Sweet Marjorum should go over the course if he had to walk.

As the horses were uncovered and brought forth, the disparity in their appearance was so great that hundreds of sad hearts noted it.

The young darky requested that he might take a standing start at the score, and this was allowed. He held his horse sidewise that he might swing him into position. As the black horse wheeled, the young lad raised his hand, signalling he was not ready, and dismounted. He motioned his father and the Indian away, unwrapped the flannel from the horse's leg, and stroked his face affectionately, talking to him in low, musical tones, his words not being distinguishable. The horse replied with a low whinney, and pawed the air with his lame leg. The black horse sprang forward, the sorrel reared and wheeled, the flag dropped.

"Now, honey!" sharply spoke the boy, and the horse leaped ahead,—a perfect start.

"Look at that sorrel run!" the crowd cried. "But he won't last, the pace is too hot for him. His lame leg will give out!"

But it had not given out at the half, for the horses were side and side, running faster than ever. The jockey was plying rod and steel to Imp o' Darkness, but the sorrel clung to him.

At the three-quarters pole the black was a nose ahead, but as they entered the home-stretch, young Eph drew a shorter rein, leaned over the sorrel's neck, and sharply spoke,—

"Now, honey, now! Sugah in de mangah waitin' fo' yo'! Run fo' mah sake?"

A tigress never sprang quicker to the protection of her young than did the sorrel horse at this. He did not seem to run. His feet appeared scarcely to touch the ground, as with tremendous strides he shot forward. The jockey on Imp o' Darkness beat and spurred, but to no purpose, for, with his great eyes bulging from his head, Sweet Marjorum crossed the line four lengths in advance, in 1.48, with the colored lad looking over his shoulder, and grinning with childish joy at his defeated rival.

The crowd did not wait for the announcement of time, but rushed in on the track, cheering, wildly cheering, the result of the race.

The yellow flag shot up, telling them at the starting-point the result.

As the horses started, Kirtley stood with open mouth, staring at the spectacle of a lame horse running with such speed; but before he had time to collect his thoughts the race was run, and his horse was winner.

Those present seized the colored lad and bore him on their shoulders, cheering again and again for him and for the horse. Kirtley rushed forward, and seizing the young rider by the hand, exclaimed,—

"You're a brick! Cum down an' take yer pick ov ther colts. As the Gov'nor ov North Car'lina said to the Gov'nor ov South Car'lina——"

"No you don't!" interrupted Wellington. "Not to-day, Kirtley. I know it's a big day for you, but don't drink any to-day, for my sake, if not your own."

"All right, Bill, I won't fur your sake; but ef I was a-goin' ter act as I feel like doin', I surely would."

It was a source of great astonishment to all that the horse so speedily recovered from his lameness. But the boy told of their strong attachment, of how he had taught him numerous tricks,—this one among others,—and that Kirtley had trusted him so much that he wanted to make all the money he could for him. When asked if he had not feared losing the race, he said he never did.

The first heat he wanted close, and during the running of that ascertained the speed of his competitor. The second heat he intentionally lost. Then he made the horse walk lame as a surprise, no one but Manulito being aware of what he intended doing.

" Ah couldn't 'fo'd ter lose," he continued, " 'caus' ef Ah did, mah pet 'd be taken f'um me, an', gemmen, Ah t'inks mo' ob dat hoss dan any one in dis wuld 'cept mah ole daddy."

As the boy disclosed these things he was cheered more than ever, for they were delighted that a mere boy should circumvent a professional gambler and beat him at his own game.

Thompson and his companions felt unusually sore over their defeat and great losses, but their bohemian life had taught them long ago to accept whatever fortune came to them. They had risked all their money and lost, and Thompson remarked, with his cynical smile,—

" We shall have to depend on the generosity of the good citizens of this village to lend us sufficient cash to enable us to reach the borders of our peaceful homes."

Almost any man would have been discouraged and disheartened after losing as much money as Thompson had on his race-horse. Not so with him. At first he appeared stunned at the result, as he had felt that he was betting on an absolutely sure thing, and the disastrous result was like a stroke of lightning from a clear sky. But he did not spend his time in bemoaning his loss. His money had come easily, and it passed out of his possession without one word of complaint from him. There was no time for sorrow or regret. The fates had been averse to him. The race was fair, he had bet and lost, and, having lost, there was no recourse. But he was a gambler, and life was the same to him whether he won or lost. His roving, wandering existence had converted him into a decided optimist, for he believed that what is was to be, and never murmured at his ill luck. He might be discouraged for the moment, perhaps, but time in its revolutions would make all things right. He had met with financial reverses many times before, but as he always kept in reserve either money, collaterals, or land, he accepted misfortune with astonishing resignation. So it was this day. His rapid imagination speedily concocted a scheme to win back much of the money he had lost. In those early days, as now, there was a fascination about a game of cards that always brought many

men, both young and old, to the table. Men filled
with ardor or conceit, oftentimes both, who thought
themselves shrewd enough to beat a gambler at his
own game. In this village were to be found plenty
of this description, only too willing to tempt fortune
at the card-table. Thompson knew this, and, with
his adherents working with him, it was no difficult
matter to arrange a quiet game of faro for the evening,—a game that lasted all night, and which resulted in the gamblers winning back their losses to
a very material extent. But Kirtley was too shrewd
for them, and could not be induced to take part in
the game.

The revelries of the day were prolonged far into
morning by the many who were fond of dancing,
when chanticleer announced the approach of dawn.

The musicians, tired and sleepy, between dances,
suddenly jerked themselves together, and strove,
with vigorous raspings, to produce from their vio-
lins music sharp and inspiring, while the tireless
floor-manager called out, in loud voice,—

" Git yer partners fur a cotillion !" or, " Now you
fellers git yer gals fur Dan Tucker !" or, when the
gentlemen condescended to give the ladies a chance
for choice of partners, he would call, " Ladies'
choice ! Come, girls, snatch some feller an' fill
the set !"

The dancing was not according to modern stand-
ards. There was no walking through a set with
listless indifference ; no faint touching of the tips

of the dancers' fingers; no minuets with their graceful movements; none of the *décolleté* abandon of the modern waltz.   But the smooth, planed pine floor coaxed many a nimble foot to greater activity, and the audience was pleased to such an extent that any extra steps, giving variations to the common ones, were always vociferously applauded.

Finally, the last dance was announced, and at its completion all departed for their homes.   Quiet crept over the village, and nothing was heard except the barking of some unsettled house-dog.

CHAPTER X.

THE DEPARTURE OF MANULITO.

" The man to solitude accustom'd long,
  Perceives in everything that lives a tongue;
  Not animals alone, but shrubs and trees
  Have speech for him, and understood with ease,
  After long drought, when rains abundant fall,
  He hears the herbs and flowers rejoicing all."
                                        COWPER.

THE seasons glided quickly by, and Wellington and his red friend were frequently seen together. A hunt intended by one meant that it would be incomplete without the other.   The pressure of business restrained Wellington from participating in many of these excursions, but it only intensified his desire to go, and the time had to be chosen when these hunts would not interfere with his legal duties.

Manulito was now an honored inmate of his household, for Wellington had told his wife how his life had been saved, and painted with the brush of eloquence the part Manulito played that day at the river. To Wellington's wife Manulito was not an Indian, but was the one who had rescued her husband from death, and the feminine kindnesses she knew so well how to show were delicately thrust on the Indian.

Manulito passed all his time at the home of his friend or in the woods, occasionally with his hound and rifle in pursuit of deer. But oftener, in the summer-time, he was a willing prisoner, as a childish hand grasped his and tugged hard and strong, beseeching him to go with her to gather the pretty flowers which blossomed so thickly in the meadow-land. His fierce heart was tamed to meek submission by the winsome maiden of four, and after they had gathered great bunches of pinks and Indian reds, and the golden lady-slippers, they would seek the shade of some large tree, and the proud, strong man, wrapped in his blanket of fiery red, his childish captor, and her older brother, would sit for hours, the boy listening with feverish excitement to the Indian's tales of his life in the woods, of his love for the Gray Eagle, and of the great chief their father was among his people. The boy could scarce restrain his enthusiasm, and the most exciting events of the stories were repeated again and again. All this time the little maid seemed lost to her surroundings, and while her brother was being wrought up to a pitch of intense excitement, she remained indifferent, and with feminine ingenuity arranged little bouquets, displaying to the best advantage the brilliant flowers they so often picked in their wanderings. Manulito had learned from this child to love the flowers as he never did before, and often in his wanderings through the forests and meadows he would stoop and pick some flower, then blow its petals into gentle quivering motion, and inhale its fragrance, while his thoughts returned to those excursions so thoroughly enjoyed with this little one and her brother. Then as he held the flower from him and gazed into its depths, its petals were transformed into a childish face with golden hair and laughing eyes, and his eyes assumed their mildest look, for his thoughts were with his heart, and his heart was with the little daughter of his friend, the Gray Eagle.

They had returned from one of these pleasant excursions on one of the most beautiful days of June, and as they neared the house, Manulito carrying his little friend in his arms, he listened with idolatrous attention to her chattering, while she laughed in childish glee and playfully tapped his face with the pink and purple flowers.

The proud Indian was a slave to the caprices of this little one. When in her presence he seemed under mesmeric influence, and she led him into contented captivity.

He hated the white race. All the wrongs his people had suffered were constantly reverting to his mind. His people were dead, he was alone, and he felt that, with the exception of Wellington and his family, no one cared for him.

In his excursions he had visited the plains and mountains of the great West. He had gazed across the wide waters of the Pacific Ocean. And when he thought, as he often did, of the encroachments of the whites, who had robbed his people and driven them from the lands they had occupied for generations, and then of the unbounded freedom, the limitless expanse of the plains, the solemn grandeur of the great hills and mountains, he longed to go away and never return. He felt chained and powerless, tied down so that he could not revenge the wrongs inflicted on his race. He lived among those who had won his undying hatred; yet he knew how he was beloved and respected by Wellington and his family. And thus he spent his days and nights longing to go, yet restrained by the bonds of love and gratitude.

The only love he had ever felt for a woman was for his mother. He had lived to see her pass away, in her last moments blessing him with maternal love. He had lived to see his father die, admonishing him of the folly of resisting the whites, cautioning him to remain their friend and ally, and prophesying the subjection of all Indian tribes. He was born free; to him the freedom of forest and prairie came as his birthright. He saw this freedom wrested not only from his people but from himself, and, at first, hatred had so taken possession of his heart that he seemed scarce able to control himself. He feared that some time when laboring under the mental strain, caused by his realization of great wrongs, he would commit some act that he would ever after repent.

But his life with Wellington had opened a new avenue of thought. With gentle simplicity he had been led to the brink of love, where fraternal affection had won him, and the bravery of his little charge,—the boy who looked to him for everything, who constantly sought his advice on all those points of woodcraft necessary to be learned, who loved to sit and listen to the story of his wanderings, whose suggestions led to a recital of the exciting and interesting portions of his life, these had all touched him deeply, but none so much as the sweet little maiden, so gentle and confiding,—too young for coquetry. She often told him he must love her, "'cause she lud him so, and always would." A touch of her hand, the clinging to him as she did, the showing of every little item of interest, the pinning to his blanket of her choicest flowers,—all such unsolicited, thoughtful deeds of her innocent love, her childish affection, softened his proud heart, and he feared for her, and loved her more than all the world besides.

It was a picture to see them together, she clasping his great hand with her tiny one, he, with his martial bearing and proud step, lagging behind and keeping pace with her, as she often said,—

"Tum, Manulito, we'll be sojers and march together." Then she would mark the time, and they would walk in step, one with the other.

She always had something new to tell him, and, as he sat beneath some great tree, she nestled close to him, and he was her confidant. A great many secrets she had for him, and as she tossed her golden curls back and looked with her deep-blue eyes into his keen, dark ones, she saw in them only an image of herself, for to her there was no fierceness in his gaze, but in its stead a confiding interest and love. And she it was, above all others, who caused him to delay his going; for the only solace, the only perfect contentment he had, was when in her cheery company. And thus it was that a hatred inherited for generations was first softened, then overthrown by an innocent child. But her influence was like balm to a cruel wound; her presence removed, he relaxed into bitter thoughts and enmity. This childish love had changed the man, and when in his bitterest moments he resolved to go to the far West and wage constant war against those who had wronged him so deeply, the sweet innocent face

14

always appeared before him, whether he was on the prairie, in the woods, or dreaming at his camp-fire. He tried to shake off this feeling, arguing that she was but a child, and that if she were told of his following the teachings of his race, and waging relentless war against his enemies, she would not sorrow over it, but would soon forget. However, he knew that in her little head was concealed more than childish thoughts, for she often asked questions that astonished them all, and he could not bear the thought of giving her one moment of pain. But though he felt that he must go away, he dreaded the sadness of parting, for it meant the deliberate separation from all that was near and dear to him. And what was he to do in his anticipated home? That he hardly knew, and little cared. His longing was to go far from the constantly-changing scenes, which warned him that time would soon wipe out all traces of his people. Already game was becoming scarce, and the rifle was fast being thrust aside for the shot-gun. The birds of the prairie, the grouse and quail, which he had always looked on as cheery companions in his hunts, were now being killed for pastime. Many of the old trails were converted into wagon-roads, and the stillness of the woodland was almost constantly disturbed by noisy, creaking wagons or boisterous teamsters.

As he and his little charge reached the garden-gate, the girl's brother bounded out, and said,—

" Why, Manulito, where have you been ? I have been looking all around for you. You promised to go with me to-day and get me a piece of hickory for a bow, and, besides, to teach me how to feather arrows."

The boy had his hands full of straight pieces of wood, some turkey feathers, and a small bottle of glue, evidently prepared to have his arrows made.

The mother caught the laughing roll of mischief in her arms, and kissed her again and again, while the Indian and his pupil started towards the woods which bordered the house. The point to which they were going was evidently a trysting-place, and they walked side by side, the boy carrying on a running conversation. He was completely enraptured with hunting, and told how he had been promised a gun on his tenth birthday, how he was going to try to profit by what the Indian and his father had taught him, how he hoped that in years to come he would be as good a shot as they, and concluded by saying,—

" Oh, how I wish, Manulito, that I may live to see what you have seen !"

" What Manulito has seen ?" quickly responded the Indian. " May the Great Manitou have pity on you, and call you to him before he permits that ! What Manulito has seen ?" continued he to himself. " I hope your young heart will never suffer as mine has in seeing my people driven from their homes."

The boy was old enough to know he had touched

a tender chord, and quickly apologized, declaring that he intended no wrong.

They soon reached the destined spot, but there were other occupants before them. These were not human beings, but the babbling brook in this sequestered spot was known to bird-life, and they saw a pair of quail, with their downy brood, gently sipping the water as they approached. A sharp chittering by the mother admonished her children of danger, and they scampered into the thick underbrush.

The Indian and the boy seated themselves beneath the great limb of a magnificent walnut-tree that cast its shade for many yards around. The surroundings had never before seemed so pleasant to the Indian. He had sat beneath this tree scores of times in the spring when the wild pigeons in countless thousands had filled the woods and usurped every tree; in the summer-time idling the hours away visiting with his young friends; in the autumn, listening for the gobbler's call; and in wild winter, watching for the deer to approach for its drink.

As he sat there, the boy respected his silence and busied himself with his arrows, whittling away, intending that Manulito should suggest the feathering and finishing touches.

It was mid-afternoon, a time when the day was at its brightest. The silvery clouds floated lazily in the heavens, obscured at times by those of a lower stratum travelling at a greater speed. The wind soughed gently, in musical tones, through the tree-tops, causing them to bend in supple gracefulness at the recurring breezes, which followed one another with sufficient regularity to keep the leaves in constant motion.

Along the borders of the tiny stream pond-lilies in their snow-white bonnets added variety and beauty to the scene, while the flitting robins, orioles, thrushes, and red-winged blackbirds darted through the openings in the woods, or favored the visitors with their choicest songs.

The air was delightful: so pure that every breath inhaled seemed laden with the perfume of forest and meadow. No wonder, then, that Manulito, ardent worshipper of Nature, revelled in the charm of their retreat. He had a vivid imagination and had seen much of life. His was not a religion of books; he did not worship according to any creed. He felt that if he lived as his father had, according to the teachings of his tribe, committing no crimes, worshipping Nature to the exclusion of all except the ever-living God, whom he recognized in the Great Manitou, then his reward would be everlasting life. Not a life of ease, of singing, of devotional exercises, but one whose happiness consisted in always having game and ponies with which to hunt.

Years before, when he had visited the tribes of the great West, and had acquired their language,

l   14*

he learned that they anticipated the coming of a Messiah; that the white race would become extinct, the Indians obtain complete possession of their lands, and game be as plentiful as in bygone years. But, as he saw more of civilization, he realized the impossibility of this, and believed that the Messiah *had* come, but that it was the Messiah of the whites, and that by His teachings and example He had shown what a Christian's life should be. Manulito did not fear death; he had nothing to live for, and really felt that death was preferable to a life passed in constant misery. Death meant to him simply a transposition of his soul to the Happy Hunting-Grounds,—his heaven,—where he would be resurrected and live again as he had lived on earth, where sorrow, suffering, and misery would be banished forever, and where, with abundance of game, he could hunt and fish to his heart's content.

The boy had nearly completed several arrows and finished them according to the suggestions of Manulito. They were straight shafts, headless arrows, precision in flight being obtained by reason of the feathered ends. These were made by taking a stiff feather of a turkey's wing, cutting in just above the quill, where the feather peeled off, taking with it a thin slice of the quill. This served as a strip or foundation for cementing it to the shaft. It was then glued to the arrow, and another piece of feather was fastened in like manner directly opposite. The feathered strips were securely tied with fine thread for the glue to " set," and the arrow was laid aside to dry, when the feathers were to be deftly trimmed to make the flight of the arrow perfect.

The boy was so absorbed in his work that he did not think that the small fly which so persistently lit on the rim of his ear, and was as often brushed away, was a straw in the hands of his little sister; but her merry laugh disclosed her identity, and with it the presence of his father and mother.

Wellington remarked that he had come home unexpectedly, and as the day was too fine to be spent in-doors, they had hunted up the truants and located them without difficulty.

As he and his wife seated themselves on the soft greensward, the little girl ran to the Indian, sprang into his lap, settled herself contentedly, and, looking archly up at him, said,—

" Did I hurt you? If I'm too heddy, I won't stay long."

All laughed at this, and the Indian made no reply, but tenderly twined one of her bright sunny curls around his strong, dark fingers, while his eyes shone with a light that denoted how deeply his heart was touched by this innocent mark of the little one's love and confidence.

" What a relief this is !" exclaimed Wellington, as he lay supported by his elbow. " To feel that one is absolutely free from the noise and confusion

of the court-room, and away from the jar and
clangor, the excitement, the wrangle of every-day
life that is thrust upon a successful lawyer. I sometimes feel utterly disgusted with life. To see what
I have seen, friends turned to enemies! Relatives
in the closest degree of consanguinity driven apart
because of some difference in money matters!
Then, again, the difficulty of telling which of two
witnesses is testifying to the truth! I have seen
such duplicity," continued he, "that I have grown
distrustful of a man even under oath. Of course,
these are some of the disagreeable features of my
profession, and they are more than offset by the
delight one feels in being an honest exponent of
that which is the foundation of the civilized world;
for the law is founded on truth and right, while
equity steps in and corrects that in which the law
is deficient, thus guaranteeing to all equal justice
and the enforcement of their legal rights. But I
don't intend to deliver a legal lecture, for I am
happy in being with you this afternoon, Manulito,
and I want to enjoy your society. Your race, Manulito, is one of dreamers. I will not say that you
idly dream your time away, but you love to seek
the seclusion, the quietude of some such place as
this, and spend the time away in some romantic
manner. That is how I feel to-day. I would like
to wander through the fields of romance, following
your trail, you to be my guide, and to disclose to
us the many things you saw years ago, when you

visited the tribes of the great West. I will be an attentive listener, so will we all; and I would like to have you tell us what you will of that land, almost unknown, but inhabited by the Indian tribes of many nations."

" Were Manulito to tell of what he saw and heard, of what he learned, of the many moons he spent among his far-distant friends, the passing day would fall asleep under the mantle of the approaching night, and the moon would smile, and the stars glisten above us before the story was half done."

" I know, Manulito, you have much to relate, but some time ago you promised that you would tell us, and you will never find a better opportunity than now, when we are all here. I would like to have you describe the country, its formation, its resources, its climate, its hills, mountains, and streams, its customs, game, and possibilities."

" And I," said the wife, " would like to hear of its people, their progress, their religion, their manner of worship, their homes, their filial and paternal love, their devotion, their nobility of soul, their generosity towards their fellow-men, and whether or not it is true that the wife and mother is subjected to menial service that makes of her a broken-hearted drudge and slave."

" And I," said the boy, " would like to have you tell of hunting the buffalo and elk, the fights with grizzlies and mountain-lions, the wars between the

tribes, and all about the braves who delighted to
fight, and didn't fear anybody; and all about their
dogs and their ponies, and everything that you
would like to have told you by a brave man that
had seen it all,—that is, if you were a boy eight
years old and about my size."

At this sweeping request all joined in a hearty
laugh. Then Wellington turned to the little girl
and asked her what she would like to have Manulito
tell a story about. At this she ran to her father,
twined her plump arms around his neck, kissed
him repeatedly, and exclaimed,—

"I don't care! He can tell what he has a mind
to, and I'll just lud you."

Manulito saw the impossibility of complying with
the requests of all, and said,—

"Were Manulito to tell of all that is asked, his
story would become tiresome because of its length.
He will tell then, in part, of what he saw on his
visit to the great hills."

As he prepared to commence, his quick ear heard
a musical tinkle. The others caught it,—the subdued chords of a banjo. Then there issued through
the woods strains that caused the birds to twitter
and sing in louder tones, as if to welcome their
serenaders in this their bowery home.

They recognized the voices as those of Uncle
Rastus and Eph. Their song was a plantation
melody, of that bright character that caused the
listeners' eyes to sparkle with delight.

The singers then changed their theme to a sere-
nade. Eph sang in his clear, pure soprano, while
his father modulated his tenor voice into a full and
mellow alto.

There was a charm about their singing which
only those present could realize. The serenaders
were hidden from view, and the wind blowing so
gently through the forest helped to soften the tones,
now subduing, now wafting in fullest volume to the
listeners the words and music of the songs.

Wellington and his wife were excellent judges
of music, and as the singers' voices floated smoothly
from majors to minors, they sat listening with
pleasure to each recurring note.

There is a power about music that carries one
insensibly with its tones, whether it be to quicken,
or to soothe and calm the feelings; and to those
who listened, one of the chief charms was the in-
visibility of the singers. There was a delightful
uncertainty as to their whereabouts, which aroused
curiosity, and made more pleasing the songs which
drifted from their hiding-place.

At the conclusion of the second song the singers
stepped into view, and were received with generous
and continuous clapping of hands. The darkies'
faces were wreathed in smiles, for they saw their
impromptu singing was a complete surprise and
was received with delight.

"Where in the world did you two come from?"
inquired Wellington.

" Jus' f'um home, Mars' Wellington! Jus' f'um home!" replied the elder. " Yo' see me an' Eph foun' a bee tree, an' ter-day Ah 'lowed we would take de missus some honey,—yer it is in dis yer bucket. Ah tole Eph 'e done bettah take 'is banjo, 'caus' w'y de chillun mought like ter heah 'm play de 'Debble's Dream' or de 'Money Musk,' or de missus hear 'm sing. So we 'lowed we'd go froo de woods. We heard yo' voices, an' jus' ser'-naded yo'. But, golly! Ah was orful skeered feer yo' would heah or see us, an' den yo' wouldn't be s'prised."

" You're just in time," exclaimed Wellington, " for Manulito is going to tell us of his wander-ings. Sit down and listen.—Now, Manulito," said he, " we are ready."

The Indian looked thoughtfully at the ground for an instant, and then began,—

" In dreary days and sleepless nights the time of Manulito was passed away,—this was many moons ago,—for in the daytime he wandered through the fields and forests, and at night he laid his tired body to rest, seeking the peaceful sleep, the renewed life which did not come. His bed was the dry leaves, his covering his blanket; but far above all was the star-lit sky, which always looked down on him. Occasionally he drifted into forgetfulness; but it was for a short time only, for with the closing of his eyelids his soul passed into another land, and sweet refreshing sleep was banished. Manulito dreamed, ever dreamed of a far-distant land where the white man did not live; where the Indians had complete possession of the earth, and roamed and fished and hunted to their heart's desire. In this manner the time slowly glided away, but the heart of Manulito was sad, for he longed to visit this unknown country. The spirit of unrest seized upon him, and one time when the spring had come, bathing the earth with melting snow and warm, gentle rains, and the buds were bursting on the trees, and the seeds were swelling in the ground, the robins and bluebirds, as they sang their song, seemed to tell Manulito to go and see this land in the distant West and learn of its people. So one night when the world was asleep Manulito, guided by the North Star, started on his journey to the West, to the land of the setting sun. His was not a journey with many people, for he travelled alone. Not that he was without friends, for through each and every day the flowers brightened his pathway, and the birds sang to him. At night he slept as he had never slept before, in sweet, sound slumber, listening to the song of the whip-poor-will and the mellow hooting of the horned-owl; for he felt that the Great Spirit approved of his journey, and would watch over him and protect him.

"The days glided quickly by, for Manulito did not feel lonely. Was he not born in the woods? Was not his whole life spent amid such scenes as these? The noise of the city was never heard where Manulito was; but instead, the singing of birds, the whistling of the quail, the drumming of the grouse, the cooing of the doves, the tinkling of the brooks, the murmuring of the streams and waterfalls, bringing the most delicious music to the ears of him who lived in the open air and called the prairies and the woodlands his home."

"Weren't you afraid of getting lost or of being killed?" inquired the boy.

"Afraid of getting lost?" replied the Indian, with an incredulous smile. "Afraid of getting lost? Does the eagle lose its way when it pierces the clouds through the limitless sky, or the elk as it traverses the pathless woods, or the wolf in its tireless runs over hills and prairies? Or does the wild goose lose its way when on its flights each half-year, or the fish in the deep and winding streams? And by the same unerring instinct which the Great Spirit has given to these Manulito, too, was guided; nor was there with him the fear of death; his rifle protected him from the wild beasts; his skill, from his enemies. And if he were killed," continued he, thoughtfully, "what of it? A man should be happy to meet death while doing what the Great Spirit intended he should, for death does not take from him his existence, but carries him to another world, where he resumes the unfinished work of this.

"After Manulito had travelled many days the land changed. He climbed great ragged bluffs, whose bare sides facing the west, and unprotected by trees, had been burnt by the summer's sun. Such was the spot where Manulito stood and gazed afar over the bottom-lands, into the winding river, —the swift-running, the ever-changing Missouri. Here he looked across into the land of the Omahas, a quiet people with whom he dwelt a welcome guest for many days.

"After Manulito left the Omahas, he visited the Loups and the Pawnees, the Arapahoes and the Sioux. As he wandered towards the setting sun the trees disappeared, and as far as he could see were vast plains of waving grass, at whose outer edges the sun rose in the morning and sank to rest at the approach of night. The Great Spirit had been generous with his people here, for the plains were blackened here and there with herds of buffaloes or brightened with curious, timid antelope. And still," he continued, in deep contemplation, "the white man had been there, for the iron shoe of his horse had made impress on the soil, and the wheels of his wagon had creased the rank grass. Like the serpent that steals in to bite and sting and leave misery in its trail, so will the white man always prove to the Indian race. They came with smiling faces and deceitful hearts to rob those whose fathers had lived on these lands for generations. There was no misery, no want, no suffering among the tribes until they were cursed by the presence and the fire-water of these white trespassers. They were happy in their freedom, their love of hunting, the abundance of game, their traditions, their religion. But the whites came with a Bible in one hand, a rifle in the other, and the Indian lost his home, his standing, his independence, forever."

The bitterness of his tones conveyed to his hearers the deep hatred that dwelt in Manulito's heart towards the white race.

" And yet," continued he, " they blame the Indian for his cruelty. It is his mode of warfare to severely punish his enemy, in order that by the death of one the many may take warning and avoid him. Is he to be blamed that he strikes for his liberty, his home, his wife, his children? Can you say that he loves all these less because the Great Spirit made his skin red instead of white? And if even the animals, the bears, the wolves, the dogs,—ay, even the tiny wren,—will protect their young, will fight for their homes, would not the Indian be lower than these beasts if he, endowed with reason, with strength, with weapons, stood still and saw his home despoiled, his father murdered, his children scattered? Would not the Indian be less than human if he refused to punish those who thus injured him?"

As Manulito paused for breath, his eyes flashed and his breast heaved in great excitement. Wellington appreciated his feelings, and sympathized with him, but he desired to change the tenor of the story, and said,—

" Manulito, I understood from what you once said to me that you settled among the warlike Sioux."

The Indian stared at the speaker for an instant, then collecting his thoughts and apparently regretting his violent language, said,—

" The Gray Eagle is right : Manulito visited many tribes, but his youthful spirit was like the Sioux'. This was before Manulito had lost his hand. He lived with them for many moons, and among all the tribe there was none fleeter of foot, none so sure with the arrow or rifle, as Manulito. They invited him to remain and become one of them. He fought with them, and so pleased were they that they made him a chief, and he has promised to return to them some day. From them he learned many things. He joined in their war-dances, the Sun-Dance, the Corn-Dance, the Buffalo-Dance, the Ghost-Dance. He learned that the customs of these people were those of his people; that good deeds were rewarded and evil ones punished; brave warriors admired and praised and cowards made squaws of as in his own tribe. They told Manulito of a Messiah that would come to earth, and that this Messiah would be for the Indians. And this is what they said and believe :

" Years ago, when these trees which now shelter us were saplings and seedlings, when herds of deer were ever to be found, when the Indian roved over this whole land, taking what he needed, but never injuring the supply, there came to the far East winged canoes filled with men. While these men were strange in appearance, pale as if they had never faced the sun in his noonday anger, or the wind in his wild wanderings, still they were received with all kindness by the tribes that dwelt near the ever-living waters. These men had ways as strange as were their faces, for though they had been received with all the kindness of a simple people, still, with no regrets, they broke their treaties and promises with the Indians. What chance had a people armed only with arrows and war-clubs against such beings as these? It was of no use now to try to drive them away. Like leeches they clung to this rich land upon which they had fastened themselves. The pale-faces did not depart, but it came about, little by little, that those who had received them with open arms were driven from their accustomed haunts.

"Who can tell how? But true it is that the story of the terrible deeds of these pale-faces soon came, no one knew from whence, to distant tribes. Perhaps the breeze that filled the woodlands brought it, or the birds as they returned in the spring. Then came surer tidings from those who had seen these strange men, and who had been driven from their homes. And at last, as they had been warned, came the intruders themselves. Their ways were pleasant and their words as sweet as the sap of the maple in the spring-time.

"After many moons there appeared a deliverer

to the red men, who came as silently as the green leaves in spring-time. From tribe to tribe, from nation to nation, he went, imploring them to resist the advances of the white men while yet there was time.

" This prophet related all the events that would come to pass were not the strangers driven away. 'Already,' said he, 'is the Great Manitou displeased; for, see, the plains which he has made beautiful with waving grass and nodding flowers they have invaded. With their strange tools they have torn the grass from the earth, leaving it brown and bare, and they have sowed seed, and the ground is covered with plants which were not intended for this country. He is not pleased that his work should be disturbed, and, as a punishment, he will drive away the game which has hitherto been so plentiful.'

" But the words of the wise man were unheeded, and when he found that it was in vain he labored, he vanished with the leaves in the autumn, as silently as he had come.

" He told them that the Great Father was dis- pleased with them because they had not answered when called, and that now he would leave them to their own devices until they were ready to accept the things that were done for their good. He would go, but he would come again when they most needed him. He taught them strange dances and ceremonies for the different seasons, and told

them that when the time was come for the new
Leader to appear, signs would be given them.
Then should they practise, night and day, these
things that he had appointed. By their faithful-
ness in this matter the time of their waiting would
be shortened, for by these dances they would become brave men, and it pleases not the Great
Manitou to keep brave men in sorrow. His teachings are followed, and the Sun-Dance which he in-
stituted has made the bravest warriors that have
ever been known.

" Among other things, this prophet told them of
a Messiah who had been sent to the white man, but
who had not been accepted by them. He had
been mistreated and put to death, so that on his
return to earth the next time he would come as a
Messiah to the red men, and would show his dis-
pleasure against the white race by driving them
from the country.

" When the invaders learned of the faith of the
Indians, they laughed at their beliefs and ridiculed
them in every way; but the Indian's religion is
as sacred to him as is Christianity to the white
man."

" I agree with you there, Manulito," interrupted
Wellington. " There is but one true religion, that
is the worship of the ever-living God. Every nation has its manner of worship, but it all tends to
the same end,—everlasting life in the presence of
the Creator. How that can best be obtained is a

question which will always be a subject of dispute.
The Catholics, the Presbyterians, the Methodists,
—each sect regards its form of worship as the right
one; but although the outward showing of their
religion is different, the desire for the ultimate end
is the same with them all. The Messiah of the
white man appeared, he was crucified, and arose
from the dead. But he is not the one whom all
nations desire, or, I would better say, accept, and,
therefore, the Jews look for the coming of their
Messiah, the Christians for their Christ, the savages
for their Mahdi, and the legends of the sleep of
the German Emperor Frederick and the Welsh
King Arthur tell of others who anticipated similar
events. I respect the religion of every man and
every nation when the devotee follows his convic-
tions devoutly and conscientiously; for while we
all claim to be right in our views, we cannot say
that others are altogether wrong, and I have the
utmost reverence for a religion which has been accepted for generations by the Indians, which has
existed for ages, and has passed down from father to
son without question. They have the same right to
believe in the coming of a Messiah, to expect the
redress of their wrongs and the reward for their
steadfastness, as the white men have. Both have
a religion of faith, an element which is essential
in every belief which promises a future reward.
While I do not agree with the red men, still I am
glad to hear of their beliefs and their expectations,

m

and in me and mine you have not only willing but sympathetic listeners."

The Indian's glance conveyed his thanks for the kindly words, and he continued,—

"One day, after the departure of their would-be deliverer, an old Indian, who had lived far beyond the greatest age ever attained by one of his tribe, fell asleep. He slept for hours, the hours lengthened into days, and still he did not waken. All thought he was dead, but the medicine-men said he was alive but sleeping. At last he awoke, and, calling all the men of his tribe together, said,—

"'Be not fearful! I have been in the land of the blessed. Call the nation together, that I may tell them what I have seen and heard. My body was with you, but my spirit was in another land, a land where buffalo and ponies were so plenty that they scarce found room to graze. As I looked with delight on the scenes in this newly-discovered country, the spirits who were my guides spoke to me. Their voices were low and soft and sweet, and they said that the Great Spirit is angry with us, and that unless we refrain from wickedness He will destroy us, and we shall never see that beautiful land. But if we follow his commands He will ever look kindly on the red men, and will sweep the white men from the continent. They promised that we should always have plenty of game, and that the white men should never be seen again; that the Indians who were dead should be restored to life, and the body of every dead white man be changed to a buffalo. These spirits then said that we must dance till the coming of our Messiah,—the Ghost-Dance, the Fire-Dance, and the Sun-Dance.'"

"But why were they to dance?" interrupted the boy. "Couldn't they fight or do something besides dancing? I don't see how dancing made them fearless."

To which Manulito replied, "Dancing is a part of the Indian's religion. He dances when he rejoices and when he mourns, when he starts on the war-path and when he returns, and he shows his penitence by self-torture in these ceremonies. When he has danced a long time and his heart is warmest, his body is on earth, but in his mind he sees a picture of spirit-land, and talks with his friends who are dead. At one time a prophet said he had been visited by a person who had been dead for years, and this person came to him and gave him a piece of fat buffalo-meat. The next night the prophet stepped into the circle of the dance bearing a wooden platter full of meat. He called up the dancers,—there were more than a hundred of them, —and after all had eaten the platter was more than half full."

"But tell us of the Sun-Dance!" exclaimed Wellington.

"One of the ceremonies in which the Indians participated when they expected the coming of the Messiah," said Manulito, "is the Sun-Dance. They were not obliged to take part in this, but all Indians want to be considered warriors, and they are always anxious to prove their bravery. Joining in the Sun-Dance is the most severe test they have. When they are ready to begin, old warriors attach long strings of rawhide to the centre pole of a wigwam. The breast of the Indian is cut and pieces of wood thrust through the opening; the long strings of rawhide are tied to these, and, facing the sun, while they all sing their low chants, the brave dances and swings his body, trying to tear himself loose. This cannot be done for hours. Sometimes he faints, but he does not yield, and tugs and pulls until he snaps the sinews of his own breast. Then he is free, and is received as a warrior, ever afterwards wearing deep scars of his torture. All the time he is trying to break loose he shows no sign of pain, nor sighs, nor groans, but swings and throws his weight against the cords until the flesh gives way. He can be set free any time if he asks it; but then he is called a squaw-man and cannot fight with warriors.

" When Manulito was with his red friends he saw much that was new to him, for his tribe had been subdued by the whites when he was a child, and these strange customs brought back to him what his father had often told him of the bravery, the cunning, and the wild life of a free Indian. But the days slipped swiftly by, and Manulito wandered farther towards the land of the setting sun. As the days grew longer, he rested in the shadows of the great rocks and trees, and journeyed at night, guided by the light of the moon and the path pointed out by the Great and Little Bear and the Pole Star. It seemed now as if Manulito was in another land, for the scenes of his boyhood were gone. The rolling prairies were no more; the deer had changed; the grouse were wearing coats of blue; the hills had grown into mountains, where the sun smiled warmly in the valleys, and the peaks were white in their robes of snow. The quail of the Mississippi Valley had disappeared, and in their stead the bushes were alive with crested quail, which ran and chatted, waving their long topknots as they hid from view. Beautiful flowers, far more handsome than Manulito had ever seen before, blossomed everywhere, and the trees had grown to such a height that they seemed to reach the clouds, while one of them was larger than any fifty that he had ever seen before. 'This,' thought Manulito, 'is Paradise,—the Happy Hunting-Grounds,—for no other world could be brighter, no air purer, no forest more beautiful than this.'

"In a few days he sat and looked far away to where the sun was just going to rest,—it seemed as far from him as ever. Manulito could go no farther, for he sat on the shore, as the day went to rest, and he saw the sun sink into the Pacific Ocean. The waters rippled, showing rainbow-colors, while the sky, blushing from the kisses of the sun, was radiant with shadings of rose and white and gold.

"But the night is coming on, and we must go. The day is nearly gone, and soon the dew will fall as the sun sinks behind the hills."

"Go on, Manulito! Go on!" exclaimed Wellington. "We are not weary of your story, and the night is hours away. But perhaps you are tired of talking, tired of telling us of your life."

"Manulito tired?" queried he. "No! no! He could sit and talk of his life not only for hours but for days, and it would but make him the happier, for Manulito has no friends, he has no home, except here. His life is like a dream,—it has been and is not. When he questions the reality his senses seem to desert him. He loves to sit where he can breathe the pure air of heaven, and sleep and dream forgetting the sad past and hoping for a brighter future. This is a beautiful spot, and here Manulito, when tired of the world, has often come and rested, listening to the sweet songs of the birds or gazing at the floating clouds, idly dreaming the time away. But there is one spot made holy to him, because it is his mother's grave, that is dearer than this. Away up on the bluffs, where from their majestic heights he can look down over the tall tree-tops into the fertile bottom-lands of the Mississippi, where the living world looks into the calm mirror of waters and sees the reflection of its thousand trees, where islands in their green suits are bound by the running river, where the meadows nestle between the groves of elm and willow, where

bluffs in broken ledges pierce the sky,—that is the
spot which Manulito loves best of all. But why
talk of this? It is time to go."

At this they rose, and as they wended their way
homeward a silence fell upon them all. Wellington felt that it would be but a short time before the
spirit of unrest would seize upon the Indian, and
he would leave them, perhaps forever. He knew
the war that was raging in Manulito's heart, his desire to leave these scenes of past sorrow, his wish to
go where he could try to bury the past and begin life
anew, and he did not intend to urge him to remain.
He had sometimes wondered at the strong friendship which existed between them. But Wellington had seen much of the world, and was broad
and liberal in his views. He was a physiognomist,
and had that keen perception which reads one's
thoughts during an apparently rambling conversation. He had seen the glitter of the world, the de-
ceit of individuals, and experience had taught him
an invaluable lesson, how to separate the dross from
the pure. Thus it was that with him time served to
strengthen and deepen the regard he had for Manulito, for in him he found both a friend and a brother.
The blood of consanguinity did not flow in their
veins, but the bond of sympathy, of respect, of
pure love, held sway in their hearts. It was seldom that their mutual affection found vent in words,
but whether in the woods or at home, their eyes
never met without speaking for them the love they

bore for each other. Wellington knew that beneath the swarthy skin of Manulito there beat as
true a heart as man ever possessed. He had taken
great delight in teaching the Indian, for he was not
only a willing but a brilliant pupil. His mind was
one of vast resources; his thoughts were poetical,
and his life infused into his mind and heart those
rare virtues learned only by those who have associated with Nature in all her moods. His voice was
melodious, and when he talked his face expressed
the feelings he sought to convey, and it was like enjoying the sweetest music to listen to him. He was
a natural orator, like many of his race; his inspiration came from his love for out-of-door life, and
when he spoke, the earth, the sky, the water, the
seasons, and animated Nature served to illustrate
his thoughts. He had for years been brought into
contact with the whites, and had acquired their
language, speaking it fluently; their words helped
him to express himself, but his manner of speech
was entirely individual. As Wellington said, "Manulito's speech is like a rivulet of water. It flows
gently, carrying one with it, until its musical tones
thrill through the listener."

And Manulito was an equally ardent admirer of
Wellington. He loved him with all the strength of
his fierce, wild nature. It was a passionate love,
founded on gratitude, and graven deeply on his
heart by reason of continued and unsolicited kindnesses. His friendship for Wellington had con-

stantly increased because of the latter's brilliancy and learning. Although the event was never mentioned between them, yet Manulito often thought of the time he had fired at Wellington in the forest, and though he knew he had long since been forgiven, he yet craved opportunities to prove his repentance and his love. He would have been glad at any time to lay down his life for his friend, and his only regret would have been that he could no longer show his affection.

As they sat at the supper-table that night, Wellington, who was usually the soul of mirth, and seemed to have a never-ending fund of jollity upon which to draw, was disinclined to talk, and the others caught his mood, so that the meal was eaten in comparative silence.

When the children were ready for bed, Manulito watched their every motion. After they had kissed their papa and mamma good-night, the little girl kneeled down, clasped her hands, and with upraised eyes concluded her prayer with the words "and God bless Manulito and keep him well." This evidence of childish affection almost unmanned him, and as she put her arms around his neck, he buried his strong face in her sunny curls to hide his emotion. Then he showered kisses on her neck, her forehead, her hair, until she said to him,—

" Who has hurt you, Manulito? Your eyes look as if you had been crying."

Her father understood all, and tenderly taking her in his arms, carried her to bed.

When the boy came to say " good-night," Manulito was himself again, and, stroking the lad's brown hair, said,—

" The years will glide quickly by. They will be years of joy and sorrow. The Great Spirit has blessed you with a kind father and mother. From your mother's daily life you will gain lessons that you will never forget, for from her you will learn to pity the unfortunate, to sympathize with the afflicted, to help the poor, to aid the sick, to lead such a life that the world will be benefited because you have lived; for the Great Spirit has been generous to her, and has given her all those virtues which make her presence as welcome as the warm sunshine is to the sick-room.

" And your father,—you will always love him, for he is wise and good. In after-years, when you become a man, the most pleasant words that can reach your ears will be those that tell you that you are like your father. You love your parents now, but time alone can teach you the depths of that love; for, when they are dead and you stand at their graves, a voice will come to you from the heavens where they will live again, reminding you of your kindness, and accusing you of every unkind word or deed of yours that ever brought a pang of sorrow to their hearts. Then love and respect your parents. Honor your father and mother. For no success you can attain in this life will console you for any act which brings sorrow to them."

The boy looked in astonishment at Manulito, for while he had occasionally received advice from him, he had never heard him speak in this way, and he said, wonderingly,—

" Are you sick ?"

" No," replied Manulito.

" Are you going away ?"

" Yes."

" Never mind asking questions, son," said Wellington. " It is time for you to retire."

The boy looked interrogatively first at one then at the other, gave Manulito's arm a squeeze, and left the room.

They sat in silence a few moments, each apparently waiting for the other to speak, when Wellington said,—

" We are not blind, Manulito, and we can see that you have made up your mind to leave this place, but the time of your departure we know not."

" To-night !" exclaimed Manulito.

" And where are you going ?"

" To the mountains and the prairies. To live again the life the Great Spirit intended for me."

Wellington arose, walked slowly across the room, turned, and, facing the Indian, said,—

" We have known each other so long that I understand why you leave us, and I do not blame you for going. You know that in this house you are as welcome as my own brother. There is nothing that I could do for him which I would not do for you. When we part with you it will be with sad hearts; but we will hope that in years to come your thoughts will turn this way, and your love for us, for our old hunting-grounds, for that sacred spot where rests your dear, dead mother, will touch the tender chords of your heart, and you will come back to us. But I can't say more, my heart is too full for speech." And Wellington bit his lips to suppress his emotion. Manulito concealed his own grief, and without a semblance of pain, a tremor of voice, looked tenderly at Wellington and his wife, and replied,—

"All that is near and dear to Manulito is in this house, and when he thinks of leaving here it seems as if he were going to tear himself from his world. When first he came here he was like a ship without a rudder, drifting before the wind. He lived,—not that life seemed worth the living, but because he had dared death many times, and it never came. His heart was fierce; he hated all men, and lived only for revenge. But by your hands the wounds of many years have been healed, and this spot has become sacred to him. At first his heart failed to receive the impress of loving acts, and when he realized your kindness his life seemed a dream too strange to be true. His brother has been so kind

that the Great Spirit will bless him for it. Manulito
has not deserved all this,—he did not expect it,—
and many times kind words and generous acts have
been like drops of molten lead poured into his heart.
He had always thought that the time would never
come when his hatred would cease towards a single
member of the white race. But the deep interest
you have taken in him—you with whom Manulito
has lived, you who have clothed and fed him—has
made his heart yours and not his own.

"But he is going away. And why not? He can
do nothing here. Then let him go, carrying with
him your best wishes and your prayers, and know
that the lessons he has learned from you will not
be forgotten. He goes to live the life of a free
man. His home will be the boundless prairies,
where he will hunt the buffalo; he will war with
the enemies of his adopted tribe, and for the sake
of the love he bears you all he will never raise his
hand against a woman or a child. He will be happy
on the great prairies, and his deeds shall win the
praises of his adopted tribe. At night, tired from
hunting, or from his wars with his enemies, he will
sleep sweetly with the stars shining above him, and
in dreams he will be with you and the little ones,
hunting with you, his brother, or gathering flowers
in the valley with the child he loves. And perhaps some day you will hear of a strange warrior,
of one who feared not death, one whose name struck
terror to his enemies, and then, if they tell you

aright, they will say that he was fair in war, and, although an Indian, was merciful to all. And this will please you, for you will know that Manulito's heart did not forget its love for you. And then, perhaps, we will meet again. You will not stay here long, for this is no place for Manulito's brother; the field is not large enough. But when you live in a great city, will you not sometimes think of Manulito? Manulito the Indian! A savage, perhaps, and yet he loves you better than man will ever love you again. And when, at times, the Gray Eagle sits in his office, he will let his thoughts wander to the Wapsie, to the bottoms where he and Manulito have so often hunted and slept together. And when Manulito strikes down a buffalo or a deer, or camps beside some beautiful stream, he will think of the Gray Eagle, and his only regret will be that his brother is not with him, for without him the pleasures of the woods will be but half enjoyed. But the moon is at its greatest height, the stars warn Manulito to start, and as he goes he prays that the Great Spirit will shower his blessings on this house."

As he said this, he advanced to Mrs. Wellington and knelt before her. She placed her hand on his head, and in a voice broken with emotion exclaimed,—

"May God bless you, and so direct your steps, Manulito, that those with whom you dwell will be blessed by your coming!"

Wellington could not speak, but grasped the Indian's outstretched hand, and they all walked out of the house. As they did, a horse neighed to them, and Wellington said,—

"Manulito, you know that horse. I bought him from Kirtley, and he is young, fleet of foot, courageous, and tireless. Take him. And may he be the means of lightening your journey and giving you pleasure."

As he concluded, Uncle Rastus, who had been passing with the horse, stepped forward, placed the reins in Manulito's hands, and Imp o' Darkness had a new owner. Manulito bowed his thanks, sprang on the horse's back, said a last good-by, and rode slowly away.

The night was beautiful, and Wellington watched the retreating figures as they threaded in and out between the trees. Then they disappeared for an instant, but in a moment were again visible on a knoll where horse and rider were sharply outlined against the sky. Manulito must have known that his friend was still watching, for he paused an instant with arm uplifted, waving a last farewell, and then disappeared over the brow of the hill. Wellington stood as if in a trance, looking with strained eyes, but Manulito was gone. Then his wife said,—

"Come, Will! Come!"

He looked at her, and said, in a voice trembling with emotion,—

"There goes the truest heart that ever beat. God bless him! God bless him!"

Then nervously clutching his wife by the arm, he walked unsteadily into the house.

CHAPTER XI.

THE MESSENGER.

"Thou art too wild, too rude, and bold of voice;
  Parts that become thee happily enough,
  And in such eyes as ours appear not faults;
  But where they are not known, why, then they show
    Something too liberal."
                          SHAKESPEARE.

IT was now nearly five years since Manulito had said farewell to his friends. Wellington and his family were still at the old homestead, but they saw the futility of remaining much longer, for a man of Wellington's acknowledged ability could not tie himself down to a place where his practice compelled him to travel with teams in a judicial circuit throughout which his services were in constant demand. His scattered practice, furthermore, necessitated his absence from home a greater part of the time, and this was peculiarly distasteful to him, for he was a man deeply attached to his family, and exceedingly domestic in his habits. During the excitement and worry of the many trials in which he was engaged, he always looked through the clouds of legal wars and saw beyond the haven of rest at his little home on the farm, where love and constancy ever welcomed him with open arms.

He knew the brilliancy of his mind, the depth of thought he possessed, the intuitive faculty of discernment, his power of analysis of any subject. But while he saw all these things which were evident to those with whom he was brought into contact, he was neither vain nor egotistical, and the light of his intellect shone brightest when struck by the spark of some opposing element.

The gift of intellect which Nature had dealt him with such a lavish hand he made the foundation on which he built his legal and oratorical successes. When he began the practice of law, he saw that, while young both in years and experience, his services were in demand in every important trial in his locality. This did not fill him with vanity, but was the spur that urged him on to merit his victories and to make him worthy of the compliments so freely given him. He was not ignorant of the influence he carried in his arguments, and constantly strove to improve his mind and to add to his store of knowledge, so that the power to create sympathetic emotion, with which he knew he was gifted, would flow from the spring of a mind which was the receptacle of truth, history, and learning. He knew that the power of a man's arguments would soon be lost unless back of them there was a mine of wisdom and learning; that wit or impassioned utterances at the bar, unsupported by legal knowledge, would have little weight; and that the eloquent lawyer, if not also profound, would be a failure compared with the prosaical jurist who had the statutes always at his tongue's command. He was a student, and his disciplined mind enabled him to retain what he read. He was literary in his tastes, and took pardonable pride in both his legal and private libraries. He wanted to probe to the bottom all subjects in which he was interested, and, therefore, when in the study of law new points were at all times being suggested, his great mind sought to grasp them all. Accordingly, he studied ancient and modern history, the classics, mythology, but especially the history of England, for in the old law-books of that country and in the Bible he reached the origin of the subject, and learned that generations before statutes existed the world was ruled by the Common Law, which was simply the established customs of the people.

Many who heard his speeches did not realize that his brilliancy of thought, the beauty of his rhetoric, was the result of profound study. They were charmed by the melody of his voice as its silver tones reached the recesses of the court-room, but when in sarcasm he tore to pieces some argument advanced by his opponent, or with judicial wisdom presented some hidden point of law, or with supreme confidence quoted some familiar maxim known principally to his profession, or with fervent eloquence swayed his audience by his beautiful comparisons, and then from brilliant similes drifted into the deepest subjects, showing the depths of his researches, they did not realize that this eloquence was the result of days and nights of the most ardent study.

He loved poetry. His favorite authors were Shakespeare and Milton, and in the poems of Burns he often found thoughts which inspired him to loftier language, and insensibly changed his words to poetical prose. When speaking, he seemed to have his hearers under mesmeric influence. When he denounced some act as deserving the scorn of honest-minded men, all were with him; and when he pled for sympathy or mercy, his impassioned speech won for him the support of judge and jury. Few could resist the power of his eloquence, and many a man who at first withstood his pleadings felt his set lips relax, and his moistened eyes told the story of the surrender of his heart. As Wellington's reputation increased with his years, the knowledge that he was to plead a cause would fill a court-room. To a certain extent his eloquence was the means of creating opposition to his client, for the jury, forewarned of his persuasive powers, would sit, not always to study the merits of the case, but determined to resist the brilliancy of his speech. This increased his labors; but if their hearts were of iron, his reasoning was a drill of steel, and soon pierced their armor.

Time in its revolutions wrought wondrous changes in the scenery where this story is founded. The dense forests were swept away by the settler's axe, while civilization, in its onward progress, converted rolling prairies into cultivated fields. Here and there little farm-houses dotted the fields. The deer-paths and the hunters' trails were broadened into wagon-roads. The creeks were spanned by bridges, primitive as yet in their construction, and the land was occupied by incoming strangers.

The hunters' paradise was a thing of the past, for big game was growing scarce, and only an occasional deer was killed. There was still an abundance of small game, both fur and feather, but to one who had for years tested his skill against the antlered kings of the forest, this afforded but indifferent sport. Wellington hunted but seldom. The journeys were so arduous, game being so hard to find, that each season he found himself less inclined to hunt. But his resolutions to quit hunting were but the outbursts of disappointed feeling, not an evidence of a change of heart, for he still loved the fields and forests and the solitude of Nature. When one has been a devotee of out-of-door life, a passionate lover of field sports, those feelings are never entirely lost. When oppressed by the trials of business, when his tired body demands rest and recuperation, the recollection of the green fields, the quiet woods, and some spot where he can rest and enjoy the, beauties of Nature, comes back to him. And he longs to be away from mankind, where, amid the solitude of his surroundings, he can dream the hours away.

So it was with Wellington. When he thought of leaving this section where so many of his happiest days had been spent, like a clinging vine these thoughts wound their tendrils around his heart, and he was loath to leave a place so sacred to him. He felt that when he made the change, the bustle and activity of city life would keep him from the places he loved so well. But he could not remain here, for he knew that it would be an injustice to his family and to himself, and he had therefore made all arrangements to leave and practise his profession in one of the larger cities.

The years had passed quietly at the old home since Manulito left, and the children were the blossoms of perfect health. The boy was sun-browned and ·dark, an expert with bow and arrow, obedient and yielding, yet so bold and fearless that he would catch some wild colt, and, with a rope for a bridle, ride it while it ran its swiftest over the rough ground, leaped the ditches, and tried to free itself of its rider.

With the little maiden the five years had but added to her beauty and simplicity, and she had grown into a lovable girl of nine. Her sweet man-ners had not deserted her, for the intervening years had only added to her graces. Her tall, slender form, her perfect teeth, her violet eyes, her golden hair, which hung in curls over her shoulders, her merry smile, her sunny disposition, attracted every one to her, and she was the light and happiness of this little home.

They all remembered Manulito well, his beautiful sentiments, his noble character; and often they sat before the crackling fire, hour after hour, while Wellington told of the exciting incidents which happened when Manulito and he were together on their many excursions. They loved to talk of this absent friend, and hoped that some day he would return to them. Each remembered him according to the individual impression received. To the boy he was chivalrous, learned, wise in the knowledge of woodcraft; to the girl, kind and affectionate, so willing to go with her to gather flowers, so generous, so appreciative when she showed her childish love; while Wellington and his wife remembered him as a man of noblest mould, possessing a heart as true as steel and of the grandest impulses. There was a charm to Wellington in recalling what he knew of Manulito, for when he talked of him it brought the sweetest recollections of his past life; and it seemed as if the veil were lifted, and he and Manulito were together, hunting, fishing, or sitting in some favorite nook in the forest. It was a dreamy retrospection in which he loved to dwell.

One night the family were sitting by the fire-place. It was in the month of May, and though the days were mild, the nights were cool enough to make the warmth of the fire agreeable. Welling-ton had been speaking of Manulito, and as he finished, the boy exclaimed,—

" And don't you ever hear from him, papa ?"

To which Wellington replied, " I have never heard a word from him until to-day."

" To-day !" they all spoke in unison.

" Yes, to-day I heard from him. It was in an unexpected fashion; but the messenger proved a most welcome one, and I have good news."

" Good news !" exclaimed the mother. " Oh, I am so glad! He is coming home !"

" No, no ! Not that! He is not coming home; but let me tell you what I heard."

At this the mother dropped her sewing, and the boy and girl seated themselves at their father's feet, their eyes sparkling with expectancy, as he said,—

" I sat in my office this morning, deeply engrossed in looking up authorities and making a brief pre-paratory to arguing a demurrer, when the door opened, a man entered the room, and, after ex-changing with me the courtesies of the day, seated himself composedly in a chair. He was a stranger to me, and from a casual glance at his dress and general appearance I took him to be a farmer. My mind was intent on the point I was studying, and therefore I gave him only an occasional look. In reply to my inquiry if I could do anything for him, he said, ' Not just now. Go ahead with your work, judge.' He was surely complimentary in the title he gave me ; but, as I dug through my books, I felt somehow that the man was making a study of me. At times I looked up suddenly, and invariably caught his eyes, though, as he met my glance, he would look indifferently away. Finally, I must confess, my curiosity got the better of me, and I began a study of my caller. He was of medium height, tanned from exposure, and his whiskers, moustache, and hair were of a faded brown color. On his head was a battered felt hat that had originally been white, but through the exigencies of long wear had acquired a shade which was indescribable; his coat was a faded yellow ; he wore a ' hickory' shirt, ' blue jeans,' and his feet were encased in brogans which were thickly covered with dust, showing what had been his mode of travelling.

" I must confess I took great pleasure in studying this specimen of humanity, and I tried hastily to form an opinion of him, his errand, and his occupation. It was evident to me that he was penniless, and yet there was an indifferent abandon about him that told plainly of his satisfaction with the world in general. I pretended to take no interest in him, but he kept me under constant surveillance, until at last, as if through with my studies, I closed my books, and, turning to him, said, 'Well, my friend, what can I do for you?'

"At this he looked at me intently, and said, 'Squire, you've been studyin' me for some time, but you don't know me. I am a tourist.' Then he laughed, and said, 'In plain words, a tramp. You can't do any law business with me, but I've suthin' to say to you that will interest you. I'll have to ask you some questions fust; but before we begin, I want to say with truth, and I'll sw'ar to it if you want me to, that I heven't had a bite for twenty-four hours; and you know how it is yourself, when a man's stomach is empty he ain't in no condition to talk. Now, if I was a millionaire, or had a few dollars, I wouldn't talk this way; but I'm bu'sted,—completely broke,—and I want you to lend me a quarter. Then I'll get suthin' to eat and come back; and if you are the man, then I've news for you that will please you.'

"Of course I gave him the quarter, for some way I felt that he had something to say which would interest me, and naturally I was anxious to hear it. He went out and soon returned, having evidently made good use of the quarter, for, as he seated himself, he took a generous chew from a great plug of tobacco, and said he was ready to begin. At once I discovered that he was to be the questioner, and I was to be thoroughly investigated, for he began,—

"'Squire, I don't want you to take offence, but

what I ask you about you will soon find my reasons for.'

"Then he asked me if my name was Wellington, and if my wife had black hair and beautiful brown eyes. I was proud to reply in the affirmative, and thank him for the compliment so worthily bestowed. Then he wanted to know if I had two children, a boy and a girl; and, next, he asked if an old darky worked for us named Uncle Rastus. I watched him eagerly as he disclosed his knowledge of our family, and tried to identify him, but I couldn't place him. Then I asked him if he had ever lived around here. He answered that this was his first visit, and, divining my thoughts, said,—

"Now, Squire, don't try to locate my phiz, for you can't do it. I'm a stranger here. This is my fust trip through these parts, and I'm simply on the back trail through the States. You wonder what I'm doin' here, and I'll tell you. I'm here to keep my word, to see you and your wife and little ones face to face, and deliver my message accordin' to promise.'

"At this I was more mystified than ever, for I could not imagine what this man might have to say to us. I could scarcely withhold my impatience, and insisted that he tell me at once what his errand was. He appeared to take delight in my eagerness, but retained his knowledge as a kind of delicious morsel, until finally I said,—

" ' Tell me, my good man, what you intend to. Please don't delay it any longer. Tell me where you came from and who sent you.'

" At this he rose, walked up to me, and said,—

" ' I come from the plains! I come to keep my sacred pledge to the Lone Chief, Manulito !'

" On hearing the name we love so much, I grasped both his hands, and asked him about twenty questions in one breath.

" I must have talked very excitedly, for he raised his hand and said,—

" ' Not now! Not now! My errand must be delivered to all of you,—yourself and your family.'

" So he promised to come here to-night, and it is time for him now. Hark! Yes! I hear heavy footsteps. It must be he."

Saying this, he opened the door, and the stranger entered. As Wellington greeted him, he asked him his name, and then said,—

" Mr. Martin, I have the pleasure of introducing you to my wife, our son, and our little girl."

" It is scarcely necessary, Squire, to interduce your family, for the description given me would tell me whose children they are."

Notwithstanding his effort to appear self-possessed, he seemed a trifle ill at ease, for he said,—

" I ain't very handsome in this outfit. What luggage I have don't bother me to carry, for I wear it all the time. I ain't much for style. Workin' don't agree with me, and my stomach is so constituted that it can be empty for a couple of days or be overloaded; it's all the same to me. My wealth don't bother me any. I don't make any debts, 'cause no one is fool enough to trust me; and if I had money I couldn't keep it. I don't worry any, 'cause worry shortens every man's life. I've got a heap of travellin' yet to do; my old legs will give out some day, and when they do, I expect I'll turn up my toes 'side of some hedge, or be found a stiff in some honest man's barn. Therefore I intend to take life easy and accept things as they come."

"You are certainly a philosopher," said Wellington.

"Hardly that, Squire! Hardly that! For I think that what you call philosophy is jest good hoss sense. We all know about what's right in this world, but it's mighty hard allus to carry it out. We don't all agree,—good thing we don't. I go my way,—got no relatives,—it's nothin' to nobody, so no complaint comin'. But I promised to tell you about your Injun friend. Say the word and my story begins."

"All right," said Wellington; "we are all ready and waiting."

At this the queer guest took in a fresh supply of tobacco, and said,—

"Appearances are not deceivin' in my case, for I'm a queer duck, and while you mought hurry me by suggestin' things, then ag'in you moughtn't;

'cause I'm like a wild-cat: you can't most allus tell which way I'm goin' to jump. So with me the probabilities are that the longest way round 'll be the shortest cut. I ain't a-goin' to tell much of my life, 'cause that's neither here nor thar, but, as the preacher says, ' in the course of my peregrinations I may refer incidentally to the subject not under discussion.' Purty big words for a man of my cut to use, don't you think?"

Wellington and his wife smiled at this, for they began to feel almost as much interest in the man as in his story, while the children thought him the oddest specimen of humanity they had ever seen.

" I've tramped through all the States and Territories, and the longer I live the funnier the world seems to me. When I fust come to your office, I didn't know but what I had made a misdeal; but you showed your hand, I felt I had as good, so I stayed. If you had made a bluff, I'm thinkin' your jags would have lost the game; but you played honest with me, and Jim Martin don't go back on no man what gives him a squar' deal. But to my story. I hoofed it across the plains with a gang of gold-hunters goin' to 'Frisco, mined awhile, made some money, and spent it a heap faster than I made it. But it wasn't no use; I wasn't contented. I prospected, but was down on my luck most of the time, and twice I had a fortune slip away from me. Once I sold a claim for two thousand dollars. For a few weeks I painted the town, but the money soon went, and I was bu'sted. And then, what do you think? That same claim that I had dug, picked, washed, and worked in for two solid years,—the same infernal one that I sold for a miserable two thousand,— witiin two weeks afterwards they sunk a shaft six feet farther, and sold out for *seventy-five thousand dollars!* Think of it, *seven thousand five hundred tenners!* In fact, that was the kind of luck I played in all the time.

"Then I drove stage, whacked cattle, fought, bled, and came mighty nigh dyin' with the Injuns; indeed, was so long with them that I can speak most any Injun language. If I couldn't I wouldn't be here, for that's the way I've got out of a good many scrapes with the reds ; and I wanter tell you, right here, that I ain't got no love for any of them,—no, it's hardly fair to say that, for I do feel uncommon kind towards your friend, and I want to tell you that he has a heap whiter heart than the average white man.

"You see, I was guide across the plains for years, and knowed all the tricks of the redskins. I'd never happened to run across the Injun they called the 'Lone Chief,' but he had the reputation of bein' the greatest warrior they had. He could outrun or outshoot any of them ; he was the biggest brave in all the tribes, and in their councils he always took the lead, while, when it came down to speech-makin', he took the cake, and would have taken the ice-cream and spoon too if they had had any. His hoss had an equal reputation, and nothin' on the plains could touch him for speed. He was jet-black, and they called him the 'Evil Spirit.' They had a high-toned name for him, 'Imp o' Darkness,' but plain words are good enough for me, and I allus called him the 'Devil.'

" Last summer I was guidin' a train across the plains. The men were the most disgusted lot you ever see, and one in partic'lar was mean as a coyote. He laid all his bad luck to the Injuns; fact was, they had relieved him of several hosses, and failed to return 'em or pay for 'em. So one night he was a little full, the boys twitted him, and he took a solemn oath that he'd shoot the fust Injun he saw. Some of 'em thought he was gassin', but I knowed he wasn't, 'cause I knowed he was a sandy cuss, and I was afeared he mought do what he threatened. So, after he was sober, I talked to him, but it didn't do no good. He said he had sworn to shoot the fust Injun he saw, and he was goin' to do it. I told him that if he did the whole outfit would be ransacked and all of us lose our headgear, but he said he'd do it. Well, two days arterwards we was camped by a little creek,—it hadn't any name then, but it's called Raw-Hide Creek. It was about three miles from the Platte, right above the North Bend. We had packed up, and some of the boys said that Pete—that was his name —had gone huntin'. Pretty soon one of the men come runnin' in and said, 'Pete's kept his oath; he's shot an Injun.' Now I knew we were in for it. We started right off, but that afternoon a cloud of dust was seen west of us, and then it seemed as if the plains was alive with Injuns. Ahead of them all, and in command, was the Lone Chief, ridin' that black hoss. I knowed the jig was up, and I told the boys so. They had sense enough to see it, so we stopped and waited. Jerusalem! I've seed many an Injun on a hoss, but such a fine-lookin' fellow and such a noble hoss I never seed before nor sense. The Lone Chief rode up in war-paint, feathers, gewgaws, etc., and said in jest as good English as I'm usin' now, 'I would speak with your commander.' Well! It almost knocked me silly to hear an Injun talk that way; but I stepped out, and he said,—

"'We seek the man who shot one of our squaws at the creek this mornin', and this train must turn back'ards and go with us.'

"That settled it; but I made up my mind to tell the whole story, and to put the blame where it belonged. We started on the back trail, and while I was ridin' alongside this warrior, he said,—

"'A lyin' tongue will bring its owner to grief. Many lives will be spared should the Pawnees know who fired that shot. If the murderer is not discovered, the innercent 'll have to suffer with the guilty.'

"I was in a box; didn't know what to say. At

last they stopped at this same creek,—the identical
spot where the squaw was shot,—and this warrior
rode out, and said,—

" ' Who was the man that fired that shot ?"

" No one spoke. Then he axed the question
ag'in, but didn't get no reply. The Injuns were
gettin' oneasy, and it was all their chief could do
to keep them from sailin' into us. Then he said,
for the third time,—

" ' Who was the man that fired that shot ?'

" I knowed the game was up now. We couldn't
fight, for they had disarmed us at the start. The
boys shut their teeth and breathed hard. Jest then
Pete stepped out, and said,—

" ' I am the man !'

" The Lone Chief said, ' You've saved the lives
of your friends, but you must answer for your
crime accordin' as my warriors desire.'

" Now, Pete was no coward, and he said,—

" ' There's no use my lyin' about it. I said
I'd shoot the fust Injun I saw, and I kept my
word.'

" ' But,' said the Lone Chief, ' she never did you
no harm. She went to the creek to get some water,
and you shot her down jest like you would a wild
beast. You didn't give her no chance to defend
herself, and when her little pappoose come to its
mother it found her—dead ! What reason can you
give for this ?'

" Pete saw now what he'd done, and hung his

o   18*

head without speakin'. Then he looked up, and he
said, ' I've nothin' to say.'

" ' 'Tis well !' exclaimed the chief.

" Then they held a confab. I saw what was
comin', but didn't know in jest what shape. Two
warriors sunk a stake, about six feet high, right at
the spot where the woman was killed. Then they
took a lot of rawhides, and when everything was
ready, the Lone Chief rode up near the stake, and
this is what he said,—

" ' Few men have suffered more than Manulito
at the hands of the white men, but to-day he forgets his bad feelin's towards them, and only lets
his warriors punish the guilty. If my braves had
their way, all of you would now be dead. Nobody
but the guilty shall suffer, but you, his friends, must
see us punish him. He took the life of an innercent person, and his own life must pay for it.
When you get back to the settlements and speak
of this day, you can say that *one* Indian was merciful towards the innercent, and saved you from bein'
put to death by his warriors.'

" When he'd finished this here speech, he made
a motion to his warriors, and four of 'em grabbed
Pete, stripped him to the waist, and tied him to the
stake. Then a big, strong buck come up with a
whip made with a short handle and four rawhide
thongs, each one braided separately. When he was
tired of whippin', another took his turn, and so
on. But, Squire, I ain't chicken-hearted or mealy-

mouthed, but I'm not goin' to tell more. It makes me sick to think of it, and I ain't any tender-foot, either. How long it lasted the Lord only knows. But Pete's crime was punished, sure enough, and he died right on the spot whar', a few hours before, he had committed murder. It was awful! But, Squire, hard as it was, we all had to admit it was a squar' deal.

"You kin bet your sweet life I wasn't in any shape for visitin', but this chief, Manulito, took me one side, and I'm willin' to admit that that Injun knowed more than any one I ever met. When he found I was goin' to the States, he pumped me to find out whar' I was goin'. I told him it didn't make any diff'rence to me. Then he asked me if he hadn't done me a good turn. I told him if we had been playin' cahoots and he held four aces, he couldn't have done himself prouder. He asked me if I would do him a favor. ' Well, I should say yes!' says I. 'Then he drew a map, directin' me how to reach you, and after he had explained things so I couldn't miss the trail, he got kinder confidential-like, and told me all about you all, how kind you had been to him, and how he loved you. When he spoke of *love* I come mighty nigh snortin', 'cause it struck me so quar for an Injun to love anybody. But he soon satisfied me he did love you all, and I found, on talkin' to him, that while he was the smartest and bravest warrior of them all, he had a heart as soft as a

woman's.   He told me to go to you, to tell you,
Squire, that he had forgotten nothin'; that night
arter night he dreams of you, and when he is successful in a hunt he wishes you was with him; when
others praise him and flatter him, he don't 'preciate
it nigh as much as he would a few words from you,
tellin' him you approved of what he had done.

"Yes," continued the stranger, "he is the wisest
and best Injun I ever run across, but his heart is
right in this house all the time, and he loves you
more than all the rest of the men in this wicked
world.

"To your wife, he said to tell her that the promise that he made the night he left your house he
had allus kept.   He didn't mention what it was,
and I was goin' to ask him, but on second thoughts
didn't consider it any of my business, and I hate a
pryin' cuss anyhow, so I didn't say nothin'.   But
he kinder let the cat out of the gunny-sack, for he
said, 'Tell her I have kept my promise, and have
saved many women and children, and seen they
reached their homes safely.'

"He sent his love to the boy, and said to tell him
that he hoped he was well and strong, and that he
would not forget the last advice he gave him, to
try to be like his father; and he said for him to be
good and true, kind and obejient.   Strikes me he
said suthin' else, but the hinges of my memory are
purty rusty, and I disremember what else he said
to tell the boy.

"To this little gal he said,—say, Squire, what do you think? Well, I'm willin' to be lassoed for a coyote if that Injun's eyes didn't grow weak and kinder watery when he spoke of the gal,—he said to tell her that he never saw purty flowers in the mountains or on the plains without thinkin' of her; and when he rested at the aidge of some stream he often picked flowers, and he loved those best that were like those she used to find. I never seed a full-grown man think so much of a child as he does of this little gal. I listened, and he talked for hours,—all about you-uns, and it struck me that he was a romantic cuss if he was an Injun."

"But tell us," said Wellington, "did he say he was coming back?"

"No, he didn't, and I don't think he intends to. He seems to be mighty happy,—that is, for an Injun; it don't take much to satisfy them. He's free to do as he pleases, hunts buffalo and antelope, goes to war most of the time with neighborin' tribes, and is a heap big Injun generally. What more could he want?"

"You expect to return again, and when you do, tell him for us——" interrupted Wellington.

"Now, look here, Squire; don't give me any message, 'cause it won't be delivered in that blasted country, for I'm a coyote if I ever go there again. There's nothin' out there I want. The Injuns don't owe me nothin', and I ruther think they have some old scores to settle with me. My headgear is a heap more becomin' to my style of beauty than a wig, and I don't intend my scalp shall dangle in a wigwam if the court knows himself, and I think he does."

Wellington smiled, and remarked, " Well, Mr. Martin, you have surely seen much of the world, and your experience has been varied."

" Seen much of the world ?" queried he. " Well, I should smile. And as for experience, Squire, I couldn't have had more at a camp-meetin'. I'm not one to force myself on any community, neither am I so awfully modest that I can't make my wants known. Indeed, Squire, modesty don't worry me, and I ain't afeerd to ask for what I want if I don't see it. I believe in the old sayin', ' If you don't see what you wants, call for it.' Doin' this has given me many a squar' meal. I've had many a tussle in my lifetime; have slayed grizzlies and mountain-lions, but when I tackled John Barleycorn, I was knocked silly the first round. And when a man gets peart, as we all do at times, John Barleycorn is the fellow that will show him up. Yes, Squire, when a man thinks he can get the best of whiskey he is goin' to get beat, dead sure. He may be strong physikerly and bright mentally, but whiskey will floor him quicker nor two jiffs of a lamb's tail. I've been there, Squire, and know what I'm talkin' about. I once got to drinkin' powerful hard, and the more I drank the sassier I got, until I felt as if I had a contract to drink all the licker in town. Well, I didn't drink it up, but I got awfully peart, and the fust thing I knew I was in the jug, sentenced to thirty days' services in studyin' geology."

" Geology?" inquired Wellington.

" Yes, geology! You see, the city authorities had a stone-pile, and us bummers, what was sentenced to break them stones for use on the streets, was called 'geology students.' Well, I graduated in thirty days. Then I tumbled to myself, and made up my mind I would brace up and be somebody. You see, I was allus handy at anything, and one day as I stood on the levee at St. Louis, a man walked up, and said he to me, ' Can you tell me whar' I can employ a second cook for this steamboat?' 'Well,' I said, kind of independent-like, ' Can I? I should say I could!' At this, I stuck my thumbs in my vest and looked at him, while I rolled my eyes and said, ' When you hires me, you gets a horseshoe, for I'll bring you good luck. I'm the seventh son of a seventh daughter, and they was all cooks, some pastry-cooks, while others was jest common every-day cooks, and wasn't ashamed to wash dishes on a pinch.' Well, I was accepted. In less than three months the head cook died of yaller fever, and I was appointed ' chef.' Well, now, Squire, talk about major-generals, shoulder-straps, etc., they ain't nowhar' compared to a ' chef.' Of course my salary was raised, and I began to feel my importance. I gained fifteen pounds in weight,

I waxed my moustache to look Frenchy, and when any strangers was round, I looked fierce, and rattled off some jargon what I picked up in Canada. Gee-whiz! but I was important. They all saluted me, from the capt'n down, and I was the biggest man aboard. Naturally I felt my oats. So one day the capt'n intrudes on me between meals, jest when I was suppin' some old Madeira and eatin' some wafer-crackers,—jest a little lunch you know,—and the capt'n said to me, 'Monsieur,'—I mought explain right here that that was the way they all had to open up a confab with me,—'Monsieur,' said he, 'a very elegant lady desires a cup of hot tea.' 'What!' said I, 'a cup of tea between meals? You know, sir, that's against the rules of my kitchen!' This riled the capt'n, and he said, 'Confound yer imperdence! Who's runnin' this boat, I'd like to know?' 'Give it up,' said I. 'All I knows is I'm chef of the culinary department, and I don't allow no one to intrude on me.' The capt'n was an old steamboat man, and of course a pow'ful cusser when he got on the war-path. Talk about Paradise Lost! Talk about 'Hell hath no fury like a woman scorned!' Paradise or hell couldn't touch the capt'n. I've heard harvest hands hold purty lively discussions. I've been with raftsmen on a tear. I've listened to cowboys expressin' their opinions about Injuns and buckin' bronchos. But never did I hear any human bein' swear like that capt'n did. I looked him squar' in the face, tryin' to look him out, and then I give him a biassed look over the arm of the chair, but it was no go. As a clincher, I looked at him catawampus-like over my right shoulder, but nixey! It wouldn't phaze him. Hoop la! but didn't he rave! He damned all the cooks that ever was born, and all that was to come. He said they was the cuss of every capt'n's life; that he had more trouble with them than all the rest of his help put together; that they allus wanted big wages, done as they pleased, and quit without notice.

" You see, I got ruther tired of the capt'n talkin' so, and I jest lassoed him with the remark,—

" ' Capt'n, you've got a big trip, and a bluff don't go. You're at least two days away from another cook, with a hungry lot of passengers. You've abused me pussonally,—that I don't care so much about,'—then I took on an offended look, and made my voice tremble as if I was greatly affected, and said, ' Capt'n, the language to me I can forgive and forget, but the insult to my perfession—never! Now, if you don't apologize, I get off at the next landin', and there'll be a mutiny aboard, 'cause the passengers ain't got nothin' to eat.'

" The capt'n saw he had kicked over the whiffletrees while he was still hitched to the tugs, and he knew I had him on the hip. About this time I rang for the second cook, and while the capt'n squirmed and tried to get out of it, I made him apologize for what he said. I knew he was inwardly cussin' me, but he had to come down off his perch or have them all howlin' for grub, so he come. Arter he went out, I turned to the second cook, and I said, ' Young man, become a chef! Then the world bows to you.' "

" But," laughingly interrupted Wellington, " I should have thought the captain would have planned some revenge for this."

" Don't worry about the capt'n. He had it in for me all right. He was awfully pleasant for days, and one day he sneaked in a new cook without notice, and watched his chance for me. The passengers knew of the jamboree the capt'n had with me, and sympathized with him. So one day, jest at dusk, they landed at an island. Two roustabouts grabbed me, and while they led me off turkey fashion, the band played the ' Dead March.' The crowd cheered and jeered. They said I should still be ' chef,' and not only chef but king, and I was fired without a mouthful of grub. I lived on that confounded island for ten days, eatin' nothin' but blackberries and turtle-eggs. The Lord only knows how long I would have stayed there if it hadn't been for a stray log that floated nigh, which I grabbed and straddled, and then paddled to the main shore, bein' in terror every minute for fear a ' 'gaitor' would grab me and pull me under."

" But," said Wellington, " I should have thought

that passing steamers would have seen you and have come to your relief."

" Relief nothin' ! They did all see me, but they knowed it all, and every one whistled for a landin', then gave me the passin' signal jest to devil me.

" Still," continued he, with a self-satisfied smile, " I still live, and my steamboat experience helped me to another job. I drifted around from place to place, workin' at my trade,—doin' nothin',—until one night I ran slap-bang up against a meetin'-house. They was holdin' revival meetin's, and as I stuck my head in, the pastor, a white-haired old man, said, 'Now let every one join in singin' this famee-liar hymn.' Then they struck up ' Rock of Ages, cleft for me.' Now, while I don't look it, I'm somewhat on the sing, and tenor is my long suit. So I j'ined in the song, and then I sang another and another. The next night I felt my shanks propellin' me towards that church as if the safety-valve was closed with one hundred and eighty poun's of steam, when I only had license for one hundred and fifty. Well, to make a long story short, I got religion, and got it bad. I never was very back'ard on the talk, and my gift of gab helped that good old man to convert many a tough sinner. It done me a heap of good, too, and I wish I'd stuck to it. I'll tell you what it is," said he, in a serious tone, " it's the only real satisfyin' thing there is in this world. Arter I had got several doses of it, I kinder felt like savin' the world and startin' out as

an evangelist; but my fust experiunce discouraged
me, for I got a position as mate on the steamer
'Grand Republic.' Now, thinks I to myself, here's
a chance to do some missionary work among a
tough set. Jest my luck! I started on the wrong
trail, and preached to them about the beauties of
heaven instead of the horrors of hell. I got one
nearly converted; he was a tough cuss,—never
wore a coat, and you could allus see his bare feet
through his old shoes. I pictered to him, as best I
could, heaven, angels, and everything good. 'Will
I be an angel?' said he, 'and hev wings, and 'sociate with decent people?' 'Of course,' said I, 'if
you repent and are saved.' 'Never expected anything so rich,' said he. 'Wouldn't feel at home.
But if you can fix it to let me in on the ground-floor
whar' I kin hev a chance to work my way up,
don't mind thinkin' it over. But I don't want
to disgrace no one in this world or the one to
come.'

"I argued with him, but he got away. I gave
chase and let out full sail,—even let out the jib,—
but couldn't overhaul him. Then I preached hon-
esty to the roosters under me, spoke kindly to
them, and thought I'd elevate them, but I found
the only true and ke'rect way to elevate them was
with my boot, for they stole my watch and money
while I was prayin' for their souls. Unless they are
swore at and punched occasionally with a pitchfork
handle, they think they're neglected, and won't

work. Nothin' like a man havin' the rations he's used to, Squire. Ain't that so?"

Wellington bowed assent, and laughed aloud at the stranger's logic, but to Mrs. Wellington he was an enigma. The stories of his strange life were to her a fascinating but distasteful revelation, and her refined nature rebelled at the coarseness of his language. She felt in constant terror lest he should say something to shock the children, who listened with bated breath to the story of his life. To them it was a tale weird and wild, an exposition of things of which they now heard for the first time. They listened with childish eagerness to the story, but were frequently puzzled to catch the meaning of many of the strange words and idioms used by this unexpected guest.

"Yes, it's a funny world," continued he, "and the people like to be swindled. Allus cravin' suthin' new, allus wantin' suthin' for nothin'. But that's what makes life easy for us. I made two thousand dollars one summer as easy's fallin' off a log, jest by bamboozling greenies. You see, I had let my hair grow long, wore buckskin clothes, claws for a necklace, kept my face stained, and passed for an Injun doctor who spoke pretty good English. Then I travelled with an Injun attendant. We cured—at least pretended to cure—all kinds of diseases with my wonderful medical discovery. To show it wuzn't dangerous, I used to taste it often. I sold a heap of it that summer, but an old Dutch-

19*

man got too inquisitive, and a chemist told him this wonderful medicine, put up in four-ounce bottles, consisted of four ounces aqua pura, a little extract of smart-weed, a few drops of ile of sassafras, with enough aniline red to color slightly. You can imagine the profit in it. But then," said he, looking wise and elevating his eyebrows, " expenses were heavy, and us perfessional men allus should be paid well for our services. My money soon went, and the next thing I was travellin' with a side-show, wrestlin' with a cinnamon bear. But one day the bear got mad, and put his arms around me so tight that two of my ribs was broke. I then—— But here, it's gettin' bedtime for these chicks. I hurried somewhat in my story, and once or twice let out a reef to make better speed, and now I'm through, think I'll get a move on myself, as I'm gettin' nigh the home-stretch."

"You will stay with us to-night!" exclaimed Wellington.

"What? Where?"

"Why, here in this house, of course!"

At this the guest laughed as if some great joke had been perpetrated, and said,—

" Why, Lord bless you, Squire, I hain't slept in a decent man's house for years. Can't sleep indoors, anyhow. I feel oppressed-like, and when I wake, unless I sniff the fresh air, I'm choked for breath. I'm jest as much obleeged, but with your consent—and if you don't give it, I'll do it anyhow

—I'll jest crawl alongside the straw-stack near the barn. I ain't afeared of bein' robbed, and if any one tackles me, their friends are apt to ask 'em whose mule they've been foolin' with."

As they reached the door, Wellington thanked him for his visit, and again offered his hospitality, but the stranger declined, and bade them goodnight.

Early the next morning, as soon as they were astir, Wellington hastened to find his strange guest and interview him again, but his search was unavailing, for he found that the wanderer had disappeared.

CHAPTER XII.

FROM VILLAGE TO CITY.

" His tongue
Dropt manna, and could make the worse appear
The better reason, to perplex and dash
Matured counsels."

MILTON.

As the days passed after this strange visitor had called, there steadily crept over Wellington a feeling of discontent, for he knew that the field for the exercise of his talents was circumscribed, and he often likened himself to a caged animal which longed for perfect freedom. But the tender ties of home and the pleasant associations with the honest people with whom he had lived so long, the affectionate interest they had in himself and family, the pride they felt in his success, the admiration they always expressed for his abilities,—all these things made him hesitate to take his wife and children from these devoted friends and place them in a city where they would miss the flowers, the hills and meadows, and the sweet accustomed scenes of village life. He felt, however, that he had already remained longer than was wise, and now that he was offered the position of solicitor for an influential corporation, he saw that his opportunity had come, and he decided to improve it.

It was no easy matter to arrange his departure, for clients were not unselfish, and begged him not to leave the village and allow the trial of their cases to fall into the hands of some other lawyer. They had engaged Wellington, and him they insisted on having. He exercised all his ingenuity to rush to trial all cases in which he was retained, but his opponents advanced the numerous excuses always at the command of ingenious lawyers who desire a continuance, so that many trials were deferred from term to term, until a year had passed before Wellington could take his final departure.

The night before they were to leave, after kind neighbors had made their final calls, the deep, soft tones of the old family clock rung out the midnight hour, and the full moon shed her softest light over the sleeping earth, Wellington and wife, whose hearts were too full for sleep, wandered out into the night, and stopped at the garden gate.

" How beautiful the night!" said he. " Such nights as these recall so many pleasant memories, nights of peaceful life, of love and hope, for on such a night as this I first met my love, and as the moon made more beautiful her loving glances, and darkened her brown eyes into softest tenderness, and her raven hair shimmered in its bright light, I knew I loved, and years have only served to make it more holy and sacred, and I feel that God has dealt most kindly in giving me such a jewel as my arms contain. You have not forgotten that night?" said he.

" Forgotten it!" she replied, reproachfully. " Forgotten it!" And her moistened eyes chastised him in their look of reproach. " There is a time in a woman's life that she will never forget, that is the time when the man she loves confesses his love to her. Her innate modesty has long fought the fight of maidenly concealment, for she strives hard to choke down a love that is devouring her, lest the one she loves does not reciprocate ; and when, that night, you plead your love to me, the world was my heaven, for I loved and learned that I was loved in return. The moon, the stars, the silent night, were witnesses to our mutual pledges of affection. I thought I loved you then,

p

Will, but that love was nothing compared to what I now have after years of marital life."

Her looks corroborated her thoughts; his right arm drew her closer to him as he continued,—

"As we stand here to-night, it seems but days instead of years since, from this same spot, we waved a last good-by to him whom we loved so much, our absent Manulito. I know his thoughts so well, and on such nights as these, when the heated day has given way to dew-laden evening, when the cool breezes float softly through the trees, and the moon has arisen and her mellow glow softens and beautifies the earth, it sometimes seems to me, as it did to Manulito, that these nights are the connecting links between earth and heaven, and I know that on such nights our absent friend will think of us, and ask the Great Spirit to watch over and protect us."

"Do you know," continued he, "I would give almost anything I have to see him again. Yes, would give anything but you and the children. I have often wondered if we will ever meet again. It seems so strange that we should have loved one another so much. Scarcely a night passes that I do not dream of him, and the dreams are so realistically true; we hunt together, fish together, but oftener sit side by side in the forest, holding long conversations on subjects of mutual interest; then I see the loving glances of his great dark eyes, feel the warm pressure of his firm hand, and then I awaken, as if he were in my room, but find it all a dream. And yet I love such dreams. I am not superstitious, believe in neither the good or evil effects arising from a dream, but it is a sweet satisfaction to be with him either in this life or in the life I lead in dreamland. We shall hear from him again. I feel assured of that. The tide of emigration is fast drifting towards the unsettled West, and some day we shall hear more of him. I read your thoughts all through the wandering story of Martin, and shared your satisfaction when we learned that Manulito was true to the teachings he received at our hands. His savage heart has been converted until it possesses the nobility, the gentleness, the purity of that of a woman. Manulito won't preach Christianity to the Indians, but he will, by his life and conduct, set an example for them that is bound to be for their good."

At this moment the clock struck one.

" Come, come!" said he. " This won't do! We must play the lovers some other moonlight night."

And then, with his strong arm around her, an appreciated but unnecessary support, this couple, whose love only increased with advancing years, returned to the house.

The next morning they were early astir, and the little caravan which was to transport such of their worldly goods as were to be taken was being prepared for the journey. The neighbors bade them farewell with moistened eyes and sad hearts. But no one was sadder than Wellington and his wife, who strove hard to keep smiles on their faces, though all knew they were but veils to hide the actual feelings they strove to conceal.

After a journey of a week their destination was reached, and the truth of the saying that ability does not long go begging was soon proved, for one day, shortly after his arrival in the city, as Wellington sat within the bar in the Criminal Court when the docket was being called, he saw in the criminal dock a young man who seemed deeply cast down and apparently friendless. When his name was called to answer to the charge in the indictment, he raised his head, and in answer to the interrogatory, " Guilty or not guilty ?" he replied, " Not guilty."

" Have you counsel ?" asked the court.

To which he replied, " I am a stranger, friendless and penniless, charged with the crime of murder. I have no counsel, and I have no means to procure any."

At this Wellington arose, and said,—

" If the court please, I would like to defend the young man. I have never practised at this bar, but am not entirely unknown to your honor, and if I am permitted to defend the prisoner, I will do so to the best of my ability and without compensation."

" Do you accept the gentleman as your counsel ?" asked the court, and the prisoner nodded assent.

Thus was Wellington to try his first case at his new home. When the day for trial came there was an intense interest manifested, for a cold-blooded murder had been perpetrated, and the supposed murderer was now to be tried. He had not been caught in the commission of the crime, but circumstantial evidence pointed to him as the guilty one.

The court-room was filled with interested parties, while curiosity, which is such a strong element in the average human mind, brought many more. It was regretted by court-frequenters that in such an important case some criminal celebrity had not been selected to defend instead of the beardless lawyer, whose personal appearance was decidedly boyish. The prosecuting attorney was bombastic and egotistical, elected to office by reason of the political majority of his party, and not because of his legal ability. He had, as he supposed, estimated the ability of his opponent, and had invited many of his personal friends to be present and see him make " a guy" of the lawyer from the backwoods.

During the impanelling of the jury Wellington gained many friends by his cool, shrewd, and gentlemanly questions, and he had not proceeded far before the court saw that this young man, so boyish in appearance, was an astute, experienced, and brilliant lawyer, capable not only of protecting his client's interest, but of taking most excellent care of himself.

In his opening address the prosecuting attorney put the case for the State, and fiercely denounced the prisoner as the guilty one, and called for the

20

fullest penalty of the law to be inflicted. Then, in sneering, caustic tones, he referred to the opposing counsel as one who had tired of bucolic life, tired of trying cases in country school-houses before illiterate justices of the peace, and had come to the city to learn the ways of civilized people. He promised him protection, at the same time he hoped that his country friend, who had left the farm to practise law, would not take to heart any rough sayings or cutting suggestions, for the earlier he received a proper initiation the sooner he would be able, if ever, to cope with those of greater learning and experience. At this the court called him to order, saying that there was no occasion for remarks of that kind. But Wellington raised his hand deprecatingly, and said,—

"No, no, your honor; don't stop him. Let the gentleman proceed. I am young, and have much to learn."

At this he again folded his arms, a cynical smile played around his mouth, and his blue eyes turned to a dangerous gray, while he calmly listened. When the prosecuting attorney had finished his harangue, and called repeatedly for the punishment of the crime, demanding the greatest penalty that could be inflicted by the law, he took his seat, and condescendingly said,—

"Now, young man, it's your turn."

Wellington arose and stepped towards the jury. As he did, his handsome physique and personal appearance, the winsomeness of his manner, and his gentlemanly carriage, won for him the sympathy and respect of all. As his lips parted and the words fell from them with mellow regularity, with delicate shade of feeling, with perfect modulation, and each syllable with rare distinctness, judge and jury at once recognized that before them stood a matchless orator. He had formed the habit of fondling his watch-chain at his vest and twining it occasionally around his finger when opening an argument, and this he did as he said,—

"May it please the court and gentlemen of the jury : No man ever recognized more fully the importance of his responsibility than do I this day as I stand before you pleading the cause of an innocent man. I have not undertaken the defence of the prisoner at the bar from any mercenary motive. He is a stranger to me, but when I sat here a few days ago and saw the sad look on his face,—that hopeless expression which is so often seen on the faces of those who are despondent because of some great trouble,—and when I learned he was a stranger, without money, without friends, arrested, indicted, and to be tried for the commission of the greatest crime known to the law, the obligations taken by me when I was admitted to the bar, the resolutions I formed years ago to at all times help the poor and friendless, came back to me with renewed force and strength, and I rejoice that I am here with health and a knowledge of the law to protect this young man, to see that he has that fair trial which the Constitution of the United States guarantees to every human being."

He then spoke of the enormity of the crime, and said that he desired the punishment of the guilty one, but denied that his client was that one. He said that the evidence would disclose their defence, and that the examination of the State's witnesses would prove the innocence of his client, as there were facts within his knowledge that precluded the possibility of the prisoner being the murderer. At this the prosecuting attorney smiled incredulously, but Wellington continued,—

" I shall ask you, gentlemen, to give your attention throughout this case as you would have others were your own son on trial for a heinous crime. Any man may, by force of suspicious circumstances, be placed in the same position as this young man. It is no evidence of guilt, for the law expressly says that ' every man shall be presumed innocent until his guilt is proven,' and if, bound as you are by the sanctity of the oath you have taken as jurors, your honest hearts satisfy you that there is a reasonable doubt as to the guilt of the accused, then the court will charge you to give the defendant the benefit of the doubt, and he must be acquitted. But I will not take your further time. 'Tis true, as my friend says, I am from the country; and if that is a crime,—to have come from a spot where the winds from heaven breathe sweet incense into the blossoming flowers; where honest men till the soil, and greet strangers with courtesy and good-will; where a stranger is welcomed with unself-ish generosity, civility, and gentlemanly conduct; where, perhaps, inelegant expressions drop from the tongues of men who never had the advantages of schools, and yet whose tongues have never uttered a falsehood, whose homespun suits enclose hearts the noblest God ever permitted to beat,—if to have lived amid such surroundings and to have associated with such men as these is a crime, then, gentlemen of the jury, I stand before you guilty.

"As a child I loved stories. What child does not? And when my friend made his unprovoked attack upon me, which called forth a reprimand from the court, I heeded it not, for men are but children grown, and his remarks brought back to me the fable of Æsop, which relates how the ass paraded in the lion's skin. He succeeded in frightening all who saw him until his conceit asserted itself,—he spoke, and the illusion was dispelled, for all found that the supposed lion was but a braying ass, and fear and respect were changed to unmitigated contempt.

"I apologize to your honor, and to you, gentlemen of the jury, for this comparison; it would have been more elegant, more refined, perhaps more palatable to the taste of my æsthetic friend, if I had used language not so indelicate; but to him who criticised me wilfully, deliberately, and without the

20*

slightest provocation, I have simply returned an eye
for an eye. Perhaps I should have paid no attention to his insulting words, for when a man so far
forgets himself as to make slurring remarks about
a stranger, nothing that the brain can conceive or
the tongue utter will bring that man to a realization
of what true and professional courtesy is. I will
drop the matter, simply telling my friend that when
again he seeks to please the spectators by allowing
himself to insult a gentleman, he should hesitate,
lest that gentleman greet him with this quotation
from Pope:

> ' Immodest words admit of no defence,
> For want of decency shows want of sense.' "

This was too much for judge, jury, and those
present, and everybody burst into a roar of laughter, after which the trial was conducted with gentlemanly courtesy.

The evidence showed a brutal murder; an old
man had been beaten to death between the hours
of ten and twelve at night. The prisoner had been
seen near the house, and was arrested as he was
leaving the neighborhood. A blunt weapon had
been used, and after the commission of the crime
the murderer had evidently run against the wall,
for there was a complete impression of a blood-
stained right hand. It was clearly outlined,—the
palm, the thumb, and the four fingers. During the
trial the prisoner sat with a glove on his right

hand. Many thought it curious, and the State made a strong point of this, denouncing the murderer, and daring him to uncover his guilty hand, for the prosecuting attorney insisted that the imprint on the wall was made by the man who committed the deed. At this the prisoner's eyes brightened, but Wellington reserved an outward calm, for this assertion he knew would acquit his client.

As the State concluded their evidence, Wellington arose, and said,—

" Let the defendant remove his glove and be sworn."

The prisoner rose and held his right hand aloft. As he did, a murmur ran through the court-room, visibly affecting the jury, for *two fingers* of the right hand were gone, the wound had long since healed, and it was evident that the prisoner could not have committed the murder. Wellington saw the effect, and said,—

" I have no questions to ask the witness."

The case was argued by the State, but when Wellington had concluded the defence, his unanswerable logic, his brilliant comparisons, carried all with him, and after the immediate acquittal of the defendant, both judge and jury complimented him on the able manner in which he had conducted the case. This trial at once gave him a local reputation, and, as far as the gaining of clients was concerned, the battle was won.

CHAPTER XIII.

THE GLADIATORS.

"No thought of flight,
None of retreat, no unbecoming deed
That argued fear; each on himself relied
As only in his arm the moment lay
Of victory."

MILTON.

IT was now one year since Wellington reached the city. The courts were to have their vacation in July and August, and he, representing a powerful syndicate of capitalists, had promised to go to the far West to investigate its mineral resources, and to purchase a large amount of wild but fertile land.

At that season of the year, when business is at its ebb in cities, many were desirous of joining the party, both from a love of adventure and a wish to get away from the activity of city life. A party of twenty was formed, and early in July, with health and abundant wealth to back them, they started, a joyous crowd of happy young men, to visit for the first time the great plains of the West of which they had heard so much.

They reached the Missouri River on the 10th of July, and at once started, under the guidance of an old plainsman, across the beautiful but apparently endless prairies. The dreams of years were soon to be realized, and they were already planning to hunt the antelope and the buffalo. When a few days out, the prairie-dogs, those odd little inhabitants of the plains, yelped and barked in astonishment and affright at them. Soon they killed large numbers of antelope, and on the afternoon of the fourth day an immense herd of buffalo was reported. This was the event for which they had been so anxious, and rapidly making their preparations for the hunt, they advanced, under the instruction of the guide and scout, to a little elevation, from which they looked down upon thousands of buffalo peacefully grazing in the valley. The scout had previously warned them not to be carried away by the excitement of the chase and become separated, but to hunt in pairs, lest some accident happen. He also warned them not to go far from camp, for while the Pawnees were friendly, the Sioux often swooped down from the north, or the Comanches came from the south, and both of these tribes were at this time on decidedly unfriendly terms with the whites.

Wellington's heart beat with rapturous pleasure, for he was once again on the open prairie and amid the scenes he loved so well. Cool as he was, he could hardly curb his feelings, but longed to test the speed and skill of the spirited broncho on which he was mounted. The little party moved quietly forward, then the horses broke into a smart trot, which soon became a furious gallop, and amid the yells of their pursuers and the rapid firing of guns, the great black mass of moving life thundered away, and as their hoofs beat the hard earth, the noise and confusion was terrific; the herd was soon broken, and, despite the warning of the scout, the pursuers became scattered.

Wellington had killed several of the animals, and, finally, his pony, wild with excitement, rushed along by the side of a huge beast, so close that he could fire only occasionally, and thus they went for miles. At last the buffalo received a shot which was fatal; it bellowed, the blood ran from its nostrils, it reeled, then pitched forward on its knees, rolled its sad eyes with pitiful glances, and fell over on its side—dead.

Wellington dismounted without taking time to reload his gun. He brushed his hair back, drank in the refreshing prairie breeze, and revelled in this opportunity of enjoying his long-pent-up desire. His pony raised its head and neighed, and as Wellington looked up, his blood ran cold, for from every direction Indians were rushing down upon him. He mounted quickly, and looked for some point of escape, but in vain, for scores of Indians with levelled spears were fast closing in on him. He pointed his empty gun at the one nearest to him, but at this the rider dropped from view, only his foot appearing over his pony, while beneath his horse's neck his dark face leered with devilish ferocity. On they came, and one, more daring than the others, sprang towards Wellington and tried to snatch him from his horse. But he grabbed the Indian's spear, and, wrenching it from him, knocked him from his seat; then, breaking through their ranks, he spurred his pony and fled for his life. But the race could not last long, his horse was tired, and only kept its pace frightened by the hundreds of yelling demons behind him. As one reached out to grab the fugitive, Wellington swung his captured spear with skilful celerity, and with a howl of pain his pursuer dropped from his horse.

They were now intent on making him captive, and seeing this, he checked his horse, and before they realized his intent he charged one of them, and the impetuosity of the charge sent the Indian and his pony rolling over in a heap. They now yelled more horribly than before, and closed in on him in a surging mass; but his terrible spear still unhorsed them. Then, driving his spurs into his pony, the animal screamed with terror, and, bounding forward, Wellington, ponies, and Indians were crowded together in a struggling mass. He fought with desperation, and seemed possessed of super-human strength. The surging horde pounced on him, but were thrust aside like children. The unequal contest soon ended, however; his arms were seized from behind, he was bent down by superior numbers, and when he was permitted to arise, it was with pinioned arms, for he was a captive in the hands of the Indians.

The sun had gone to rest, and twilight was fast coming on, when all was ready for a start. Wellington, as yet, had not heard an intelligible word. All to him was a monotonous jargon. He knew not to what tribe his captors belonged, and he was utterly ignorant of their intentions towards him. When they were ready to go, he was lifted upon a pony, an Indian mounted behind him, and then in single file the cavalcade started in a southwesterly direction. Despite his condition and the fact that he was a prisoner without any probability of immediate rescue, he did not give way to despondency, but nerved himself to make the best of his situation and to attempt to escape at the first opportunity. A resolution of this kind was easily made, and under the circumstances was a natural one, but his captors appreciated their prize too highly to give him any chance of obtaining his liberty.

After a few hours' travel they were joined by another band, equally as large, and from their painted faces and the trimmings of their ponies Wellington inferred that they were not only on a buffalo-hunt, but were also on the war-path. After three days and nights of almost constant travel they reached an Indian village, where they were welcomed by men, women, and children with noisy demonstrations of joy, while dogs of all ages, sizes, and descriptions howled their approval.

Up to this time Wellington had not heard one word in his own tongue, and was therefore pleasantly surprised when an Indian approached and in broken English informed him that he was in the hands of the Comanches. It was not encouraging, so far as the realization of his situation was concerned, but it was a satisfaction to feel that at least one person in the ferocious and motley crowd could partially understand a Christian language.

As was the custom with all Indians after the return of a party from a successful hunt, their joy must find escape by ceremonies peculiar to their tribe, expressive of gratitude and devotion to the Great Spirit who had led them to find game in such great plenty. They therefore decided that on the second day after their arrival they would participate in their Buffalo-Dance, since other parties which were out would have returned by that time.

Wellington was advised of this decision, and was also told that the tribe considered him a great warrior, that he had shown his skill in fighting, and that during the day of the Buffalo-Dance his bravery would again be tested. He tried to discover their intentions regarding him, but all his appeals were in vain, for his interpreter had the faculty of failing to comprehend when he did not wish to enlighten the captive. Wellington told him that he had never harmed one of them, and had always entertained the kindest sentiments towards them. To which his listener responded, "Now?" intimating that the captive found it advisable to have kindly feelings just at that time, then burst into a

L   q   21

laugh, and walked away, saying, " Pale-faces great liars."

On the following day Wellington was permitted the freedom of the village, although he was under the constant guard of two braves, who walked at his side. He thought this a concession on their part, but he little imagined that this exercise was not to please him, but to keep his limbs and muscles supple, that he might afford them the greater sport at the proper time. At night he was firmly bound and securely guarded. During the day he saw the enthusiasm of the Indians in their preparations for the fête of the next day. Every little ornament of copper, brass, and tin was subjected to the brightest polishing; beads and ribbons were selected and assorted to make the greatest combination of striking effects; ponies were groomed, painted, their manes and tails plaited and adorned with ribbons and feathers of hawks and eagles, and each brave tried to outdo his neighbor in painting his face and breast.

At night a council of the chiefs and warriors of the tribe was called. An accurate account was given of their hunt, the enemies they had killed, and the narrator dwelt with especial earnestness on the capture of Wellington, his skill, and the great strength of which he was possessed. This was the most pleasant music to their ears, for the Comanches were brave, delighted in anything striking or mysterious, and now that they had a fearless man in their power, they foresaw that his tortures would add to the enjoyment of the day. They intended that he should die, and they were now to determine the manner of his death. Ordinary torture was considered beneath the dignity of a warrior of his standing, and as they recognized in Wellington almost the perfection of bravery and of physical strength, they resolved that before he met his death his skill and fortitude should be tested. They therefore decided that, according to the code of their tribe, he should fight a warrior selected by lot, and if the prisoner was the victor, which he could be only by killing his adversary, then he should be set free. This proposition was hailed with enthusiasm, and every one present hoped that *he* might be the one chosen to represent his tribe.

As this decision was reached, another party, which had just returned from a hunt, entered the council. They were all painted and bedaubed, with the exception of one tall Indian, who strode in with dignity and seated himself near their chief, showing that he was recognized as one of their head men. The story of the capture of the pale-face was related to the new arrivals, who heartily concurred in the decision of the council. The braves then approached the chief, who held a bag containing as many wolf's teeth as there were warriors present, and each man thrust his hand into the bag, and, taking one of the teeth, held it in his closed palm. Then the chief, Running Water, arose and said,—

"When the sun is at its height to-morrow one of my braves will fight the stranger for his life. The pale-faces are the enemies of the Comanches; they try to rob us of our lands and our ponies, and they kill our people. The pale-face that the Comanches have captured is strong and brave and cunning. He will fight for his freedom, for his life, for it has been decreed that if he survives he shall be set free and returned to his people. Then let the warrior on whom this honor falls ask the Great Spirit for strength and skill, so that when the sun sinks to rest at night our tribe will rejoice because its honor has been protected, and because at the rising of the sun, after the battle has been fought, one less pale-face will curse the earth by his presence."

This speech was received with nods and vigorous grunts of approval. Continuing, the chief said,—

"In each warrior's hand there lies a tooth of the wolf, whitened by the suns of many moons; but in one hand there lies a tooth stained by the damp and darkness of ages. Unfold your hands, and to him who holds the darkened tooth, to him falls the honor of representing our tribe in the coming battle."

At this all hands were opened, and many flung their white ballots to the earth in disgust when they found that they had lost. But when the warrior who had lately entered, and was seated near Chief Running Water, opened his hand, there was exposed the stained and darkened tooth, and therefore, by the decision of the council, he was to be the champion of their tribe on the morrow. It was further decided that the combat should be on horseback and with spears. A Comanche Indian was more at home on his horse than afoot, and the height of his ambition was to display his agility and skill in the carrying out of some startling or presumably impossible feat of horsemanship. They owned not undersized bronchos, but horses of full growth and stature, combining the qualities of speed and endurance. These animals were trained to obey the will of their masters almost without command, and they always considered that when mounted they at once had an enemy at a disadvantage.

The Indians rode bareback, with a lasso or strip of buffalo-hide fastened to the under jaw of the animal. Still, this was more ornamental than useful, for they guided their horses by a pressure of the knees or by a swaying of the body, the rein lying loosely over the animal's neck. Therefore, when a Comanche was mounted on his favorite horse, he was ready to bid defiance to the world.

Wellington had spent years in the saddle, both as a boy and after his maturity, and he had yet to see the horse he could not bring into subjection He was an athlete, and to him it mattered not what arms he wielded; all he asked was that he be placed on an equality with his opponent. When, therefore, it was announced to Wellington that he was to fight for his freedom, fight on horseback with spear and shield, he inwardly breathed a prayer of thankfulness because of his early training and the study he had made of heraldic encounters. When a youth, his paragons of perfection, his ideals of knighthood, were Ivanhoe and Richard Cœur de Lion. He knew by heart the history of the Crusades, the march of knighted men, their bravery, their sacrifices for the cause of Christianity; and often, when deeply engaged in the perusal of incidents in which armed knights advanced among the ranks of infidels and battled for the cause of Christianity, he longed for such an opportunity, and could not restrain his disappointment because he had not lived at such a time. And now, to find among wild, untutored men the same ideas of personal encounter which had existed for ages, but of which they could not possibly know, seemed to prove that people are controlled by the ideas of men of whose very existence they are ignorant.

Wellington's surprise was still greater when he learned that he and his antagonist were to fight with their features masked. This mask was made of the softest and most flexible skin, covering the head and face, with apertures for the eyes and mouth, while the crest was adorned with eagle's feathers; the face was painted with black bars, and the head was decorated with stars and crescents in yellow and red.

During the greater part of the night preparations were being carried on for the fête of the coming day. The chattering of the squaws, the cries of restless children, and the whining and barking of dogs rendered sleep almost an impossibility. At last the morning dawned, and with it a gray mist spread over the village, threatening a lowering day. The wind howled dismally, and the spirits of the inhabitants were in consequence depressed; but the summer sun was too strong and warm, and his rays speedily dispelled fog and mist, the winds veered to the north, the threatening storm disappeared, and instead of a rainy day, the hours increased the promise of the most delightful weather. As the clouds rolled away and the mist disappeared, the Indians showed their joy in divers ways: ponies were decked with gaudy ribbons; squaws clothed themselves in petticoats of striking colors; chiefs were arrayed in their war-bonnets, their faces streaked and daubed with paint, while necklaces of the claws of birds of prey and of various wild animals made a rattling accompaniment to the jingling of beads and tiny bells.

Wellington passed a night of restlessness, and his broken slumber only increased his misery, for while he slept he dreamed of home, and his awakening intensified the suffering caused by his surroundings. At last, the Indian who acted as interpreter came to the tent, and Wellington arrived at a partial understanding of what was expected to happen. As yet he had not been advised of their intentions, and had supposed that the passage at arms was to be for the gratification of the tribe, and that no serious results would happen, unless possibly by accident. His visitor told him that each would be armed with a shield and a blunted spear, for in that manner they could show their skill, agility, and horsemanship without endangering each other's life. Wellington, as yet, had not seen his antagonist, and when he asked to have him pointed out, he was told that neither was to see the other until they met in the arena; that his adversary had not seen him, and that when they met, they would be on an equality. "And," the visitor added, laconically, "the pale-face may never see the face of the brave he fights with."

"Very well," rejoined Wellington; "if your warrior is afraid or ashamed to fight except with his face concealed, I will not ask to have it otherwise. It makes no difference to me."

The hour of noon was drawing nigh. The scene was a delightful one, for the eye could see the silent flowing river, the green waving prairie grass, in the distance the indistinct mountains reaching to the blue skies, while the teepees of the village and the constantly-moving forms of the Indians added picturesqueness to the view. At any other time, if free from the dreadful uncertainty which now oppressed him, Wellington would have been charmed with the scene; but now his anxious eyes watched every move, his alert ears listened to every sound, awaiting—he knew not what.

As the shadow of a warrior indicated the hour of noon, a cry went up, and a circle, perhaps one hundred and fifty feet in diameter, was formed. The scene was full of animation and color: first the squaws encompassing the battle-ground; at their feet nestled children of all sizes; then came half-grown boys and girls; then old men, and warriors standing, men who were too poor to own or too friendless to borrow a pony; back of them hundreds of ponies stood facing the ring, their riders painted and streaked with glaring colors, while above horses and riders sharp-pointed spears glistened in countless numbers. It was a wild, weird gathering, and such as could be found only among savage tribes.

As Wellington viewed the romantic spectacle through his soft and yielding mask, his horse was led to him. It was sleek with summer grazing, compactly built, with fire shining in its dark eyes, while it sniffed and pranced as if anticipating the contest. In truth, the horse was accustomed to these mounted battles, and, as the interpreter told Wellington, should be guided by the pressure of the knees and the swaying of the body, for he was thoroughly trained, and could be depended on for guidance without the use of the reins. The spear which was given him was made of hickory, with a blunted end covered with some soft material, which prevented any serious injury arising from its coming into forcible contact with a person. This spear was used only in mimic contests, and in practice where injury was to be avoided.

The warrior who was to contest with Wellington now appeared, splendidly mounted, and wearing a mask which was the counterpart of his opponent's. He was naked to the waist, while gayly-beaded trousers of fringed buckskin covered his limbs. In his right hand he lightly held his spear, while his left arm was thrust into loops of leather, which held his shield firmly to his forearm. His shield was oval in shape, studded in the centre by a brass head, while the frame was covered with several thicknesses of buffalo-hide, dried and toughened, making it almost impossible of penetration. The surface was artistically painted, depicting a wolf at bay, while Wellington's shield represented an eagle swooping down on its prey, a fleeing bird.

The warrior was mounted without a saddle, but with straps suspended from the surcingle holding stirrups, by reason of which he could strike with greater force. Wellington was permitted the use of his saddle.

When the attendants lifted their hands, signifying that the contestants were ready, the chief, Running Water, advanced, raised his spear, and said,—

"All pale-faces are not cowards. All do not flee at the howling of the wolves, the screech of the wild-cat, or the war-whoop of the Comanches.

Such a pale-face we have among us to-day. IIe is brave, but has no experience in our mode of warfare. Our champion will teach him how *warriors* fight."

This was interpreted to Wellington, who smiled in reply. As the chief raised his spear as a signal for the struggle to begin, a wild yell arose, and the brave who was to do battle wheeled his horse and went to the farthest limit of the circle, in order to increase his speed and the strength of his attack. Wellington's horse sprang forward, and they met with levelled spears, but the Comanche swerved, and their weapons rattled harmlessly on their shields. This seemed to arouse the enthusiasm of the Indians, and they yelled with delight in anticipation of what was to come. The Comanche underestimated his opponent's skill, for, when they again met, he aimed at Wellington's face, and in doing so left a portion of his body unprotected. Wellington was quick to take advantage of it, for he deftly changed the direction of his spear, and before the savage could move his shield the blunt head struck him in the side, almost unseating him. At this the Indians, although completely surprised, raised a howl of congratulation in their own dialect.

The warrior was now on his mettle, and, at the next advance, both horses came at fullest speed, and the spears struck each opposing shield in the centre with such force that the riders almost fell backward from their horses.

Wellington now urged his spirited steed to its best, intending to unseat his antagonist, but his spear passed harmlessly over the horse, for the Indian had slipped over its back, and was looking at his rival from beneath the animal's neck. This exhibition of horsemanship by one of their tribe gratified the Indians beyond expression, and the braves showed their delight by jumping up and down, howling, and kicking their dogs into a yelping chorus.

At the next charge, Wellington aimed low, not intending that his adversary should play the same trick again, but in doing so he left himself a trifle exposed, which resulted in a bruising graze on his side, while his own spear clattered against his adversary's shield.

The chief now raised his spear as a signal for a cessation of the hostilities. Honors were even, and both men and horses needed rest, for their attacks had been frequent and spirited. They were both congratulated on their skill, while their horses, breathing fast from their running and flecked with foam, were watered and vigorously rubbed down.

And now, for the first time, Wellington learned the intention of his captors, for Running Water made a speech reciting the treachery of the whites, their attempts to deprive the Indians of their lands, their broken treaties, and reminding his men that each tribe had determined to put a stop for all time to come to the advances of the whites in their territory, and that, in order to do this most effectually, every white man who came into their power must die. But of Wellington, on account of his bravery, they would make an exception, and would give him his liberty on condition that he was victorious in a life and death contest with his adversary.

When Wellington heard this, he tried in every way to alter their determination, for he did not wish to gain his liberty in this way. But when he learned that if he refused he would be turned over to the squaws, he inwardly prayed for success, and determined that if his liberty must be gained as they said, he would win, or die fighting for his freedom.

The antagonists were then handed spears with points of sharpened steel, while around their waists belts were placed, in which were thrust long hunting-knives with stag-horn handles, wrapped with small thongs of the sinews of the deer to keep them from slipping in their hands.

As the determined men took their places, each was again told that it must be a battle to the death. Wellington was reminded that he was to fight for his liberty. While the Indian was admonished of the honor of his tribe, which he would either sustain or suffer to pale beneath the banner of disgrace. The signal for the battle was given, but the first contest had served to enlighten the combatants concerning each other's skill, and each guarded

22

against the agility and the cunning of his foe. The horses appeared to know that the contest was one of life and death, for their dilated eyes, their quick movements, seemed to indicate their desire for the success of their riders.

While, in the preliminary battle, the onlookers chatted and were at times inattentive, there now reigned the stillness of night, as each one looked on with closed lips and bated breath, for they knew that with those wicked spears the battle would be of short duration. The horses wheeled and circled, dashed forward at lightning speed, then, before a blow could be struck, suddenly veered to one side. At last, they charged directly at one another. The Comanches held their breath, for they expected the battle was ended. Not so! for the shields received the spears at a slight incline, and, instead of piercing through, they glanced aside, leaving a long white seam on each shield.

The Indians did not expect such skill as this on the part of Wellington, and when they saw it, they were generous enough to acknowledge it by a yell that could have been heard for miles. All their love for strife and blood was now aroused. They wanted the fight ended, and urged their champion by words and vigorous gestures to finish the battle. But he recognized too well the skill of his antagonist to do anything rash. At the next sally, just as the stroke was made, Wellington's horse stumbled slightly, and the Indian made a quick pass that would have been fatal had not Wellington thrown himself far to his horse's side. He saved himself, but the spear slightly cut his arm, tearing the sleeve from his shirt in a great broad strip, and exposing his white muscular arm with blood trickling from it. At sight of this, pandemonium seemed let loose, for the air was hideous with yells and whoops. But Wellington was more determined than ever, and rushing forward his horse at its greatest speed, his spear grazed the Indian's side, from which there sprang a great red welt, out of which the blood slowly oozed.

Now the Indian sought revenge, and as they met in mid-arena, his charge was so impetuous that Wellington swung far to one side. As he did so his heart sank, for the girth had severed, he fell heavily to the ground, and his spear, which was under him, snapped with his weight. As the Indians saw this they were wild with delight, for victory now rested with their tribe. Their astonishment, however, was intense when they saw their champion leap from his horse, cast aside his spear, draw his knife, and advance to meet his foe. They could scarcely believe their eyes, and howled their condemnation, for an Indian does not believe in open warfare, and thought that now, when their champion had the white man at his spear's point, he was needlessly risking his life in prolonging the battle. Wellington was as much astonished as they were, for he had thought his time had come.

Seeing the Indian advancing, he drew his knife, and then they who had fought so long on horseback continued their battle on foot.

As they advanced, then circled or retreated, their shields swayed up and down like limbs moved by the wind, and yet their movements were in perfect rhythm. They were a pair of warriors fit for any arena. Their deep breathing was plainly heard,—a sudden crash—the quick glittering of knives—and then, as they sprang back, they appeared unhurt, for their shields had received the blows, and their skill had saved their lives. Again the attack was made; their left limbs were intertwined, and through their masks their eyes glared with deadly ferocity, for each was determined to end this equal contest. Blow after blow was given, but the broad shields protected them. Down the side of one, down the arm of the other, the blood trickled. With a parting blow and a strong backward push they separated. Such a battle as this the spectators had never seen before, and the Indians were now too interested to yell, but earnestly watched every movement of the gladiators.

As they stood panting for breath, Running Water advanced, and said,—

"Two greater warriors never lived! Remove their masks, that when one is struck in death he may go before the Great Spirit remembering the face of the warrior who sent him."

At this the masks were removed; but as they

were, both combatants stepped back in astonishment. One exclaimed,—
"My God! It's Manulito!" while the other
sprang into his arms and said,—
"The Gray Eagle! Oh, my brother, we meet
again!"

CHAPTER XIV.

MANULITO.

> " By Heaven! it is a splendid sight to see
> (For one who hath no friend, no brother there)
> Their rival scarfs of mix'd embroidery,
> Their various arms that glitter in the air."
> BYRON.

THE spectators were amazed, and cries of rage
and disappointment filled the air, but the reunited
pair heeded them not. Wellington stood with his
arm around Manulito, the tears trickling down his
face, while the Indian seemed trying to devour him
with his loving glances, and tenderly brushed the
hair from Wellington's perspiring forehead, and
softly said, his voice trembling with suppressed
emotion,—
"At last the prayers of Manulito are answered,
and the Great Spirit has permitted him to see his
brother again!"

As is often the case when one becomes so interested in some pleasure as to fail to note the coming
of a direful event, so in the excitement of the moment these two were entirely unconscious of the
rage and baffled desires of the disappointed Comanches. The exhibition of their feelings was
like the approach of a storm; murmurs half suppressed reached the ear at uncertain intervals, like
the wailing of the winds through the forest, or its
whistling down the cañon; then came deep mutterings, like the distant reverberation of thunder,
the angry flash was seen, and then, when Wellington and Manulito raised their eyes, they were
startled at their situation, for they were within a
circle of levelled and steel-pointed spears.

Astonishment and indignation were depicted on
the face of Manulito.

"What means all this?" said he, in the Indian
language, while his form trembled with suppressed
rage.

"It means," said Running Water, "that the Black
Wolf has forgotten the vows of his adopted tribe!
It means that his heart is changed, for, instead of
upholding the honor of his people and defending
their rights against the whites, his heart is softened,
—he has become a squaw! It means that instead
of killing his enemy, as he agreed to do in the
solemn council, he forgets the pledge intrusted to
him, and like a squaw who has been parted from
her sister for a week, seeks his arms! It means

that my tribe and my warriors are disgraced! Your battle was to be to the death, and to the death it shall be, not with the white man, but with my braves!"

" He is a coward!" exclaimed a voice.

" A coward!" exclaimed Manulito, as he violently broke his necklace and flung it to the ground. " A coward!" he repeated, fiercely, as if he had mistaken the word, and his voice choked with violent emotion. " Who calls the Black Wolf a coward? Is there a man among you who dares to step from amid these walls of pointed spears and say to the Black Wolf, 'You are a coward'? Around the Black Wolf there are hundreds of warriors; then let not an unknown voice from the midst of this armed array accuse him of being a coward. Manulito a coward! Let him who dares to speak that word step from the ranks of his tribe! Let this wall of steel open, then close, and in the closing leave him and Manulito within its circle. Then shall a just vengeance be wreaked, for by the spirit of his dead father, the Black Wolf swears that he will cut that warrior's tongue from his throat, and while he yet lives will hang his reeking scalp to his belt! Coward? Oh!" he sneered, as he glared at one, then another, " it is safe to call a warrior such a name when he who dares not show himself is hemmed in and protected by armed warriors! The Black Wolf has not forgotten his vows. He never took oath to wage war against the whites. Has he not at all times

and places upheld the honor of your people? Has
he disgraced you? If so, in what? For he stands
before you alive and strong, ready to battle for
your rights, or to defy your vengeance, but not to
injure one hair of this man's head. Injure him?
Why, he is my brother! And the laws of your
tribe demand the life of him who slays his brother.
My brother? Yes, in the sight of man and in the
sight of God! You know him not. He is the
Gray Eagle, noble, generous, brave, good, and his
soul is possessed of all the virtues that are given to
men! And even if he did not possess all these,
still Manulito would protect him, because he is *his*
brother! And when your warriors insult the Black
Wolf,—confined as he is, unable to fight as warriors
love to fight,—when they revile and upbraid him,
they are like squaws, who, when a warrior is captive and cannot defend himself, cut him with
knives, pierce him with sharpened sticks, or flay
him with raw-hides, though were he free, they
would flee in terror! They are like wolves, who,
when alone, are afraid of the stag, but when that
stag is at bay, and there are scores or hundreds or
thousands of them, will worry it to exhaustion and
tear it to pieces! They are like pappooses who flee
at the cry of the mountain-lion, but when once it
is captured, its fangs removed, and it is bound
with thongs, are brave, and can torture it!"

His cutting words enraged his hearers, and it
seemed as if they would pierce him with their

spears. He read their thoughts, but was absolutely fearless.

" Strike, if you will!" continued he. "Manulito fears not death, and death alone will keep him from protecting his brother. And this is his reward for what he has done for his adopted tribe! Who among you dares to say that Manulito ever shrank from any danger? Who among you can say that Manulito dared not lead where others hesitated to follow? Who among you can say that he ever lost a fight, whether in single combat or at the head of his warriors? Who was it that, when sick at his lodge, scarce able to walk, mounted his war-horse, and in command of old men and squaws, defended your village against the picked warriors of the Apaches? Who was it that, when your tribe was scourged with the small-pox, remained from the war-path and nursed and cared for your sick? Who was it that, when clouds burst from the skies and flooded the village with water, defied the storm and saved your people? Who was it that, when captured by the Apaches and bound to his horse, escaped and fled, while his pursuers were like cows chasing a deer, when they sought to overtake the Imp o' Darkness? Who was it that saved the warrior, your interpreter, the Big Elk, when in the hands of the Arapahoes?"

" It was Manulito!" thundered the voice of the Big Elk.

" And for all these things," continued Manu-

lito, " for months and years of service and friendship and teaching of methods of warfare and leading you to victory and saving your village and
nursing your sick,—yes, for all these his reward is
to be—death! It matters not to the Black Wolf,
for he has long sought death! He has no home,
and has long been ready to die! But his brother
shall be saved." And then he told the story of
his life with Wellington, speaking with the deepest
emotion as he recalled the many kindnesses he had
received at his hands. His speech had a visible
effect, and yet there were some who could not allow
their love of strife and bloodshed to be overcome
by sympathy for an adopted member of their tribe
and for a white man, whose race they hated, and
these insisted that the fight be renewed.

" It shall *not* be renewed!" exclaimed Manulito,
glaring around him; "for sooner than raise his
hand against his brother, Manulito would die by
his own knife. You want to see me fight," said
he, his veins swelling with anger. " You shall be
gratified. Stand back, that the Black Wolf may
have room!"

Appalled by his terrible anger, they insensibly
fell back before him, as he stood, his shield in position for battle, his left foot advanced, his right
arm extended far above his head, his hand waving
his glittering knife, while his eyes were raised as if
calling Heaven to witness his awful threat of vengeance as he defied his tribe.

"And now that you want blood shed, it shall be so, for Manulito challenges every warrior in your tribe to single combat. *Let the strongest and the bravest come first,* for Manulito will fight for his brother, and the Great Spirit will give strength to his arm, and when his body is covered with wounds and he is weakened from loss of blood, he will strike again and again, and when his strength has failed him, and his willing heart cannot longer upraise his tired arm, he will receive his death-blow with a smile on his lips, and *thank his God* that he died fighting to save his brother."

"No! no! This shall not be!" exclaimed the Big Elk. "For if the Black Wolf fights one of you, it must be over my dead body!"

"The Black Wolf is right," interrupted Running Water. "The pale-face *is* his brother, and who shall say that the brother of Manulito is not *our* brother?"

"He shall be our brother!" exclaimed scores of voices.

Like an avalanche which hesitates, then starts, and gathers increased force each moment, so the warriors flocked to Manulito's support, until soon all were with him.

During the fierce and impassioned speech of Manulito, Wellington tried to read the thoughts of the Indians, for Manulito spoke in their language. When he recalled to them the many things he had done for their tribe, the benefits arising

from his coming among them, their features softened, and when later he told of his fraternal love,
and of his willingness to sacrifice his life in defence
of his brother, their eyes brightened with sympathy, they approved of his generosity, their chivalrous spirit was touched, the battle was won, and
Wellington's life was saved.

The weird and picturesque scenes were for the
time lost to Wellington's observing eyes, for as he
stood surrounded by those who were so recently
his avowed enemies, the incidents of the past few
days seemed like a dream, and now the ferocity
which had darkened the faces of his captors gave
place to an expression of interest, made still more
pleasant by eyes which extended to him good-will
and a welcome.

Now that the strife was ended and the Comanches had extended to Wellington the hand of
fraternity, they considered him a guest who had
honored their tribe by his presence, and they
sought the opportunity of showing him how truly
welcome he was among them. Manulito appreciated this, and while his adopted tribe were showing their delight in salutations and in various ways,
expressive of their friendship, his face was wreathed
in smiles, for in honoring his friend and brother
they were doing that which touched Manulito's
heart to its depth. As Wellington looked around
and saw the wildness of his surroundings and
recognized that he was free, and that those who

had sentenced him to death were now his firmest
friends, ready to serve him, to honor him, and if
need be, to die for him, his heart thrilled, and his
soul went out to these people. Manulito seemed
to read his thoughts, and he caught the spirit of
inspiration as he said, "As when the weary day
has gone to rest, soothed to sleep by the stars of
night, and the dew from heaven falls to the earth
like tears from thousands of angels' eyes, so is this
sympathy and generous interest to my tired brother
after his trials and sufferings. When the sky is
darkest, and the wrath of the Great Spirit seems
centred in the angry clouds, and the thunders
strive to split the heavens, allowing the forked
lightning to escape,—when all seems lost,—the
clouds break away, the darkest ones are fringed
with silver and gold, reflected from the light of the
sun; the thunders subside into distant mutterings;
the sun shines again, and the drops of rain sparkle
on the prairie grass; the birds sing more sweetly,
and all the earth rejoices: storms and past dangers
are forgotten, and the happiness of the present
banishes the threats of the past. So is it with my
brother's life."

"Yes! yes!" exclaimed Wellington, "you are
the same Manulito; the same philosopher; the
same dear friend; you make the same beautiful
comparisons, wherein the sky, the earth, the seasons, and all nature serve to better illustrate your
thoughts. But your friends are looking askance at

you and me, wondering, perhaps, of what we are talking. We have much to say, but not here. Let us show them our appreciation of their hospi-. tality, and to-night, in the seclusion of your lodge, we will live over again many of the incidents of our lives."

As Wellington finished, Running Water and his warriors were waiting deferentially for the conclusion of the conversation, and Manulito, who spoke both the Comanche and the English languages, acted as interpreter, and said, "My white brother, the Gray Eagle, awaits the pleasure of our chief, the warrior Running Water."

"Say to the Gray Eagle," said Running Water, "that the brother of Manulito is our brother; that our lodges are open to him; that we have venison and buffalo-meat in plenty; and that we hope he will remain with us for many days, for then he can see our dances, can see how we welcome a brother from another tribe, and, great hunter that he is, can join us in our buffalo-hunt."

Manulito interpreted the speech to Welllington, who smilingly said, "Well, Manulito, I guess you will have to talk for me this time; but tell him that I thank him for these manifestations of kindness, and appreciate the generous sentiments expressed, but that I fear my visit must be short, as I must return to-morrow."

"To-morrow!" exclaimed Manulito, in deep surprise, while his tone conveyed the depth of his feelings. "To-morrow! And must the separation of years be renewed so soon? Must Manulito in so short a time have dashed from his lips the cup of happiness which is now overflowing? To-morrow? That is but a day. The sun will sink to rest, the stars shine through the night, the gray of dawn appear, the sun rise over yonder hill, mount to the highest heavens, and then—my brother will be gone, perhaps forever, for *to-morrow* will be here. What Manulito has prayed for for years has happened,—his brother has come. But like the will-o'-the-wisp which flashes in the lowland on a summer's evening and then as suddenly disappears, so would my brother's visit be. To-morrow? No! that cannot be, for Manulito could not talk when the day was turned to night, the night to an hour, and the hour to fleeting moments. Let Manulito say what his heart prompts him to." And addressing Running Water, he said,—

"The Gray Eagle thanks you all for the kindness you show him in asking him to dwell with you for many days. He knows how welcome he is, how much he would enjoy being with you. He has not decided how long he can stay, but at least will remain until he may see how the children of the prairie hunt the buffalo."

To this Running Water replied that he hoped the Gray Eagle would conclude to make them a long visit, a wish in which the heart of Manulito fervently acquiesced.

The afternoon was passed by Wellington and Manulito in visiting the villagers, and Wellington soon became a stanch favorite, for he had a kind word and a pleasant smile, for all. Active preparations had been made for the Buffalo-Dance which was to occur that night, and as twilight came on the chiefs and warriors seated themselves in a semi-circle in readiness for the coming ceremony. The buffalo-hunt had been decided on for many days, for at this season of the year provision was always made for the following winter. The success of the hunts was more or less dependent on chance, for at times game was found in great abundance, and again it was quite scarce. As their winter stores depended largely upon these hunts, the most ample preparations were made for them. These people were firm believers in the existence of a deity, and to him they constantly appealed, not so much by personal intercession as through the pleadings, sacrifices, and prayers of their medicine-men, whom they believed had occult power with their Manitou. These medicine-men had fasted and made sacrifices for a number of days, and now the common people and the warriors were to offer a last plea, which consisted in a supplicatory dance, showing their humiliation and their craving for the aid and support of the Great Spirit. As the spectators sat or stood in the glare of the fire which was reflected on the many dark but earnest faces, the scene was impressive beyond description. There was a deep solemnity about the occasion which conveyed to Wellington the sincerity of the participants. Manulito gazed at his white brother interrogatively, and then, as if satisfied with a silent answer, looked steadily forward, knowing that his friend sympathized with these earnest men, who were illiterate, untutored, savage, but were still controlled by the love for one whom they could not see, but in whom they had implicit faith. As the fire blazed higher, twelve buffalo-skulls were placed on the ground in a semicircle, while near them stood medicine-men with bows and arrows, consecrated by frequent invocations and the use of sacred herbs. The medicine-men bowed their heads in silent prayer, or in low tones besought the Great Spirit to sanction the hunt and lead the band to success. The petitioners showed their humility not only in their attitudes, but in their quivering voices as they asked that their prayers be answered. When these old men had finished their invocations, a drum sounded with a rumbling noise, and there sprang into the circle a number of almost naked warriors, who danced with noisy demonstrations of delight, as if the hunt was an assured success. When these were exhausted others filled their places, and so the dance was prolonged throughout the night.

Wellington and Manulito remained until midnight, and then they repaired to the lodge of the latter. As they entered the door, Wellington turned and said, " And this, Manulito, is your home. I never thought to visit it, but now that I am within its portals, I have a feeling of security that I have not experienced before. How natural everything seems! Natural, and yet all these beautiful trophies of your skill with the rifle are strange to me. But there is about your lodge an evidence of civilization which would convince any one that its owner was accustomed to a home among the better class of white people. How contented I am!" continued he, as he seated himself on a divan of skins of the mountain-lion, while his feet rested in the long white fleece of the wild goat. "And how beautifully you have adorned your lodge! As I look around and see the evidences of your skill, the robes of deer and wolves, of antelope and bear, and on your walls the feathers of the golden eagle and the great bald eagle, it seems as if the birds and beasts have all paid tribute to you. And then, how natural the head of that grizzly, with its horrid teeth!"

As Wellington proceeded, Manulito had seated himself at his visitor's feet, and each complimentary word was like music in his ears. He looked up into Wellington's face as a slave would gaze at his beloved master. "And so you like my home?" inquired he.

"Like it!" said Wellington. "It's grand! It's beautiful!"

"Oh, I thank you for those words!" said the Indian. "For whenever Manulito added a trophy to his wigwam his heart always went out to his brother, and he longed for him to be here to see and enjoy these things. But my brother is tired. He must sleep, and when he sleeps Manulito will ask aloud, as his heart has always asked, that the Great Spirit will watch over him and protect him." At this Manulito drew the curtain; but when Wellington had fallen asleep the Indian softly entered and sat with folded arms beside his sleeping brother, while a smile of satisfaction played over his noble face.

Wellington slept soundly until the morning was far advanced, and when he awakened he was dazed for a moment, uncertain of his situation; but his faithful friend was waiting for him and cheerfully greeted him. All through the morning the tribe waited with anxious expectation the return of the couriers who had been sent out to locate the wandering herds of buffalo. It was late in the day when they returned, and then they told of an immense herd that was grazing many hours' travel from the village. Distance, however, was no obstacle to their hunt, for hours frequently lengthened into days when they were on the chase, and the hope of finding game was the delicacy that whetted their appetites for the excitement and pleasure they anticipated. It was therefore decided that they should begin the journey at once, approach within a few miles of the herd, and then at break of day advance on their errand of destruction. Officers were selected and put in command, for any indiscriminate hunting or unsystematic pursuit would result in simply frightening the game, and would destroy their chances of success. Very soon the cavalcade set out,—a joyous crowd, for at the start there was no necessity for silence, as the game was too far from them to render any precautions necessary.

First rode the warriors on their horses; then came others, fleet of foot, but not owning ponies; then squaws and boys, mounted and leading pack-horses, while all were provided with the materials for the immediate care of the skins and meat. Far in advance of this immense train, scouts stood on elevated points and beckoned the hunters to advance. The sentinels were guided by a system of silent telegraphy, whereby others, who were still farther advanced, signalled the condition of the outlook. Thus they travelled along until the hours lengthened ; but, strange as it seemed, those on foot were tireless, and walked and ran with comparative ease, apparently incapable of fatigue. They questioned not the distance, but trotted along, at times flogging the lagging ponies or jerking them by their rope-bridles to quicken their speed. The squaws chatted, and, riding astride their ponies, seemed to keep up a continuous thumping of their heels against the ribs of the patient animals.

As Wellington and Manulito rode side by side, the former said, "I have wished so many times, Manulito, that you could look in at our fireside

and see the beautiful picture of domestic happiness
that has always blessed my home. And so many
times in the fall, or more especially in mid-winter,
when the crackling fire threw out its generous
heat, and when the twilight was fast usurping the
light of the dying day, we found our greatest delight in talking and thinking of you. Imagine a
room furnished with rich but not gaudy furniture;
with curtains, carpets, walls and ceilings, blending
their colors with perfect harmony; beautiful pict-
ures seem to fill each niche and vacant spot; the
mantels are ornamented with dainty bric-à-brac,
while curiosities from other climes add to the
beauty and variety of this, our sitting-room. Before the fire, which sputters and crackles, just as
our grate fire did at the old homestead years ago,
there are seated father, mother, sister, and brother.
Our boy is quite a young man now, and he remembers you so well, and hopes to see you; and
our little girl, you would know her anywhere; she
is still the pure, good angel she always was,—grown
taller, of course, and more beautiful. On those
wintry nights when the winds shriek through the
trees and wires I appreciate most my pleasant and
happy home. And when I see and enjoy those
sights, although I am not what the world calls a
Christian, Manulito, I am willing to admit that I
have many times secretly thanked God for those
blessings.

"In that room, Manulito, is a picture which

we prize more than anything we possess. It hangs over the mantel, and when, as is often the case, our home is thrown open to receive our friends, including among them men wise in jurisprudence, renowned in literature, and skilled in art, there are none so high in positions of honor that they have not been fascinated with it. It is my inspiration, Manulito, and seems to lead me to greater thoughts, and surely to better deeds; I love to talk of it, and when I am before it, and speak of him who gazes down on me with such quiet dignity, my soul is in sweet communion with him, for I know the purity of his heart. It's only a picture, Manulito,—only a picture. But every line is a mine of pleasant reminiscences to me.

"The picture," continued Wellington, "is one of the most perfect I have ever seen. The figures are so accurately drawn that they seem imbued with life; the moonlight streams through the trees, giving the shadows a denser gloom; the leaves seem to tremble in the night air, while one almost feels the soft balm of the summer night. It was painted, Manulito, by a celebrated artist who had never seen the landscape or the figures, but I had seen both, and the sight was so indelibly impressed on my heart and mind, that each tree, each bush, every vein on the horse, even the position of his flowing mane and the curve of his sweeping tail, were before my sight. And if I could remember these minor things, so as to depict them to this artist and point out to him each trifling variation between his work and the picture in my mind, always suggesting a correct alteration,—if, as I say, I could do this, is it strange that when the rider's face was so indelibly engraven on my very soul, I could tell how he looked,—his forehead, his eyes, his nose, his mouth ? They were photographed on my heart, and my eyes, as agents of my heart, were able to recognize any defect in the painting. It is a picture of *you*, Manulito,—of you and Imp o' Darkness, the night you waved us that last sad farewell, the night you left our home, as we believed, forever.

" And when I look at the painting, it seems as if my eyes see you just as you looked that night, slowly threading your way among the trees, then temporarily disappearing. And my anxious ears hear, then lose again, the footfalls of your noble horse, until at last you are on the brow of the hill,—yourself and steed in distant outline against the sky,—as you give a last wave of your hand. When I look at your picture my ambition is greater ; my thoughts purer and nobler ; my life better. That painting is my guiding star, for in it you seem to beckon me ever forward to greater deeds. So in years to come, when you think of that picture, let that love for us grow stronger, for you will know that you are not forgotten. My successes and triumphs, the pleasures that money bring, will not change my love towards you. Those things are

temporal and secondary; for this strange friendship which has existed and united us in life will be
severed only by death. And should it please the
Great Spirit to take you first, I want your trusted
friends to know the place of your burial, that I
may visit that sacred spot; for I know that the
gates of heaven would be opened, that you might
look down and see him who was faithful in life
weeping at your grave."

It seemed as if Manulito's heart was too full for
speech, as he listened to this avowal of love from
the man he idolized. And he rode along, his head
bowed, as if he could not find words to express his
feelings.

Suddenly the signal to halt was given by the
advance sentinel, and at once they all became as
silent as death, for that signal indicated that the
herd had been found. The silence was too oppressive, however, and the Indians began to indulge in
subdued talk, as if they were unable to restrain
their ardor. Just then a warrior, who was recognized as one of the scouts, was seen riding hastily
towards them, and he reported that the herd was
resting quietly within a few miles from there.

As it was not yet light, they concluded to rest
for a few hours.

CHAPTER XV.

THE CHASE.

"Like yelling fiends the tribes are out,
   With flourish'd lances, with frantic shout!
   Each plume of feathers, each scalp-lock tress,
   Streams in the breeze of the wilderness;
   While fast and far, in desperate race,
   Speeds on the bison, speeds on the chase."
                                    McLELLAN.

AT break of day, the Indians selected their ponies, and preparations were made for the advance. The scouting-parties reported that the herd was still at the same place, unsuspicious of danger and quietly grazing. Couriers were again sent out, and the band was at once placed under the strict orders of their commanders. No firearms were permitted to be used, except by Wellington, for they desired to do as much execution as possible without more noise than was absolutely necessary. All were armed with strong bows, lances, and a quiver containing many arrows, but Manulito, on account of the loss of his left hand, could use only lances.

As the Indians approached they displayed great ingenuity, for it was necessary to surround the herd and to disconcert them so that they would run distractedly about. First, the fleetest footmen crawled through the high grass and stopped at the spot

24

designated for them. There they lay concealed, awaiting orders. While they were waiting, others stealthily surrounded the herd, and remained ready to advance at the promised signal. Behind a rise of ground which was quite near, the rest of the party stood beside the ponies, ready to mount at a moment's notice.

It had been previously arranged that those on foot should begin the attack, and continue it as long as they could keep the buffaloes within their range, and then, after the beasts had stampeded, the mounted Indians were to join in the pursuit. But in order that the buffaloes should not gain on those who would be waiting, the mounted assailants intended following closely those who preceded them on foot. While the carnage was expected and desired to be great, those who slew the animals were not to claim the meat, which went to the first one getting it; but the robes belonged to the slayers, who were easily known by their arrows, which always bore some private mark for identification. Therefore, after the animals were killed, the squaws removed the hides and carefully rolled them up, leaving sticking to them the fatal arrows, by which the owners afterwards claimed them. Thus it often happened that some brave who had killed the greatest number of buffaloes would at the end of the day have an immense pile of skins coming to him, but not a pound of meat, because he had no squaw to provide for him, while some lazy hunter with a tireless squaw would return to camp with his ponies laden with meat. While this rule was far from equitable, still it was the custom and entirely satisfactory to the parties interested.

When all were ready for the attack the signal was given, and hundreds of anxious eyes noted the result of the first movement. Immediately there were seen, skulking through the grass, several Indians, who hopped along on their hands and knees, imitating as closely as possible the motions of wolves. They advanced, then hesitated and sat on their haunches, following closely the movements of those animals, for they knew the buffaloes were accustomed to them.

At first the buffaloes paid no attention, but quietly and indifferently grazed along, or now and then raised their heads slightly, as if the boldness of the intruders was worthy of some trifling notice. But soon their indifference changed to interest, and that interest to alarm, for they saw that the decoys were different from the wolves which they were accustomed to seeing, and they shifted uneasily and walked faster while grazing, rolling their great eyes in watchfulness towards the intruders. Their alarm grew to consternation, and those on the outer edge surged and crowded against their neighbors, who, not seeing the cause of the excitement, peacefully submitted, or offered mild resistance by hooking or bunting those nearest them.

Curiosity has a strange power over animals, and they will often defy danger for the moment in order to investigate some mysterious sight. So it was with these buffaloes : they recognized a danger, feared it, and yet courted it; for, instead of fleeing when it was at a distance, they waited until it was upon them, and several of the bolder ones advanced at times with lowered heads, as if defying their strange visitors, and then hastily retreated to the herd, as if astonished at their own lack of discretion. By this time the Indians were almost within effective arrow-shot, and, simultaneously jumping to their feet, they ran towards the closely-packed herd. Each Indian picked his victim, and the twanging of their bows, the thudding of the arrows as they sank into the affrighted beasts, was speedily drowned by the shuffling noise which accompanies the getting into motion of a large body of animals. The buffaloes squeezed together, trying to crowd over one another in their anxiety to run, and it was but a few moments before all were in motion, and with lowered heads dashed away. They had but fairly gotten under headway, with their route determined on, when, to their astonishment, scores of Indians rose from the grass ahead of them, and, waving their blankets and yelling wildly, changed the course of the affrighted animals. As the hunters saw this, they cheered louder than before, and ran to the side line of the herd to take their part in the slaughter. Whichever way the poor brutes ran,

Indians arose as if by magic and changed their course, until the prairie was a confused mass of buffaloes and Indians on foot and on horseback.

The buffaloes were wild with terror, and the Indians, crazy with excitement, forgot the element of danger connected with the chase and boldly charged into the midst of the herd; then, when it seemed as if they would be run down and crushed, they would give a joyous whoop and drive their wicked spears viciously into the panting brutes. For a long time the coolness and cunning of the Indians kept the buffaloes running in a circle, but as they seemed to be getting away again, Manulito saw the necessity of a bold move, and called to his companions, " Turn them! Turn them a little to the.east! To the river!" The orders passed from mouth to mouth down the line; and, as all recognized what would be the effect, individual pursuit was almost entirely stopped, and, like drilled soldiers, they strove to obey orders. There was a strong swerving and shying, but, when the buffaloes saw before them an opening, the leaders darted towards it, and the Indians increased the gap, yelling in great glee, for the buffaloes were now running straight for the river.

The formation of this stream was peculiar. At a distance it could not be seen; then its first appearance was a dark but narrow seam. Its banks were precipitous, reaching from the river-bed to a height of from twenty to forty feet. It was very low at

this time of the year, being only from two to three
feet in depth, while the transparency of the water
plainly showed the sandy bed. As the buffaloes
neared this high bank, the leaders noticed it and
tried to shy from it, but hundreds were at their
heels, with noses trailing the ground, and pressed
those in advance firmly and swiftly forward to the
brink of destruction. Those at the extreme front
tried to avoid being crowded over the precipice,
but an avalanche of their wild companions rushed
upon them, and they struggled but for an instant,
then plunged into the river below. It seemed like
a black and shaggy stream falling into this unexpected abyss, for buffaloes are like sheep, and, wildly
following their leaders' footsteps, they poured over
this steep wall to fall upon a struggling mass of
their unfortunate fellows. As they extricated themselves from the dead and wounded, they followed
the narrow winding stream, wading slowly down
with the current, and their life-blood reddened the
water as they were slain by their pursuers, who had
congregated on the bank above them. This immense slaughter elated the Indians, for, aside from
the sport of the chase, the success of the hunt
promised them sufficient meat for the entire season's supply. Wellington watched with increased
interest the different manœuvres of the day, and it
was a sight he never forgot. The Indians continued
their labor until long past midnight, preserving and
caring for the meat and hides secured during the

day. They camped that night on the bank of the river, and the following morning started for their village. It was a motley sight, for almost every pony was laden with the results of the chase, and here and there some sedate Indian, the personification of dignity, sat on a great heap of robes which had been piled on his pony's back, giving it the appearance of a camel with its great hump.

The second day they arrived at the village, and as Wellington sat in Manulito's lodge, he said,—

"Manulito, I have been with you for several days, and you can imagine the anxiety of my friends, who doubtless have given me up as dead, or think me a captive without prospect of release. Out of regard for their anxiety I ought to return to them without delay. My stay with you has been all my heart could have wished. I have visited with you, slept beneath your blankets, and now that I must leave you, it will be with a sad heart, for somehow I feel that this parting between you and me must be for a long, long time. We will hope to meet again, and I know that with you, as with me, a separation does not mean a severance of friendship, but, instead, our absence in the flesh will only strengthen the golden link of love which binds our hearts together."

"My brother speaks the truth," said Manulito, feelingly, "and his words are full of tenderness and love far sweeter than the voice of the thrush singing to his mate. My brother's visit has been like a dream, too good to be true. And when he has gone, Manulito will sit at night gazing at the stars, and recalling each word, each look, each thought; for when he can bring back these, even though it be as in a dream, it will make the heart of Manulito glad. It seems," he continued, thoughtfully,— " it seems as if the happy hours in our lives are too far apart. The anticipation of their coming is one of our sweetest thoughts; then the event takes place, and in our happiness we forget everything; then when 'tis over we look back, craving again the anticipation and longing for what has been. So with my brother's visit. It will be the bright spot in Manulito's life; and the prairies and the brooks, the mountains and the rivers, and every spot where he wanders, and sits to think, or lies down to rest, shall be silent witnesses of the sweet thoughts which will warm his soul as he thinks of the Gray Eagle's visit.

" And so my brother must go. And when he does, it will be with that same blessing which years ago he gave to another. Manulito will not urge his brother to stay longer, but at his departure asks him to take with him something for the wife, something for the children, that they may know that they still live in the heart of Manulito."

" It would not be necessary," replied Wellington, " to send presents, or mementos of any kind to my wife and children to remind them of you or your affection. For your noble deeds have been so thoroughly impressed on their minds that time will not efface them, and in imagination I can see how, when I return and tell them of the exciting incidents that have transpired during this journey, their excitement and alarm will quickly yield to softened expressions of relief when they find that it was you who befriended me. But it is thoughtful of you, Manulito, to send testimonials of your love to those who are nearest and dearest to me; and although a man, I can understand a woman's heart, and I know that the surest way to win a mother's gratitude is to show kindness and affection to her children. Your sending these presents to them will be greatly appreciated, not so much for the intrinsic value of the gifts, but because they came from you. I tell you, Manulito, it is such little tokens of tender affection, or pure friendship, that let down the bars of our dreary lives and permit us to enjoy a knowledge of the unselfishness of others. And if the good deeds we do live after us, as you and I believe, then for years to come this kindly remembrance which you show will be as a lamp lighted by yourself, and kept burning, for the spark will be renewed and the flames rekindled by my children and grandchildren. And as they see the mementos of your generosity, they will tell how these things were given to their grandfather, years and years ago, by a great Indian chief, whose name was Manulito. It is pleasant for us to think of this, isn't it, Manulito?"

The Indian had been listening with a sad heart and head bowed down, but now he raised his eyes, which glistened with emotion, and feelingly said,—

" When the sky is at its brightest and the day is in its greatest beauty, oftentimes a cloud creeps from the prairie and hides from view the warm sunshine, chilling the earth. So this departure of my brother touches the heart of Manulito. The visit of the Gray Eagle was like the coming of the most perfect day, but now the dark cloud arises and darkens the heart of Manulito. But when my brother says that these gifts will be kept sacred by his children's children, he pierces through the clouds and lets a ray of sunshine appear. It is sweet music to Manulito to hear his brother speak as he has, for it is his only wish that, when he is dead, all who have known him will speak kindly of him. And he will ask of his brother only one thing,—that when he dies, over his grave a stone may be placed with simply the name ' Manulito' cut upon it."

" I promise," said Wellington ; "but I hope we will both live for many years, for my ambition is far from being reached, and you can do so much good with your adopted people. I wish I could unfold my plans to you. I believe that there is a time in the life of every man which if properly improved will lead him to prosperity and renown. I think that with me that time has arrived, and

I want to leave a competency for my family and a name of which they may be proud. Should I live——"

"Should you live!" earnestly interrupted Manulito. "May the Great Spirit give you many years in which to gratify your ambitions! But no man can tell. Storms and floods, diseases and death, come everywhere. My brother is mortal, and death spares no one."

"Well," laughingly responded Wellington, "you speak the truth, and I will take good care of myself and try to reach a good old age, striving each year to ascend step by step the ladder of fame. But to-morrow I must return. You will not object to my leaving then?"

"No," responded Manulito. "To-morrow you can go, and Manulito and his warriors will conduct you to your people; but to-day, and to-night, my brother is still our guest."

During the day and evening Manulito was busily engaged in preparing for the journey of the morrow, and Wellington was left to the hospitality of the chiefs. On the following morning, when the band was ready to march, Wellington bade farewell to his late captors, and amid hearty handshakes, and interpreted good-byes, and invitations to come and visit them again, he mounted his horse. As he did he looked around, and his admiration was stirred to its depths at the appearance of his guard. Fully one hundred of the bravest and finest-looking warriors were under the command of Manulito. They were superbly mounted on black horses, their lances all at the same upright angle, while they were armed in addition with bows and arrows. Manulito showed his pride in this invincible army. They were soldiers, and looked with supreme confidence on him who had never failed to lead them to victory. Wellington gazed in admiration on them as he said, "With his followers Spartacus fought his way through the streets of Capua, and defied an army in the mountains of Vesuvius, and the world never saw braver men than they; but I believe this squadron here to-day would be equally invincible, for victory would not rest with their antagonists until the last man was slain."

This pleased the Indian, and he said, " They have faith in Manulito as their leader, and he has never permitted an enemy to say that he was not first in battle, for others shall not advance before him until the hand that wields his spear is powerless in death. These warriors' horses are beyond price, for they are all descendants in some degree of the noblest and swiftest horse that was ever on these plains. Manulito means the Imp o' Darkness."

For three days the party rode, camping wherever night overtook them. During the day Wellington and Manulito constantly rode side by side. They discussed the problem of the future of the Indian race, and Manulito agreed with Wellington, that it was but a question of time when the white race would obtain possession of all the lands, and the Indians would be dependent on the generosity of the government for support.

It was a bitter anticipation for Manulito, and, while admitting its probability, he hoped he would not live to see it realized. Anxious as Wellington was to return to his companions, his pleasure in doing so was not without pain, for it involved a separation from his best friend. Manulito shared his feeling, and at times they rode silently along, each thinking of their past and future. Occasionally Wellington assumed an air of jollity and burst into a soft laugh, and then as speedily checked himself, for he felt that laughter at this time was a wanton sacrilege to his actual feelings. These men were capable of enduring suffering, fatigue, or physical torture, but their sensitive natures felt most keenly an inexplicable heaviness of heart which seemed at times almost to suffocate them.

When they came in sight of the fort, one of their party was sent forward with a flag of truce, and soon arrangements were made for Wellington to leave his escort. The Indians were invited to remain for a short time, but they declined, saying that their mission had been performed, and they would return to their people. Wellington begged Manulito to stay with him, but he gently but firmly refused, saying, " No, no ! Were Manulito to re-main the hours would swiftly pass, and the bitter-

N   t   25

ness of our parting be the same. Manulito has not seen much in his life for which to be grateful, but he thanks the Great Spirit for permitting him to see his brother once again. He is prepared to say farewell now, and live the life the Great Spirit intended for him, thinking by day and dreaming by night of this visit of the Gray Eagle. And, perhaps, some day Manulito will return for a short time to see the friends and the places which are so dear to him, for his heart longs to behold once again the spot where he first saw the light."

"And," interrupted Wellington, "you will surely come to see me then, will you not? I will never forgive you if you don't."

"Yes," responded the Indian. "Should Manulito ever return to the place of his birth, he will first visit those scenes so dear to him, in the bottom-land, on the prairie, by the swift-running Wapsie, and then he will keep his promise and seek his brother."

"And God knows how pleased I will be to see you," feelingly replied Wellington.

"The time is gliding by," spoke Manulito, "and we must part, for the day is drawing to a close, and soon my warriors will have only the stars to guide them on their way. And here," said he, "is something for your wife, my white sister. Take it to her, and tell her it comes from Manulito. It is of great value, but its worth is not to be compared to the richness of the gifts of her kindness, her love, her teachings, which she gave to Manulito. If the Great Spirit permits a man to have a guardian angel on this earth, then tell her that such she has been to her red brother. Take this watch and chain, Gray Eagle, and give it to her. It was given to Manulito by a miner whose life he saved, and he took it only because he thought some day he might send it to her.

"And to his brother, the Gray Eagle, Manulito gives these." At this he motioned to an attendant, who came speedily forward with a pony laden with furs. From its back he untied a great robe, which contained war-bonnets, arrows, knives, and implements most valued by the Indians. "These," said he, "are for my brother, and when he sees these robes he will always remember that they were gained by Manulito's skill; and these war-bonnets, knives, and tomahawks belonged to the enemies whom Manulito conquered. And these two shields, —one of them my brother carried, the other Manulito, and the traces of our skill are visible on each shield. Let them hang side by side on your wall, and when you see them you will remember that Manulito and the Gray Eagle each thanked his God that he had not slain his brother. And this broken spear,—the one upon which you fell that day,—hang it beside the shields. It is like our lives will be when old age will have broken our strength.

"And now," continued Manulito, a smile light-

ing his face, " here is something for your children."
And, turning, Wellington beheld a pair of beautiful
ponies. One, a brilliant black, with a coat like satin,
pranced and neighed as if conscious of its beauty,
and, laying his hand on its neck, Manulito said,
" This one, Gray Eagle, is for your son. It is fleet
of foot, handsome as the heart of a boy could wish,
and wild enough to please one who fears no danger. And when the little warrior rides him through
the parks, the other boys will not be less jealous, or
he less happy, when he tells them that the pony
was once wild on the prairies, and was caught by
an Indian and given to his father for him.

" And this one," said he, and his eyes grew moist,
—" this one is for your little girl, your sweet Helen."
As he approached the pony, which seemed accustomed to constant petting, and was as playful as a
kitten, it nibbled at Manulito's arm until he satisfied it with a bunch of grass.

Wellington could not avoid an expression of
admiration, for the animal was as white as snow,
and this whiteness was made more noticeable by
reason of its great black eyes. Its mane fell in
sweeping folds, and the winds curled it gracefully
far below its arched neck, while its tail fell almost
to the ground.

" It pleases Manulito," said he, " to send this
pony, for, like the softening influence of the rain
to the parched earth, so was that child's love to
Manulito. Many times, when all seemed black and

dreary, and he wondered why he lived, this little girl came and took him by the hand and led him through the forest and the meadow, that they might gather flowers. At such times Manulito forgot his sadness and was happy again. And since that time the blossoms he gathered at her command have always seemed the sweetest and the prettiest.

" She loved best of all the beautiful lady's-slipper, which was to be found only on the hill-sides, hidden in the recesses of some shady spot, and, child that she was, it was to such places that her little footsteps broke the trail for Manulito to follow. And although in the valleys of California he has gathered perhaps the most beautiful flowers in the world, yet none of them touched his heart so tenderly or seemed to breathe such sweet perfume as the lady's-slipper plucked by the hand of that tiny girl.

" And as we often see in flowers something that reminds us of our friends, so Manulito sees in the beautiful pond-lily the features of this innocent child. Its snow-white face, like frost in its purity, sparkles with the dew from heaven, great beads of water glisten in the light of the morning sun, and its petals stand upright like spears of gold. That is the flower which Manulito loves best of all, because its soft whiteness reminds him of the face of your sweet child, and its petals are like the golden hair that falls in ringlets over her shoulders. -

" And so this pony seems like herself, pure and

spotless, gentle and obedient, one whom all must
love and be proud in loving. Take it to her, Gray
Eagle, and with it the love of Manulito."

As he finished, he stepped resolutely up to Wellington, and said, " Now we must part. Words
cannot prevent it. Manulito hopes his brother will
have a pleasant journey."

It seemed as if he wanted to say more, but he
only folded his blanket closer around his shoulder
and looked affectionately at Wellington.

Wellington seized his hand and said, " We know
and understand each other, Manulito, and we cannot help what is to be. May Heaven bless you!
Good-by! Good-by! I must say farewell! Then
he turned hastily and walked away; but some instinct induced him to turn again. As he did he
saw Manulito standing at the same spot as if in a
trance. Wellington quickly sprang to him, folded
him in his arms, and, as they embraced, many a
stern warrior bowed his head, appreciating the
feelings of these strong men. A touch on Manulito's arm by one of the warriors electrified both,
and with their hands placed fondly, each on the
shoulder of the other, their moistened eyes met
for an instant, and, with an affectionate clasp of
the hand, they simultaneously breathed " good-by,"
and parted.

CHAPTER XVI.

DESTINY.

"Across the threshold led,
And every tear kissed off as soon as shed,
His house she enters, there to be a light,
Shining within, when all without is night;
A guardian angel o'er his life presiding,
Doubling his pleasures, and his cares dividing."
ROGERS.

ONE can easily imagine the delight of Wellington's friends because of his safe return. They had
used every effort to find him since his disappear-
ance, but as the guide reported that war-parties of
Sioux had been seen in the vicinity, the searchers
at last came to the conclusion that Wellington had
been captured by them. And now that he had returned, their joy was without bounds. He spent
the greater portion of the night in recounting to
his friends the episodes that had happened since he
left them, and the story was so weird, that in this
case truth was indeed stranger than fiction.

The party had delayed their return because of
the absence of Wellington, having unanimously
decided that they would remain until they found
definitely what had become of him. They did not
believe he was dead, for they had thoroughly
searched the prairies where they had hunted, and,

not discovering his body, felt positive that he had been captured. This belief was strengthened when the guide found the spot where Wellington had struggled with the Indians. He then positively announced that Wellington had been captured by some roving band, but who they were, or to what tribe they belonged, could be ascertained only by cautious search, and, believing that Wellington had been captured by the Sioux, the party sent their scouts to the north towards the lands of the Dakotas, instead of in a southerly direction, where the captors and captive really were.

They were all anxious to return home, fearing that exaggerated reports might precede their coming, and, therefore, on the following day, they started for their Eastern homes. They never tired of recalling the scenes and incidents of the trip, and especially enjoyed telling of those times when some one, more unfortunate than his companions, had met with some slight accident,—nothing severe, but just ludicrous enough to have its mention bring hearty peals of laughter at the expense of the unfortunate, who had perhaps been unceremoniously dumped from the back of some docile-looking but very uncertain broncho.

Wellington's return preceded but a few weeks the opening of the different courts. His trip had been of great benefit to him physically, and now that he was to again assume the active practice of law, he did it, as he did everything else, with eagerness and a desire to honorably succeed. This trip to the West had been the realization of long pent-up wishes. He was progressive in everything, and one of his greatest desires was to travel and visit places renowned for their romantic beauty; it did not afford him merely temporary pleasure, but those scenes, although he did not know it at the time, were indelibly impressed on his mind, and in after-years, when making some of his most brilliant oratorical efforts, his thoughts insensibly drifted towards his knowledge of nature, and the instincts and habits of birds and animals, and the lessons he learned from the fields and woods served to make his comparisons more touching and more beautiful.

His success as a trial lawyer was what might have been expected of the man. He held few offices, for his heart was in his profession, and thus the years passed by, time increasing his labors and adding to his reputation. He heard but seldom from Manulito, but what he learned showed that the Indian was the same self-sacrificing man, devoting all his time and energies towards the advancement of the tribe by which he had been adopted. Many years had flown since they had last met, and the changes predicted by Wellington were occurring faster than he had anticipated. Great corporations were reaching out and securing belts of the finest land. Railroads were spanning the continent; and Wellington had heard that surveys had been made marking the line for a railroad near the lands owned by the Comanches for generations. This did not surprise him, for he had long foreseen the future of the Indian race and the wonderful progress of the whites.

Wellington had promised Manulito that he would be careful of himself,—a promise never kept by an ambitious man. Those whose lives are passed entirely in mental work, craving that profound knowledge which alone can place them at the head of their profession, forget that they are mortal. Their ambitious eyes are cast towards some star which rests in the zenith of their ambition. They believe that *labor omnia vincit*, and believing this, the days are too short for them, the nights are usurped, recreation is denied, the delicate chords which bind their constitutions are snapped, and then they recognize their mortality when too late, for their ambition is still unsatisfied, and death, not they, claims the victory.

For some time the friends of Wellington had noticed a haggard look which was occasionally to be seen on his face. They cautioned him not to overwork himself, but he merely laughed at their anxiety. At the same time he often became fatigued and easily caught cold, something that had never happened to him before. His physician admonished him to lessen his work, and advised him to take a long vacation; but Wellington plead the importance of his cases, the impossibility of others attending to them, and promised to take his much-needed rest the following year.

One day an important trial was in progress; Wellington had acquitted himself with great brilliancy, and the lawyers crowded around him, congratulating him because of his effort. The room seemed unusually close and warm, and his face was flushed. Suddenly he raised his hand to his head, asked for a drink of water, then, before they could bring it to him, sank fainting into a chair. They carried him to a window, bathed his temples, and when he returned to consciousness, he smiled again, saying, "I don't feel very well; perhaps I had better go home for a little while. Accordingly they took him home, and when his alarmed wife met them at the door, he gave her an affectionate glance, saying, "It's nothing; I will visit with you for a few days, for I am so tired." The family physician was called, and said, "He is worn out. He must have absolute rest." And then Wellington was put to bed. As his wife tenderly tucked the coverlets around him, he wearily dropped his hand, and said, "Oh, how good this seems!" Then, while she softly stroked his hand, he, like a tired child, fell asleep.

She had for a long time dreaded that something was to happen, and a sad feeling at times possessed her, a feeling which cast a heavy burden of sorrow upon her, something she could not define, but which frequently depressed her in spirits, and still she could not tell why. She felt her sorrow more keenly now, for it flashed upon her mind that this sickness of her husband was the fulfilment of the forebodings which had so long threatened her. And now that she was to face the event which had so continuously come like an apparition before her, this frail woman, tender, loving, confiding by nature, modest, unassuming, and timid in disposition, assumed her true character and showed herself as she really was,—a noble wife and mother, possessed of all those attributes that have made men better and that have blessed the world.

The tears which flowed so copiously came from the spring of her affection, and as she sat and fondled the hand of the man whose every ambition found sweet accord with her own, her tears ceased their flowing; she breathed a long sad sigh, and then, as if some secret resolution had been made, she moved with that soft grace which only love could make, and her life was devoted to her husband. She anticipated everything. If his heart craved something, it seemed as if some angel secretly conveyed to her the intelligence, for without disclosing his desire his wish was gratified. Like all men who have been devotees of Nature, or who are of culture and refinement, Wellington loved flowers. It was not possible to supply his sick-room with those he had so many times gathered in their wild state; but his devoted wife supplied the want, for the room was constantly beautified with handsome roses, whose delicate perfume was a constant gratification to the sick one.

The days had glided into weeks, and still Wellington was confined to his bed. He had treated his sickness in a jesting manner, and had frequently set the day when he would be at his office, but when that day came, the sick-room still claimed him. Then he would seem to improve, and the happiness of the household was unlimited, but the improvement would be only temporary, and built up hopes only to cruelly dash them away, leaving their sorrow greater than ever. The cold had developed into pneumonia, and all realized his danger. He had suffered much through the day, was at times delirious, and at night his condition was still more critical. As his mind wandered, his wife and children were told of his danger. At last the crisis was passed, and he lay dying before them. At times he was conscious, and then he calmly begged them not to weep for him, and smiled in sweet affection at his wife and children who sat near him. His voice seemed unusually strong, and he spoke of dying as if it was but a pleasant journey. His conscious moments came less often, and in his delirium his thoughts strayed back to incidents that had happened in his early life, and when he spoke of them, his eyes flashed or softened and his face expressed his rapidly-changing thoughts. Finally he dropped into a peaceful sleep, propped

26

up with pillows, while his wife also supported him with her arm.

Suddenly he awakened, and with a startled expression exclaimed, " What's that? Somebody fired at me! Oh, no, he wouldn't do that, for I gave him the gun." Then he sadly said, " Let Hector loose; he will come to me. Yes! Manulito, I do forgive you fully and freely. Shoot the buck, Kirtley! Shoot the—— I respect every man's religion—I—— And I would like to have you tell Manulito of——" Then he smiled contemptuously and said, " Very well, if he is afraid to show his face, it makes——" His thoughts were fleeting fast, as he continued, " If the court please—I wish to——" Then, as if astonished, he exclaimed, " My God, it's Manulito!" He was growing weaker. His words dragged. There came a flash of consciousness; he realized his condition, and calmly whispered good-by to his wife.

Then his eyes were centred on Manulito's picture which had been brought into the room. He gazed at it intently, seemingly lost to his surroundings, shaded his eyes as if to obtain a better view, raised himself on his elbow, and said,—

" Perhaps with your spirit in the land of your God you can look down and see me weep for you—for I have sometimes wondered if those in heaven — if— those — in — heav — if— those — in — heaven——" His voice grew weaker, and he clutched nervously at his throat; then hesitatingly

spoke, "Yes — Manulito — I — forgive — you. I—
have—forgiven——"

Giving his wife a last fond look, he breathed a
long deep sigh. His head sank wearily on her
shoulder. They listened for his breathing, but
nothing was heard but the sobbing of the heart-
broken family. The physician tenderly touched
the weeping woman, but she knew it all,—the
noble husband, the kind and generous father, was
dead.

When in health, Wellington had often told
where he wished to be laid to rest when dead. His
wishes were adhered to, and his body was interred
near the scenes of his early manhood, for the successes of his later years had not weaned him from
the places which former times had made so dear to
him.

All the honors that could have been accorded a
man of his prominence in life were shown him at
his death. There is a sweet satisfaction to every
honorable man, who belongs to some civic, mili-
tary, or secret society, in feeling, when he is sum-
moned to cast aside the garments of mortality,
that his life has been a lesson to those with whom
he has been associated as a friend and a brother,
and that there has been something in his life
worthy of emulation.

There is no fraternity which holds its honored
members by stronger ties of affection than the legal
profession. So it was that, in recollection of Wel-

lington's life, from the courts of limited jurisdiction to those of last resort memorials were passed and spread upon the records eulogistic of the man. For it was truthfully said of him, "None knew him but to love him, and those who knew him best loved him most."

Taken away as he was, just after the summer of his life had past, and when the autumn-time promised so rich a harvest after his years of labor, it brought forcibly to mind that—

> " Leaves have their time to fall,
>   And flowers to wither at the North wind's breath,
>   And stars to set, but all—
>   Thou hast all seasons for thine own, O Death !"

CHAPTER XVII.

THE WANDERER'S RETURN.

> " Oh ! couldst thou but know
> With what a deep devotedness of woe
> I wept thy absence—o'er and o'er again
> Thinking of thee, still thee, till thought grew pain,
> And memory, like a drop that, night and day,
> Falls cold and ceaseless, wore my heart away !"
>   MOORE.

A FEW years had passed since the death of Wellington, and the recital of our romance carries us back to the scenes where he and Manulito spent so many happy days.

Time had wrought wonderful changes in the vicinity, and wild forests and unbroken prairies had given place to cultivated fields. The ox-teams and the prairie "schooners" were things of the past, and railroads traversed the land from ocean to ocean. The village where Wellington first practised law had grown to quite a little city, and rejoiced in all the modern improvements.

As the train came in one summer afternoon, there was one among the passengers who by his dress and bearing, as well as his features, commanded admiration. He was advanced in years, and the strong form, the dignified walk the wealth of iron-gray hair which swept over his shoulders, or was carelessly tossed by the winds, gave additional interest to this personage.

The crowd looked at him with undisguised curiosity, but he heeded them not, and alighting from the train, stopped for a moment as if in uncertainty, and then, having taken his bearings from the sun in the western sky, started in a southerly direction. His tread was as elastic as that of a youth. His advanced years seemed to have been cast aside, for, buoyed up by joyous anticipations, he walked briskly forward, occasionally pausing as if to drink in the scenery which surrounded him. "How sweet the air!" he said. "These hills seem as they did years ago, except that the forests are not so dense as then. And there, away off to the south, the sky stoops down and softly touches the tops of the trees at the Wapsie or loses itself in the bluffs across the stream.

"The night is hours away, and the heart of Manulito directs him to the spot where he saved the life of his brother. That was years ago,—years in time but only hours in memory, for the earth, the sky, and the forest are the same. But the winds bring sweeter fragrance from the meadows to-day, perhaps because it is the summer-time, or perhaps because the heart of Manulito is so glad to be here again."

He entered the bottom-land, neared the river which he knew so well, and soon emerged through the timber and stood at the water's edge,—at the precise point where Wellington had had the struggle with the buck. It seemed to bring to him a flood of recollections, for he stood for a few moments in deepest thought. "Oh, how good it is to be home again! Home?" said he in a doubting manner. "Yes, home again; this is the home of Manulito, for 'twas here he spent his childhood days and passed the happiest hours of his life. Manulito has said he had no home, but his heart tells him of his mistake, for now that he has returned, he sees that here and on the banks of the Mississippi are the dearest spots in all the world to him. Years ago, Manulito thought he would not care to return to these places again, but he has changed, for when once the thought came to him, his love for these well-remembered spots burned like fire into his heart. He could think of nothing else by day, and at night his wandering dreams brought him here, until the hills and streams, the prairies and the forests, the secret caves, and each familiar place, seemed to come before his sight, and the stars beckoned and the winds whispered for him to return again to the old home of his brother.

"And stronger than all these was the desire to see his brother, for years have passed since last we met. Manulito will keep his promise and go to see him, and then the Gray Eagle will show Manulito his home, his family, and his people, and the picture of which his brother spoke. And when the friends of the Gray Eagle come," he will say to them, 'This is my red brother,—this is Manulito, of whom you have heard me speak.' They will be glad to see Manulito because he is the brother of the Gray Eagle. And the boy, now a grown man, and the girl, now a woman, they will talk to Manulito. Oh!" he exclaimed, "the heart of Manulito is bursting with joy, for he sees so much happiness in store for him."

The sun was going down. He noticed it, and said, "The years are swept aside by the setting sun, for it goes to rest in the same spot, and casting the same colors, that it did the night Manulito saved his brother. And now Manulito will go to the place where, years ago, the Gray Beard lived. No doubt he is dead, for he was an old man then. His log cabin has doubtless been torn down, and his children will have built a larger home, but Manulito will go, for the Gray Beard once thought kindly of him."

As he stepped from the forest into the road, where he could obtain a clear view, he stopped in astonishment, for there, on the hill-side, he saw the identical cabin he knew so well. It was unchanged; the great hickory-tree shaded it as of old, while the ivy clung to its sides as it did when Manulito was a young man. He stopped, placed his hand over his heart, and involuntarily raised his eyes in thankfulness at the sight. It was just dusk as he reached the door. He hoped the place had not changed hands, and stood for a brief time thinking what he should do or say. As he knocked he heard a shuffling sound, and then, if a spectre had arisen from the grave he would not have been more surprised, for the door opened, and Kirtley stood before him. He did not recognize Manulito, but called to the boys,—

"Here, you fellers, whar be ye? Git a light. Thar's a stranger here, an' my ole eyes ain't no good 'thout a light this time o' day. Come in! come in!"

At this Manulito entered the cabin and seated himself, trying to recover from his surprise, and wondering if Kirtley would recognize him. As the light was brought in, Kirtley scanned him closely, but his eyesight had failed to such an ex-

tent that he merely saw that his caller was an
Indian. At this discovery, he said,—

" Wall, I'll be gol darned ef it ain't an Injun !"

Manulito could not help smiling, for he well remembered the farmer's opinion of Indians. He
appeared to be much the same Kirtley as of old,
except that his extreme age had deepened the
seams on his face, and his once strong frame was
but a feeble semblance of its former self. His hair
and whiskers were as white as snow, but his independence was as marked as ever. Staring at his
visitor, he spoke as if to himself,—

" Wall! wall! An Injun here at this time ! Hungry, no doubt, penniless, an' beggin' fur a livin'!"

Addressing his conversation directly to his
visitor, he said,—

" Be yer hungry ?"

" Yes."

" Wall, now, thet seems good ter hear an Injun
speak United States in thet way, an' not grunt
an answer. Do yer expect ter stay here ter-
night ?"

" Yes."

" Wall, thet settles it; an' while I hain't no love
fur your race, an' never seed but one thet was half-
way decent 'cordin' ter my notion, at the same time
yer kin stay."

At this moment Manulito's supper was brought
to him. He sat where the light shone on his face,
and as he ate, he expected that each moment

would disclose his identity, for Kirtley was very inquisitive both in words and glances.

"Must have had quite a tramp," said he, "the way yer gettin' outside thet grub. Don't live 'bout these parts, do yer?"

Manulito smiled, and said, "No."

"No? I thought as much. Come from out West perhaps, eh?"

"Yes," responded Manulito.

"Yes? Wall, now, as Bill used ter say, yer comin' in with yer rebuttal. Ever been in these parts afore?"

"Yes."

"Yes? The devil yer say!" And he drew his chair nearer his visitor. "Been here afore, eh? How long ago?"

"About thirty years."

"About thirty years," said Kirtley, musingly. "I come here nigh forty years ago, an' I was here at the time yer say. Say, just begin at my feet an' foller the trail ter my face, an' tell me if yer ever seed me afore? All Injuns look alike ter me, an' mebbe thet's why I can't place yer."

"Yes," responded Manulito. "At one time you knew me well; you were my friend."

As he said this, Kirtley opened his mouth in astonishment and stared at the speaker.

"I knowed yer well?" said he, incredulously. "I knowed yer well? Where did yer ever see me?"

"Listen and you shall hear. Once, when the buck was going to strike him you loved better than a son. Once, when at the village, you gave me control of your horse. Once, when——" But he did not have time to complete his sentence, for the old man tottered to him, placed his hand on his shoulder, while his voice shook with emotion as he said,—

"For God's sake don't trifle with me! I'm an old man, nigh eighty-five, an' I don't want ter be deceived."

Manulito rose and grasped his hand, saying, "You are the Gray Beard, and before you stands Manulito, who has returned after an absence of many years to visit his old home, to see his old friends."

At this Kirtley seated himself, and with childish fervor exclaimed, "Wall, I'll be blowed ef this ain't ahead o' my time! So it's you, is it? Wall, but I'm powerful glad ter see yer! But I'll tell yer, you 'll find a heap o' changes here,—most the old timers dead or moved away. Goin' ter stay long 'bout here?"

"Only a few days," responded the Indian. "And then, after Manulito has visited these places so well known to him years ago, he will continue his journey and seek his brother——"

"Say that last ag'in. 'I don't know thet I jes' caught wot yer said."

"Manulito said he would seek his brother."

" Yer brother !　Where ?" asked Kirtley, in surprise.

" Where ?　Where but in the city, which is his home.　For Manulito has promised to visit him some day, and now the time is near, and Manulito's heart beats with continued joy, and he counts the days and even the hours before he will see the Gray Eagle again."

Kirtley had turned his face from the light, and exclaimed, " Oh, Lord, this is awful !　I s'posed he knowed it !"

But Manulito continued : " And when he goes, he will call just in the early evening at the home of his brother, and perhaps he may be permitted to look in and see him and all those so dear to him sitting by the grate fire, reading, or perhaps thinking of the war chief, from whom they have not heard for years."

" Stop right thar !" interrupted Kirtley.　" How long since yer heard from—from——"　His voice seemed to fail him, but giving a great gulp, he continued : " Yer know who I mean."

" How long ?" repeated Manulito, meditatively. " About three years."

" Three years ?　And ain't yer heerd from none ov 'em fur three years ?"

" No ; not for three years."

" Oh, Lord !" sighed the old man ; " then he don't know it !"

" And then," continued the Indian, " when Manulito steps to the door and it is opened,—just as the Gray Beard opened his door this night,—and the soft light shines out, my brother will spring to meet me, saying, ' Here is Manulito ;' and then he will take me in his arms, just as once, on the prairie, I took him in mine, and then——"

He did not finish his speech, for Kirtley sat with bowed head, sobbing like a child. The Indian approached the old man, and stood waiting for him to speak; but, as he did not, Manulito said,—

" The Gray Beard is tired, and the heart of Manulito is sad, for he thinks he has said something to offend him, but what it is he cannot recall, for, as the Great Spirit is his judge, he did not intend to wound the man whose guest he is."

" Oh, no, yer hain't offended me,—but—but— three years air a long time, yer know; an' these times, thar's a heap o' things might happen. Banks fail, an'——"

" Manulito understands : his brother has been unfortunate and lost all. So much the better, for Manulito has lands, and they will be given to his brother. Does he want riches ? Then he shall have wealth until his heart is satisfied, for once when the mountain storm raged its fiercest, Manulito sought refuge in the cañons; the earth trembled with the violence of the storm; the floods rushed down the mountain-sides, leaving the rocks at the feet of Manulito ; and when the storm had ceased, and the

o   27

waters had fallen, the rocks were traced with ledges of gold. No white man knows the spot, but Manulito will guide his brother to the place by night, and when the morning sun peers over the mountain, the gold will glisten in its light, and he will say, ' This is Manulito's, and what is Manulito's is his brother's !' "

"Oh, yes," responded the old man, " yer intend all right,—yer intend all right; but there air other things in this world wuss than losin' prop'ty,—sickness, fur instance, an'—an'——"

"Death," whispered Manulito, as if horrified at the mention of it.

"Yes, death," responded Kirtley.

"My poor dear brother! the heart of Manulito pities the Gray Eagle! And when was it?"

"A year ago," said Kirtley.

"His boy?"

"No," responded Kirtley.

"His girl?"

"No."

"Then it was his dear wife, the noblest woman that ever——"

"No, 'twant his wife."

"What!" ejaculated Manulito, as if a sting had penetrated his heart. And seizing Kirtley by the shoulder, he hissed,—

"A death in his family—and not his boy? his girl? his wife? Then it must be—oh, God! my brother!" And he stood trembling like a strong tree in a storm, then, with a piteous moan, sank unconscious into a chair.

Poor Kirtley was wild with grief and piteously begged him not to take it so to heart. He dropped on his knees before the Indian, rubbed his hands, and pleaded with him not to give way to his grief.

As Manulito opened his eyes and beheld the old man kneeling before him, he looked intently at him, and softly said,—

" And so Manulito's brother is dead!" and then he closed his eyes again. " Dead? Oh, that is a bitter word to speak of him whom Manulito loved so much! And now the sweet dreams of days and nights, of months and years, are brushed aside. The star in the heaven of Manulito's life is set, for he whom he longed to see is no more."

He sat for a long time as if in a dream, and then, turning to Kirtley, he said,—

" Tears soften the sorrow of those who suffer, but Manulito cannot weep. 'Tis said the Great Spirit does all things for the best, but Manulito regrets that he lived to see this day." And then he sat and calmly listened to Kirtley's account of the sickness and death of Wellington.

All night he paced the floor, and when in the morning they invited him to stay and insisted on his remaining with them, he replied, " Manulito came to fulfil his promise, to seek his brother at his home. He will keep his word, for he will visit his brother's grave."

When breakfast was called, Kirtley said, " Come, Manulito. Come, old friend, yer must eat somethin'. Goin' on an empty stomach won't help matters."

The Indian tried to obey, then said, "Manulito cannot eat. It is his soul, and not his body, that cries for food."

" Wall," said Kirtley, " s'pose yer want ter ketch the fust train ?"

" No," responded Manulito.

" Thet's right ! thet's right ! Ye're like me,— ain't got no use fur trains. I'll hev the boys hitch up an' drive over."

" No ; Manulito will walk."

" Walk ?" exclaimed Kirtley in surprise. " Walk ? Yer ain't goin' ter do no sech thing. Walk ? Thunder an' lightnin', man, it's nigh on ter twenty mile."

" And if it was forty, what of it ? From daylight till darkness Manulito has walked, tiring out many horses. He has not become so old that he is weak. He knows the spot he seeks, and the day will give him time to think. To think ? Oh, that Manulito were like a tree or a plant, that lives, but cannot think, for to think is to suffer !"

Late in the afternoon he arrived at the cemetery, and gently lifting the latch of the gate, he softly let it fall again, as if he feared he might disturb those resting so near him. Slowly he wended his way, until his shadow darkened the turf where the old sexton on bended knees was using the sickle. The good old man looked up, and then dropped his sickle in surprise when he saw an Indian. He noticed Manulito scanning the different stones, and said, "Can I be of service to you?"

"Yes; Manulito is looking for his brother's grave."

"Your brother's grave? Surely, my good man, you are being deceived by some one. Your brother isn't buried here. I have been sexton here for thirty years, and to my knowledge there has never been an Indian buried here."

"Manulito's brother was a white man."

"A white man? Oh!—ah!—yes—I see: a half-brother, I suppose."

"No!" said Manulito, indignantly. "He was my brother because he was my best friend; because he was good to me and true to me, and because I loved him better than all the world."

"Oh, I beg pardon, I didn't mean to hurt your feelings. Do you remember his name?"

"Remember his name! Remember his name, whose looks and words and thoughts are part of Manulito's existence! Do you remember your son's name, your mother's, your own? Yet you will forget them all before Manulito forgets the name of Wellington."

"What!" said the sexton, in surprise; "Judge Wellington?"

"Yes," said Manulito.

27*

"Right over yonder, on the brow of that hill,—
a big square monument,—you will find it all right."
As Manulito started in the direction pointed, the
sexton continued in a low voice: "That must be
the Indian I heard of."

When Manulito first saw the monument, he
quickened his steps, read the inscription, and then,
sinking on his knees, said, "And this is his grave."
Then he knelt for a long time in silent grief.

Wellington was as much a child of nature as
Manulito. He loved to wander over the hills and
through the shadowy glens, and his mind was in
the sweetest communion with their quiet and solitude. As Manulito stood at his grave that afternoon, a panorama of varied beauty lay stretched
before him. Far to the south the spires and lofty
buildings of an active city could be seen; to the
west, a continuation of rolling hills, dotted here
and there with little bunches of trees, farm-houses,
and cattle quietly feeding on the hill-side; to the
north, a solid body of ancient oak-trees defying
the eye to penetrate it; far to the east, overlook-
ing the nearer bluffs, one saw a valley of green,
threaded here and there by the silvery creeks and
streams that meandered through it; while at his
feet the Mississippi River rolled along in circling
eddies or seemed as calm as a breathless night,
while its surface was as polished glass. The dew
of evening had begun to fall, and carried to Manulito the sweet incense of new-mown hay, which lay

in rows in an adjacent field. The birds were singing their evening songs as he stooped and picked
from the grave a clover blossom and a stem bearing four leaves, emblematic of good luck, and
bringing to completion any wish of its finder.
Raising his eyes to heaven, he said,—

"Manulito believes as his brother did. Oh, may
the Great Spirit pity him, and here at this time
grant his prayer! May the window of heaven
open, that his dear dead brother may see him
weeping at his grave, for Manulito believes that
those in heaven are permitted to look down on
earth and see those they love weeping at their
graves!"

Darkness was spreading over the world. The
birds had gone to rest,—all except one mourning
dove, which cooed its plaintive song as if its sad
notes would heal the broken heart. The crickets
chirped in the meadows. The awakened owl
hooted his thrilling cry. The stars glittered in the
sky. But Manulito was on bended knees at the
grave.

He took the clover-leaf and some wild flowers
which he had gathered, kissed them lovingly, and
softly laying them on the grass, turned to depart,
but suddenly prostrated himself and kissed the
grave where his dead friend rested. Then he rose,
walked slowly away, and soon darkness hid him
from view.

A few days later, Mrs. Wellington and her children were surprised on seeing Manulito ushered into their home. He had long been given up as dead. His once proud spirit seemed crushed. They tried to induce him to make them an extended visit, but he would not consent. On the night of the second day, just such a moonlight night as when he bade them farewell before, the spirit of unrest seized upon him, and he said, " The footsteps of Manulito must follow the trail defined by his heart, and his heart bids him seek the prairies and the mountains, there to pass his last days among his adopted people."

Years afterwards they learned that he had died a peaceful death. His declining years showed the nobility of the man, for his character was such that he was loved in life and idolized in death. And when chivalrous deeds are mentioned as having been done by members of his adopted tribe, or the names of their greatest warriors pronounced, the name of Manulito takes precedence of all. He was an Indian, and yet

> " His life was gentle ; and the elements
> So mix'd in him, that Nature might stand up
> And say to all the world, " This was a man !"

THE END.